A Kiss For the Cameras

HOLLYWOOD REBELS AND ROMEOS
BOOK ONE

OLIVIA JAYMES

A KISS FOR THE CAMERAS

Copyright © 2017 by Olivia Jaymes

A Kiss For The Cameras

Purely Business. No hearts involved…

That's how this public relations romance – a showmance – was described to best selling author Paige Mitchell. Dating Hollywood heartthrob Nate Mason is all for the publicity. He'll hold her hand down the red carpet and in return she'll let him star in the movie based on her book. It's a win-win for both of them.

Nate is charming and sexy with perfectly polished cheekbones and a smooth as chocolate British accent. She's an American soccer mom who has had less than good luck in the love department. They shouldn't have anything in common except ambition.

The more time they spend together, the more Paige begins to see the man behind the spoiled movie star façade. In private, he's a different person and things are starting to get very personal. It's going to be difficult to remember…

They're only kissing for the cameras.

CHAPTER

One

PAIGE MITCHELL NEEDED a cup of coffee and a slice of lemon cake, and she needed it right away. She'd spent the last hour of her life in a meeting with her agent Kris Hamilton, and nothing had been good news. All her dreams were beginning to evaporate before her very eyes. She'd hoped she was close, but it didn't look like it was going to happen.

"We'll get a couple of coffees, and you'll feel better," Carrie Johnson said, patting Paige on the shoulder. Carrie handled the business side of Paige's writing, but most of all, she was a friend.

"Lemon cake," Paige sighed. "I want lemon cake, too. Then, at least this entire day won't be a bust. I'll have had sugar."

"Lots of lemon cake," Carrie laughed. "And lots of fancy coffee. No better way that I know of to make a day suck less. Why don't you grab a table, and I'll order?"

There were a few empty ones near the back, and

Paige made a beeline for the cleanest, setting her purse on the empty chair beside her. She was checking the messages on her phone when the raised voices on the other side of the shop caught her attention. Sucking in a breath, her entire being was on high alert when she saw who it was.

Nate Mason. Movie star. Sex symbol. British Prince Charming.

The handsome actor was currently surrounded by fawning women - no surprise there - and was signing autographs and taking selfies with them. Laughing and smiling, he appeared to be quite at home with his adoring fans.

"Did you see who's here?" Carrie loudly whispered, placing two plates of lemon cake on the table along with two large vanilla lattes. "It's him. Flynn."

Not even close.

"He's not Flynn. Flynn is a character made up in my warped imagination and brought to life in a series of books. Nate Mason is an actual live human being."

Settling in the chair across from her, Carrie studied the actor. "Are you sure? Because damn, he is fine looking. Almost too good to be true."

He was an exceptionally good-looking man. A few inches over six feet, he was tall and lean but still muscular, with long arms and legs. His perfectly chiseled face had a firm jaw and impossibly high cheekbones along with clear blue eyes. All that gorgeousness was topped off with a mop of golden curls that lately he'd kept cut short on the sides.

"He's real," Paige affirmed, trying not to stare. "But he's

not Flynn. He's too...something. And he's not enough... something else."

As a bestselling author for the last ten years, Paige had created too many characters to count, but none had stuck with her like Flynn had. He was a hero with all the traits that went along with that role, and he was the lead male in her most successful book series. He was also the reason Hollywood had come knocking. There was great interest in turning her books into a feature film. Maybe several feature films.

Or there had been interest. After the meeting today with her agent, it didn't look like any movie was going to be made. Paige was a self-admitted control freak, and she wanted to play a part in the making of the film - casting approval, director choice, and more. Kris had broken it to her today that her hopes were a pipe dream. She simply wasn't a big enough celebrity to get that kind of control. Not enough clout, Kris has said. If only Paige were more famous. More in demand, then she'd have more bargaining power.

"Why don't you go over there and get a picture with him?" Carrie suggested. "I heard that he loves to read. Maybe he's read one of your books."

The idea was horrifying.

"Heavens no," Paige replied crisply. "I couldn't just walk up to him and say hello. That's crazy talk."

Carrie pointed to the half dozen panting women that had formed a circle around him.

"They did."

"More power to them, but that's not me."

Paige took a big bite of her lemon cake and smiled.

She'd needed this all morning. She liked New York City, but she was a homebody normally, puttering around her Florida home in her pajamas and working on her books. Being around all these people was stressful. She'd had to put on a bra when she'd dressed today.

"He looks happier than he did a year ago when he got caught cheating on Stella Riley with those two women," Carrie observed. "In fact, he always looked miserable whenever they were photographed together. He looked like a hostage being forced to play for the cameras. I wasn't surprised when they broke up ugly."

Paige had vague memories of the incident, but she didn't pay much attention to the press when she was in the middle of writing a book. The one thing she did remember was that he'd been thrown under a speeding bus by that America's Sweetheart Wannabe.

"It was his own business." Paige took a sip of her hot coffee. "A grown man had sex. Big deal. The press didn't let up on him."

"Stella said he cheated on her, and those two females said he's a kinky bastard. So much for that British gentleman image he has."

"Honestly, no one can be that perfect, so that wasn't a shock." Paige shook her head. "And we don't know what was really going on between him and her. As for those two girls, I think it was awful that they spilled all his secrets online. It was a gross invasion of privacy. No one deserves that."

"I'll agree with that. The way Stella Riley went on and on for weeks, you'd have thought they'd been together for years and not months. Some people said the relationship wasn't even real."

Paige frowned. "What do you mean not real?"

"You know, a *showmance*. They did it for the publicity and didn't even like each other. You can't cheat on someone you aren't really dating."

"I've never heard of such a thing, and it honestly sounds stupid. You'd have to be pretty desperate to get your name in the paper to do something like that. Now, what's on the agenda for the rest of the afternoon?"

Carrie shook her plastic fork at Paige. "Eat up because you have a meeting with your new publicist in an hour. You're going to follow her advice, aren't you?"

No matter how painful.

"I already am. We're going to that movie premiere tonight. Something I normally would never do, but she's said my appearance will help raise my profile so I can have more clout with the studios."

The look Carrie gave Paige spoke volumes. They both knew it was going to take much more than one movie premiere. Paige had been warned. It was going to take a concerted effort over the next year or so, and she was going to have to move out of her comfort zone. She couldn't wear her beloved pajamas on the red carpet.

Paige followed Carrie's gaze to where Nate Mason was now accepting his coffee and taking a selfie with the barista behind the counter.

"I know you don't agree but I think he'd make an amazing Flynn," Carrie sighed, her brows raised as they watched him thank the swooning girls and exit the coffee shop. Paige was almost positive she could hear the female hearts breaking as they stared at his gorgeous ass exiting. "Do you think he'd want to play him in the movie?"

"Right now there is no movie unless I cave and just hand it over to the studio to do whatever they want with it, and I can't do that, Carrie. I just can't. Flynn is...special. As for Nate Mason? It's not worth discussing since I would never choose him. Besides, I'm sure he turns down offers every day. What would make this movie look enticing to him? In a completely theoretical world, that is."

Carrie tapped her chin. "He plays a lot of bad guys. Flynn is a hero. That might be a nice change for him."

"You're getting way ahead of yourself. There is no movie. Not yet, and maybe never."

Still staring at the door, Carrie sighed. "There has to be a way to make this film happen. I know that somehow it's going to work out."

Paige looked out of the front window at the bustling city street. "Let's face it. Something drastic is going to have to happen to get this movie made, and at this point in my life I'm not sure I'd even survive it."

But she wouldn't give up.

CHAPTER
Two

PAIGE TAPPED her foot impatiently as her publicist painstakingly reviewed the document in front of her. It was a schedule of upcoming interviews, appearances, parties, and award shows she was expected to attend and the mere thought of all those people staring at her was already raising her blood pressure and making the back of her neck sweat. She didn't like being the center of attention.

Call her an introvert. Call it social anxiety. Call her stuck up and shy. Paige didn't care what label was slapped on her as long as she was left alone to do what she wanted to do. Shunning an active social life had turned her into one of the most prolific authors on the bestseller lists. A fact she was quite proud of. She was living her dream.

Her life was beginning to become slightly surreal. In her wildest dreams, she'd never imagined sitting in the posh New York City offices of an entertainment publicist talking about raising her profile and selling more books.

"Paige, are you listening to me?"

Oops. Not really.

Helen Bailey was one of the best in the business. Paige knew she was lucky to have the older woman in her corner but that didn't mean she also had to be thrilled by everything that was suggested. She could be around people when she had to be. But dammit, it was exhausting to be "on" all the time.

To be *her*. Paige Mitchell. Famous author.

Sighing, she shook her head in defeat. "Actually I think you lost me a few events back. Do I really need to attend all of these, Helen? I have a huge production schedule planned for the next eighteen months and all these events are going to put a crimp in that. The fans are screaming for new books faster than I can write them. A few days ago my dry cleaner spent fifteen minutes telling me what should happen in my next book and how I needed to write it."

Helen gave her a sympathetic look. "I know you think all of this won't make a difference but I promise you it will. Hollywood wants your stories and you want creative control. You need the fans screaming for those stories so the studios don't have any choice but to give you what you want. This is the way to make that happen."

Paige grimaced as she perused the multi-page schedule. "Whatever happened to just writing a damn good book?"

"It was never like that, my dear. Writers have always needed publicity and marketing. You're just seeing how the sausage is made, so to speak. It's not pretty but it is necessary."

"Maybe I should just take their money and give them

the books. Walk away and let them do whatever they want. It might be easier."

Helen laughed and shook her head. "Ask Stephen King what he thinks about that."

"Stephen isn't taking my calls," Paige smirked.

"You follow my plan and I guarantee that within two years Stephen King is going to ask to meet you."

Laughter bubbled from Paige's lips. "Right. Like that will ever happen. Well, as long as I'm dreaming I'd like to meet J.K. Rowling as well. Might as well swing for the fences."

Looking down at the neatly laid out schedule, Paige's stomach twisted into a tight knot. Could she really do this? Could she pull it off?

"Helen, I'm not sure I'm up to this. I don't see other authors running around to movie premieres and parties. I don't see them doing a lot of interviews and magazine covers. Why would anyone be interested in me? I'm a middle-aged widow with a teenage son. I like to read, eat chocolate, and binge watch cooking shows. I'm not exciting or glamorous."

Helen smiled and tapped her chin as she sat back in her chair. "I'm going to tell you the truth, Paige, because I think you deserve it. There were a few reasons I agreed to take you on as a client. One of them was that I love your books. You're a great writer. The second is that the minute I met you, I adored you. You're funny and smart. You make people feel at ease and you think quickly on your feet. You're very attractive and personable, and people like to buy books from pretty, happy people. If you'd been a depressed alcoholic with two noses and three eyes, I would have declined the opportunity. Does that confession bother you?"

"I'm not sure," she replied slowly. "But it still doesn't help me at all these functions. There's nothing special about me."

Snorting, Helen rolled her eyes. "You're a lovely woman inside and out, Paige. People are drawn to you because you are also smart and funny along with a dose of down to earth. But I know that you're concerned about this schedule. Which brings me to my next agenda item. There's been an offer."

"An offer?" Paige frowned. "Shouldn't they contact my agent?"

"Not that kind of offer. It's a publicity arrangement. Are you interested?"

"I don't know enough of what that is to say yes or no."

Helen rubbed her chin, her expression neutral. "A friend of mine who is also a publicist is aware that you are my client. They've made an offer that I think you should consider. It would be of benefit for you and for his client as well."

Paige was more confused than ever. "What's the offer?"

"A relationship for publicity between you and his client."

Paige's brows pinched together. "What kind of relationship? You mean like a writing partner? I work alone, Helen."

"Not that sort of relationship. A personal relationship for the cameras. You go out together all sorts of places, get your picture taken together, and snag some much needed press for yourself. The public loves a love story. Celebrities are more interesting when they're a couple."

She was beginning to see. Maybe. But surely not?

"Carrie mentioned something like this to me earlier today. She used the word *showmance*."

Nodding, Helen scooped up the papers on the desk. "That's it exactly. You and he would pretend to be a couple. You'd go to parties together, walk red carpets, basically be seen as a couple in love."

"I'll tell you what I told Carrie. That sounds crazy. Why would anyone go to all that trouble? No, absolutely not."

Helen sighed and pointed to the sheaf of papers. "Don't discard this out of hand. Think about it. Think about having someone help you through all of these social engagements. Someone who knows the ropes. Having a strong arm walk you down the red carpet and helping you when you want to hide in the limo. Think about having someone on your side when it all feels like too much. That's what they're offering and frankly I think you should seriously consider it. Or you can go it alone. It's up to you."

"I'm fine with the way things are."

"No, you're comfortable with how things are. You're so comfortable you're stagnating. I can't help you unless you help yourself. You need to think about what you're willing to do to get this movie made." She held up the schedule. "You're going to have to put yourself out there. You're going to have to admit that you're ambitious and that you want this. Think about how hard you had to work to get your first bestselling novel. You're going to have to work ten times as hard or more to get your first movie deal on your terms."

Paige groaned. She wanted this movie made so much she was dreaming about it at night.

"You're killing me here. If I didn't want it I wouldn't be agreeing to all these personal appearances. You know how much I want this."

Helen sat back in her chair and smiled. "Then meet him. Just one meeting. Talk to him. See if he's someone you could spend time with. If the answer is no, I'll drop this whole subject. But it might be yes. One meeting, Paige."

Wavering back and forth, she contemplated Helen's words. Paige had worked damn hard to get where she was and she'd been warned this movie deal wasn't going to be easy. She'd learned a long time ago that if she wanted something she had to be willing to do the things no one else wanted to do.

In the past, that had been working twelve to sixteen hours a day, seven days a week, even vacations and holidays. She'd worked harder, longer, and smarter and it had paid off.

Surrender wasn't her forte but she tried to be gracious. "One meeting. One hour. Just who is this man anyway?"

Did he even know what he was getting into? She was no day at the beach.

Helen smiled. "You'll love him. All the ladies do. It's Nate Mason."

CHAPTER
Three

NATE STARED out of the large hotel window that overlooked the New York City skyline. All he wanted to do was go home to London for a few weeks - see his friends and family and sleep in his own bed. Maybe even grab a pint down at the local pub with his best friend Max. But first he had a little business to attend to. Important business that couldn't wait.

"I'm not going to beg, Garrett. I won't do that."

Garrett had worked for Nate since "the incident". Nate hadn't wanted to change publicists but hadn't had a choice. When the entire debacle went down last year and his public profile had taken a huge hit, he'd needed someone to come in and do major damage control. Garrett had done that and more, re-shaping Nate's image as a serious actor who was so naive about Hollywood he'd had no idea what he was getting himself into. It wasn't much of an exaggeration. He was more book-smart than street-smart. Nate hadn't known what kind of backlash he was in for nor had he realized that the lady in question was going to throw him to the wolves. It was only with Garrett's help that they'd been able to change the narrative from him being a cheating cad to one of an intensely busy actor who simply couldn't give a relationship the time and attention it deserved.

That wasn't a lie either. Nate had a fire in his belly that pushed him to work harder than anyone else in the business. Ambition was a weak word for the drive that consumed him day in and day out. It was murder for any sort of a relationship to survive, let alone thrive.

Sure he'd had girlfriends on the down-low since he'd hit in the first *Thunder* movie, but there was never enough time to just be a regular boyfriend. Eventually the girls all realized that Nate wasn't Kai, the bad boy biker. He was simply himself, an Oxford-educated actor who liked fine wines and good books. Things usually ended soon after.

"I'm not expecting you to beg, Nate. But you need to know that Paige Mitchell is incredibly new to this. Helen said she had to explain the entire concept to her and it didn't go over well. The only thing that even got her to agree to this meeting was that her image would get a huge boost being linked to you. She's serious about getting this movie made."

Nate snorted, knowing full well he could walk Paige Mitchell through the minefield she was facing. If she'd let him.

"After we all get comfortable with each other, why don't you and Helen leave us for a little while? I'd like to talk to her, just the two of us, without an audience. If she's as shy as I expect she is, then that might make her more relaxed. Plus. it might make this feel a little less like a business deal."

Garrett shrugged. "That may be a plus to her, Nate. Remember, she's a widow and from what Helen has told me, she's as much or more of a workaholic than you are. If that's even possible. She's only dated a few times since the death of her husband three years ago. I'm told she's almost as boring as you are but I find that hard to believe."

Nate held up his hand. "I'm proud to be a snooze. It's made your job much easier."

Once that nasty incident was taken care of Nate had embraced his inner geek and spurned the Hollywood scene. Now his name wasn't in a tabloid unless he wanted it to be. He found he was far happier that way.

A knock on the door saved Garrett from having to respond. "I'm sure this is them. Are you ready to turn on the famous Mason charm? If she hasn't had any male attention in awhile she should be easy pickings. You should have her falling at your feet in less than ten minutes."

Inwardly rolling his eyes, Nate stood straight and tall, knowing he looked good in the dark trousers and blue long-sleeved sweater. Casual but not messy. His hair was back to its natural blond at the moment and he'd even used a bit of gel to tame his unruly curls. They'd grown out a bit since his last role that had finished a month ago. He wanted to make a good impression today. Paige Mitchell had something he desperately wanted. No, make that needed.

The door opened and two women entered the hotel living room, Helen first, a smile on her lined face. Tall and lanky with graying hair, Helen Bailey was something of a legend in publicity circles as was her incredible energy levels. She could put in an eighteen-hour day without blinking an eye.

Nate grinned and took her hands before giving her a kiss on each cheek. "Helen, so good to see you again. You look gorgeous as usual."

The older woman chuckled and patted his face. "I see you still have your silver tongue. It's good to see you too. Now I want you to meet someone very special. Nate, this is Paige Mitchell. Paige, this is Nate Mason."

None of the photos he had seen had prepared him for just how petite Paige truly was. If she was five-foot-two he'd be shocked; she didn't even come to his shoulder. Curvy where it counted, the red dress paired with brown boots showed off her assets nicely. Quite nicely. Shoulder length blonde hair framed a heart-shaped face with stunningly vivid green eyes. She was currently smiling widely, and he noticed that she had deep dimples in her cheeks that made her more cute than beautiful or exotic. Paige Mitchell had an all-American girl-next-door quality that Nate found very attractive.

That lovely woman was currently staring at him as if he was an alien from outer space, eyes wide and mouth open.

"Is there something wrong?"

Paige Mitchell took a few visible deep breaths. "Yes, Mr. Mason, there is something very wrong. Does anyone honestly think that people would believe that you and I would be a couple? Jesus, Mary, and Joseph, I'm a widow with a kid. No one is going to buy that."

Since it had been Nate's idea to choose her he was

slightly insulted, but he understood her skepticism. They weren't the most obvious couple and that's what made this so brilliant. "I don't see it that way."

Her brows shot up. "You don't? Really? On what planet do British sex symbols date and fall in love with frumpy middle-aged housewives? They're going to laugh at the very idea."

Nate grinned wickedly, his gaze raking her from head to toe which turned her pink cheeks a bright red.

Hmmm...married, baby, widowed, and she can still blush. Now this is interesting.

"I don't see anything frumpy about you, darling. And no one is going to laugh. They're going to ship us. Hard. Trust me on this."

Paige threw up her arms. "This? This is a stylist picking out my clothes. This is a fresh haircut and me actually sitting down and putting on some makeup. I spend most of my time in pajama shorts and a tank top with my hair pulled up into a ponytail."

"Sounds delicious, love. I have no objections."

Her mouth hung open but no sound came out. He'd rendered her speechless. This was better than he'd thought. Now came the charm offensive. She had something he wanted and there was one thing Nate was unashamedly. Ambitious. Luckily he had something to offer her in return. He just needed her to listen with an open mind.

"Have a seat and let's chat. We have so much to talk about."

CHAPTER

Four

THIS HAD TO BE A JOKE. Ashton was going to jump out of a closet any moment and tell her she was being punked, because none of this could actually be real.

There was a contract.

Helen and Nate's representative had put the fake relationship parameters down *in writing*. On paper and everything. With very little legalese but it was still a contract that they expected her to sign. She was completely out of her depth.

"It looks...interesting."

The first page was fairly simple. As long as she didn't have any conflicts, she'd be expected to be there for any of Nate's social engagements and vice versa. It designated which publicity team would be responsible for making statements at certain times. Paparazzi walks, etc. Nothing earthshattering.

It was the second page that almost made her gasp and

want to run screaming from the hotel room. They'd put this shit in writing.

First was the statement that if she was caught by the press with another man Nate would have the right to basically ruin her reputation. He could say anything he wanted whether true or not to make himself look better. How sweet. Of course she could do the same to him if he was caught dipping his wick where it didn't belong so it was at least fair.

Of course Nate had a better chance of finding a frisky playmate than she did. Even at this insane moment, he looked good. Oh so good. It looked like he'd put on some muscle for his last role and his sweater strained at the seams over his shoulders. His abs were disgustingly flat and taut, his runner's thighs powerful in the tailored trousers he wore. And those cheekbones. Shit, photos didn't do them justice. He was a good-looking man and she was...ordinary.

"Do you honestly believe anyone is going to buy us as a couple? Where are we going to tell them we met? Do we even have anything in common?"

She sounded sarcastic and she didn't care. This was ridiculous. She was a grown ass woman talking about a game of make believe that no one was going to buy.

Nate's gaze flickered to Garrett. "Mate, can you..."

The man smiled and stood. "Of course, Nate. Helen, how about you and I get a drink down in the bar and let these two get to know one another a little bit?"

Don't leave me!

Helen may have noted Paige's panic but she simply patted her shoulder and followed Garrett out the door.

Skippy wanted them to get to know one another. Okey dokey.

First lesson. She was blisteringly honest and blunt.

"All three of you have lost your fucking minds. Give me one good reason not to walk out of here."

She may have gone too far with that last part. Instead of replying Nate stood and went behind the bar, pulling out a bottle of wine and uncorking it. Fucker was taking his time, making her cool her heels.

"Darling–"

"Just stop that shit," she broke in, her nerves making her more brusque than she'd normally be. "I barely know you so I think calling me darling is overkill. Yeah, I get that you're a charming bastard but I'm not one of your young Barbie dolls. I won't fall backward with my legs open when you speak with that smooth British accent. I'm a little past all that."

He poured them two glasses of red. She thought she saw his cheeks flush but she might have been imagining it. "Fine. Although I think every woman deserves endearments. Women should be treated like queens."

Queens? Yep, she was the royal highness of laundry day at her house.

"Dear Lord, what kind of woman do you usually date?" Paige asked in wonderment, studying him from head to toe. He looked serious about what he'd said but there was no way he could be. "Do they fall for this shit?"

His brows rose and he smiled. "Yes, they usually do but it's charming that you don't. Now let me speak for a moment about the contract. It's for our protection, honestly. I know some parts of it are personal and rather distasteful but a year from now I think you'll be glad this was all addressed in the beginning."

"You sound so sure."

"I am sure." Nate sat down next to her, his thigh brushing her own, the tang of his body wash tickling her nostrils. He smelled damn good. "Paige, we are going to be one another's almost constant companion for twelve to eighteen months. Maybe more. We're bound to become close friends, confidants. I want to make sure we finish this contract as friends no matter what happens."

"You really think we could pull this off?"

She couldn't believe she was having this conversation.

He nodded. "I think we can. We have enough in common that the relationship is believable. I think we can become good friends as well."

Friends? Was she looking for more friends? She might not be the most social being in the world, but she had several. Good ones, too. Adding Nate Mason, movie star to that list was an interesting proposition. But she still wasn't sure this was a good idea. In her entire life she'd never thought of herself as a fake romance type of person. It seemed phony and that was one thing she tried to never be.

And this contract brought up more questions than it answered.

"What if you fall in love with someone else during this contract?"

Shaking his head, he took a sip of his wine. "Highly doubtful. I'd barely have any time to date a woman, let alone fall in love. Of course if I do meet someone I want to date I promise that no one will ever know. I would never embarrass you that way."

"So we can date other people?"

"We can, although it won't be easy or recommended. That's why I said what I did about us. We'll be spending most of our time together."

She picked up the contract and pointed to one of the paragraphs. "Apparently I'm not to mention marriage, children, or love of any kind. Wow, you must have a king-sized commitment phobia. You should see someone about that."

He rubbed the back of his neck and sighed. "It doesn't say we can't mention love. Personally I think it would be wonderful to be in love."

So did she, but she was surprised to hear it from him.

Her long-term marriage hadn't always been the happiest but they'd managed to keep it together. Then Noah got sick and any marital issues they'd had were put on the back burner; permanently, it turned out. For a long time after he'd passed away, she couldn't even think about another man and relationship but lately she had to admit it had crossed her mind. Was there a second chance out there for her?

Sadly, the odds weren't in her favor. She'd have to make do with a great career and that's why she was so determined to have this movie made.

"But," she prompted. "I hear a *but* in that sentence. You think it would be wonderful to be in love but..."

Nate grimaced. "But I don't fancy the idea of marriage or children. I'm very career focused and it would be selfish to marry and have a family at this point in my life. I just feel I need to be up front about that as some women haven't believed me in the past and that can get very ugly."

She tossed the contract onto the coffee table. "You needn't worry about me. Been there, done that, worn the t-shirt. I'm not looking to get married again and I just sent my kid to college. I don't need to go back to diapers and formula so you can relax. But I do have a question for you, Nate, and I want you to be brutally honest."

He nodded, his expression sober. "I can do that."

She was terrified of the answer but she couldn't stop herself. "I know what I'm getting in this deal. I get my name in the press along with yours. I get you to hold my hand when I want to have an anxiety attack. I get someone who has been there and knows what to do. What do you get? What do I have that you want?"

His smile widened and his blue eyes flared with life. Whatever he wanted, he was damn excited about it.

"I get to play Flynn and direct as well. That's our bargain."

He wanted to play the main character from her books? He wanted to become a director?

That she hadn't expected.

CHAPTER
Five

NATE HAD SHOCKED PAIGE. That was clear from the way she was looking at him, which wasn't exactly a compliment. She didn't have to say it out loud but obviously she'd never pictured him in the role. Her gaze was a little glassy and she blinked a few times as if turning his words over in her mind before replying. He needed this and her. He only hoped she didn't know just how much power she held in her hands.

"You want to be Flynn," she echoed. "Really? Why?"

He'd rehearsed this part until he could recite it in his sleep. "He's a fascinating character. Part past, present, but also future. He's heroic but not overtly so. He's quiet, loyal, and uses his intellect as much as he uses his muscles. I also believe that you've only scratched the surface of who he truly is and that there are layers to be peeled back with every book and hopefully movie. I'd like to be a part of that, Paige. I'd like to bring his persona to the big screen. Your character come to life."

Frowning, she didn't seem to like what he had to say. "But you're not him."

He wasn't sure what he was supposed to say to that. Of course he wasn't actually Flynn, just as he wasn't actually Kai.

"Give me a chance and I can become him for the cameras. I don't know how you've pictured him–"

"Not you," she broke in, still frowning. "He has reddish gold hair and it's longer. You're also a little taller."

Ah, the author had a specific picture of Flynn in her head which was going to be an issue. It always was when a book was being made into a movie. Somebody wasn't going to like the casting no matter what.

"Give me his words," Nate urged, leaning closer to her, his pulse speeding up with excitement. There was nothing he loved more than bringing a character to life, giving them a heart, soul, and breath. Flynn had been calling to him since the moment he'd read that first book. "Give me a chance to speak as Flynn and I swear that you will see that I can embody his true essence. By the time I'm done, when you close your eyes you will see my face when you think of him."

Her brows shot up. "That would be an accomplishment. You're very sure of yourself, aren't you?"

Only when it came to acting but that wasn't a subject he was going to discuss with her.

"I'm sure of this. Give me a chance, Paige, and you'll never regret it. Together we can bring him to a whole new audience."

Sighing, she shook her head and stood, putting distance between them, and his heart sank. She was going to say no. "Listen, I know you're a good actor. I've seen your movies and I've enjoyed your performances. You're very talented."

But... she didn't want him. Her expression said it all.

"And if the contract for this movie ever gets signed I hope you audition because you seem to have a great deal of passion for the role."

Hold on. Maybe his hopes weren't dead after all. Could she be persuaded?

"But I'm not looking for a fake relationship in my life. Frankly, I have enough problems between trying to get this movie made, dealing with the schedule of appearances they've set me up with, writing books fast enough for my readers, and the long list of other things I need to deal with but can't remember. My assistant Carrie would be able to tell you but right now I'm drawing a blank. Dealing with a man, even one that isn't my real boyfriend, just sounds like too much work."

He couldn't let this go. It was everything he'd wanted and hoped for. "I can help you with some of that. Not all of it, of course, but some of it. I can be the shoulder you lean on when walking down a red carpet. I can be the hand you hold when you need your name in the papers. We can help each other, Paige. Together we can get that movie made."

He could see the wheels turning in her head. She was thinking about it. There was a part of her that wanted the film deal so badly she was willing to do anything. But he could also see the fear in her eyes, the self-doubt. She was scared and because of that she was standing in place, frozen in position, instead of moving forward.

Rubbing her temple, she closed her eyes for a long moment. "And that's tempting. I'm scared about the next year, Nate, I won't lie. To do this I have to go so far out of my comfort zone I may never find my way back. I don't even know if I'm capable of this but I don't think a relationship for publicity is the answer."

"Is it me?" he heard himself asking. This was his insecurity talking. "Do you not like me?"

Smiling, she shook her head. "Not at all. You seem like a really nice guy. Much nicer than your character Kai in those *Thunder* movies, if you don't mind me saying that. He can be a little scary sometimes."

Those words were literally something he'd never heard. She liked him more than Kai. Normally it was the other way round.

"But you don't think it's a good idea?"

His fingers tightened on the arm of his chair, frustration making his voice tight. He'd been so sure he could convince her. That she'd be thrilled with the offer and gladly take him up on it.

"I'm no actress, Nate. In fact, I'd soon go broke playing poker. Lying is not a skill I possess. I'd fail at this and then drag you down with me. We'd be the laughingstock of Hollywood. Believe me when I say I'm doing this for you." She came closer and laid her hand on his shoulder, the heat from her palm penetrating his sweater and warming his skin. "I meant what I said about the part though. If you want it, you should go for it. I'll be your biggest cheerleader when the time comes. Anyone with that kind of passion should have a chance."

Sadly, he gazed at her. She'd made her decision, that was crystal clear. It was hard to give up though. All the things he'd been hoping for and planning on were slowly melting. Defeat was not in his nature when it came to his career.

"Is there anything I can say or do to change your mind?"

"I'm afraid not but please let me say thank you for thinking that the public would believe you and me. It's the nicest compliment I've had in years."

"I'd be a lucky man to have a woman such as you."

Laughing, she pushed at his shoulder playfully. "You and your British charm. I'm not falling for it. Now I really should be going. Thank you for the offer but I just don't think I could pull it off."

He stood and led her to the door of the suite but he couldn't let her go without one more plea. "I understand you don't think this is a good idea but I beg you, please think more about it. There are so many benefits to both of us and I'd be honored to walk you down your first red carpet, Ms. Mitchell."

She made a soft groan but her lips were turned up in a smile. There was a part of her that wanted to say yes. She lacked the self-confidence to see the decision through.

"Okay, I'll think more about it but I don't think I'm going to change my mind. You've got persistence, I'll give you that."

"Just like Flynn."

"He also knows when to give up."

He leaned down closer to her ear, his voice soft. "I do as well, and I think this is not one of those times."

He heard her laughter trailing behind her as she strode down the hall. Paige Mitchell was lovely, charming, smart, and exactly what he needed. If only she'd say yes, they could make good things happen for both of them in their careers. She had the ambition but she also had the fear.

So far fear was winning, but not by much.

———

Panic crawled up the back of Paige's neck and her chest tightened painfully, making it hard to catch her breath. She was wearing a brand-new designer dress and shoes, her hair and makeup done by a professional, and now she was sitting in a limousine waiting in the car line to be dropped off at the red carpet.

She was expected to walk down that red carpet and have her picture taken by dozens of paparazzi, maybe even do a few interviews. Knowing this all week, she'd given herself multiple pep talks and she'd thought she had this under control. Not so.

Her palms damp, she clutched the tiny black velvet purse as it if was a lifeline. In a way it was because it gave her something to do with her hands.

"You're going to be okay," Carrie said, her tone as calming as possible. If anyone understood what Paige was going through it was her best friend. Carrie had walked her through multiple occasions like this, although not all of them were this public. Sometimes she simply became over-whelmed with all the expectations her private life and career placed on her and she needed to retreat for a few hours to be by herself.

"Eventually," Paige agreed, her throat tight. "But I'm scared as hell. There are so many fucking people out there. I can see the flash of the cameras from here."

Reaching for the switch, Carrie rolled up the car window. "Does that help? How about doing some deep breathing exercises? Or some imaging? Think happy thoughts about puppies and chocolate."

Those things usually helped but Paige was too far gone. Every muscle in her body had frozen into place and she couldn't move when the limo slid to a halt and the car door opened. Helen stuck her head in and smiled.

"Are you ready? It looks like a good crowd."

Paige's legs were shaking and she had to press her high heels to the floor of the vehicle to keep them steady. "I don't think I can do this."

Carrie leaned over Paige, her gaze darting around the crowd waiting outside. "She's a little panicked. She just needs a minute."

Patting her arm, Helen tried to look sympathetic but Paige could tell the older woman was slightly agitated. "I wish I could give that to you, honey, but there is a long line of limos behind you. Let's get you out of the car and then we'll deal with the red carpet."

Paige wanted to move but she wasn't having an easy time of it. Her limbs didn't want to cooperate and she feared she was going to lose the contents of her stomach at any moment.

Tears burned the back of her eyes. She hated being this scared but the screaming crowd and the flashing bulbs were freaking her out. "I can't. It's too much. Everybody will be looking at me."

She couldn't do this. Helen would fire her as a client, and her dream of making the movie would die.

She'd barely begun and she'd already failed.

CHAPTER
Six

NATE HAD JUST FINISHED an interview with a cable entertainment network when he spied Helen Bailey out of the corner of his eye. With a reputation for being unflappable, he was surprised to see the woman looking more than a little upset, her hands wringing together. A pretty redhead climbed out of the limousine Helen was standing next to and both females seemed to be speaking to an occupant of the vehicle, wearing concerned expressions while they were doing it.

Paige? Could it be? She hadn't mentioned coming to the movie premiere tonight but then neither had he. If that was Paige in that limousine, her publicist and friend were having a hell of a time getting her out of the car.

He wouldn't lie and say he wasn't disappointed after their meeting earlier in the day. He'd been counting on that role, and on the opportunity to direct as well. He needed to build a resume behind the camera as his leading man days were numbered. Acting was a tough business and the

industry was always looking for the next big thing, preferably younger and more handsome... with a full, luxurious
head of hair. That was something Nate wasn't sure he was
going to be able to boast for much longer.

Not letting himself think too much about his actions, he
strode back down the red carpet to the limousine. He
might be able to help and not because he'd get something
in return. His mother had raised him to be a goddamn
gentleman and every now and then he tried to act like it.

"Helen, is everything alright?"

The publicist turned around and looked relieved to see
him. "Nate, I'm afraid Paige has panicked a little." She
glanced at the parade of limousines waiting behind them.
"But I've got to get her out of the car."

He'd only met her today but it was worth a shot.
Nodding to Helen, he stuck his head into the limo
expecting to see Paige in tears or worse. He was surprised
to see her looking rather calm, which immediately made
him more wary. She was keeping her emotions all tightly
bound up. Bad move.

"Paige, darling, it's Nate. You have to get out of the
limo. There are people waiting."

Her gaze darted to the flashing lights that she could see
from her vantage point and she shook her head. "I don't
think I can do this."

"Of course you can," he assured her, his tone as
soothing as he could get it. He was a stage trained actor,
after all, and this was a test of those abilities. "I'll tell you
what. Let me help you out of the car and you can hold my
hand. I know a way into the theatre that skips all the
cameras and fuss."

He had her attention. Her eyes had widened but she'd moved closer to him, sitting on the edge of the seat. "You do? Can I do that?"

"Absolutely. You don't have to walk the carpet unless you want to. But the movie is supposed to be really good. You don't want to miss it, love." Then he held out his hand and smiled as encouragingly as he could. "Come with me. We can get popcorn if you like."

He held his arm there in midair as her gaze darted from him to the lights, then back. He held his breath as she thought through her options, none of them very good. Just when he was about to give up, she tentatively reached out her hand and placed it in his.

Quickly, before she could change her mind, he closed his fingers around it, noticing how small it was in comparison to his own. The palm was damp with nerves but that didn't matter now. He needed to get her out of this limo.

Helping her from the vehicle, he admired her graceful moves even when under so much stress and fear. Her black cocktail dress with the silver beaded neckline set off her pale blonde hair. Tonight she was taller than their first meeting courtesy of sky high silver heels that matched her jewelry. Paige Mitchell cleaned up quite nicely.

With his left hand holding hers and an arm around her waist, he led her away from the crowds and cameras to an area where the families and publicists usually hung out while the celebrities walked the carpet. When they were safely behind a large pillar, he stopped to let Paige catch her breath. So far she'd been acquiescent but he wasn't going to press his luck.

"See? It's quite private back here. No photographers."

Helen and the other young woman were giving him the most grateful looks he'd seen in ages. The redhead stuck out her hand and smiled widely.

"I'm Carrie, by the way. I'm Paige's business manager, assistant, and friend, for want of better descriptions. Thank you so much for your help."

"I was happy to do it." Nate inclined his head but his attention was still on Paige, who was looking much better as the color returned to her cheeks. "How are you feeling, love? The fresh air helping?"

Taking a deep breath, she nodded. "I'm better, thank you. Helen and Carrie, can you give me a minute with Mr. Mason?"

The two women bustled over to a group of publicists leaving Nate alone with Paige, who was looking at him curiously, her brows knitted together.

"Why did you do that?"

Her quiet question wasn't what he'd expected. He'd thought she might thank him again privately before heading off with her friends to watch the film.

"First, please call me Nate. As for what I did... I did it because it looked like you needed it. Are you alright now?"

"I am," she confirmed. "But I guess I'm just surprised. I turned down your proposition today and you still helped me."

She must have a really low opinion of him, or maybe it was all actors.

"One doesn't have anything to do with the other. My mum would be very disappointed in me if I didn't give you a hand."

Paige didn't say anything for a minute, simply studying him as if memorizing his features.

"Thank you. Did you say something about popcorn?"

His grin widening, he laughed at the unexpected query. She was quite unpredictable.

"I did." He held out his arm so she could take his elbow. "Shall I lead the way, my princess?"

She was smiling as well and she was breathtakingly lovely when she did. It reminded him that she hadn't smiled much before in his company.

"Lead on, Nate. I suddenly have a craving for popcorn and Sno-Caps."

Once again he felt the crushing disappointment he'd experienced when she'd turned him down. He genuinely liked her as a person and they could help each other. He could raise her profile and hold her hand down all those red carpets. They could make this work if only she'd give him the chance. He opened his mouth to make one more desperate plea but quickly snapped it shut. She'd turned him down already and his ego couldn't take the bruising of her doing it again.

He had to face the reality that sometimes, no matter how famous, he wasn't going to get everything he wanted. No matter how much he needed it.

CHAPTER
Seven

PAIGE THREW the covers back and sat up in bed. It was hard to sleep in hotel rooms and harder still when her mind was whirling, her thoughts too numerous and varied to let her rest. The movie premiere had been as horrible as she'd predicted but then had turned rather pleasant. Nate Mason had somehow managed to pry her out of the limousine and get her to her seat without a zombie apocalypse starting.

He'd been...nice. And comforting. A strong arm she could lean on when she was overwhelmed. She hadn't seen much of him after the movie began; he'd been seated far away from herself in the Hollywood star section while she'd been in the "minor celebrity and no one knows who the hell you are" section but once or twice she thought she'd felt his gaze on her when she wasn't looking.

Because she'd felt so badly about her panic, she'd even attended the after-party with Helen and Carrie where her publicist introduced her to a few movers and shakers in the film industry. Paige called on all the charm she possessed to be friendly and entertaining, hopefully gaining the attention of a few powerful producers while also watching Nate from the corner of her eye.

A man who was not only used to being the center of attention, he clearly reveled in it. A circle of pretty and giggling women had formed around him, just like at the coffee shop that morning and he'd danced with each female one by one. The hard partying man who flirted and charmed every woman in the place was in stark contrast to the gentle and encouraging man who had talked her out of the car.

Even Helen had been smiling by the end of the evening. Paige later apologized and the older woman had been kind but blunt. If she wanted control of the movie she was going to have to learn to play the game. If she didn't think she could do that, they could part ways. No hard feelings. Helen had urged Paige to take a few days to think it over.

She wanted it so badly. Flynn brought to life was a dream she wasn't willing to give up on. Not yet anyway. Her agent had assured her they were close but Paige had some work to do with her public relations.

Swinging her legs down to the floor, she stuffed them in a pair of slippers while she reached for her bright pink hoodie she'd thrown on the chair next to the bed. Slipping it over her head, she padded out to the living room and pulled a bottle of water from the small refrigerator.

Nate. She couldn't stop thinking about him. How he'd helped her. For no other reason than he was a gentleman. He hadn't done it because she had something he wanted.

He hadn't pleaded with her to sign the contract, hadn't listed all the reasons she should. He'd just been there when she really needed him. It said a great deal about the man that he was.

It was there, staring out over the New York City skyline that she made her decision. She'd been playing it safe in her life for so long and if there was ever a moment to go big it was right now. If she wanted her dream to come true she had to be willing to do something she'd never done before to get it.

Grabbing her room keycard, she shoved it in the pocket of her hoodie and headed for Nate's room, just one floor up where they'd met earlier. As she raised her arm to knock on the door, she hesitated for a moment. Not because she was unsure as to what she wanted, but because he had no idea she was coming. He might not even be back from partying. Or worse, he might have a...guest...in there with him. That would be mortifying.

What's the worst that can happen?

Inwardly rolling her eyes, she made six sharp raps on the door, holding her breath the entire time, her heart beating against her ribcage. No one came to the door and she was about to turn and flee when it swung open, a sleepy-looking Nate standing in the doorway.

He looked adorable and it wasn't fair. Dressed in sweat pants and a t-shirt, his hair was standing on end and his eyes were squinty and unfocused. She'd woken him up.

"Paige, are you alright?"

Sucking in a breath, she nodded. "I'm sorry to wake you up. Can we talk?"

He blinked a few times and then stepped back so she could enter his room. "Of course, come on in."

He flicked on a lamp in the sitting area and motioned toward the sofa while he sat on the coffee table right in front of her, their knees brushing. "Now why don't you tell me why you're here? You look a trifle upset, love. Did something happen at the after party?"

She'd completely forgotten the party already. "No, I wanted to talk to you."

He sat there and waited patiently, his warm scent wafting around her. A little citrus, a little whiskey, and just a touch of fabric softener. "I'm listening."

He was too, watching her intently as she tried to form a coherent sentence. "I've been thinking. You know…about what we talked about yesterday afternoon."

That famous brow quirked up but he still didn't say anything, although he looked like he was dying to. It said something about his self-control that he stayed quiet.

"I've been thinking," Paige said again, her fingers tangled in the cord from her hood. "I think that maybe I'd like to say yes."

His smile was immediate and he reached out to clasp her cold hands, his large and warm and comforting. "That is wonderful news. I can't tell you how happy I am to hear you say that. What changed your mind?"

She was about to tell him that he had, the way he'd acted, but for some reason she didn't. This wasn't an emotional free-for-all. This was a business deal and there wouldn't be hugs and cookies when they inked the contract.

"Clearly I need help at these social events," she said

instead, happy that her voice sounded normal when inside she was shaking like a leaf. She was scared to death. "I don't think I can do all of this by myself. Plus, these events will raise my profile which in turns help me in contract negotiations. It's a big win for me."

"And for me," he said deeply, his blue gaze shining with happiness. "I promise you that I will bring Flynn to life in a manner that you'll be proud of."

She believed him, although that might be foolish. He appeared completely sincere but he was an award-winning actor. He was paid to convince people that lies were truth. It was a detail she needed to remember in the coming weeks and months.

"I think you will. We have the same goal basically. Get the movie deal and then make the film. I think if we work together we can get it done. I know I can't do it alone."

He shook his head. "I think you could actually but it might take longer and it would be harder. But why go through that all alone when I can be by your side?"

Like a team but not quite. Business partners, maybe. Yes, that's how she'd think of them.

Paige pulled her hand from his grasp, slightly trembling but hopefully he wouldn't notice. "Shall we shake on it?"

His smiled widened and his big hand engulfed hers. "We shall. It's a deal, Paige Mitchell. We're a couple."

A couple of idiots. There was one fly in this ointment. No one was ever going to believe they were together.

CHAPTER
Eight

THEY ENDED up not signing the contract, deciding a handshake was good enough. Helen was thrilled when Paige told her the news, but Carrie was a bit more subdued, withholding judgment for awhile. Her assistant was the careful, methodical type.

Paige still thought the idea was slightly ridiculous and no one was going to believe it but Nate's assurances had her saying yes. All Nate wanted in exchange was an acting role and to direct, which wasn't an outlandish request. He was a great actor and he did have the enthusiasm to bring Flynn into existence. He didn't have much directorial experience - just a few short films - but she didn't want a director that might be experienced but who was determined to do it his or her own way, her vision be damned.

All she had to do was keep a safe distance from him. Not get too close. Don't get attached. Keep things light and casual. He'd said they might become friends and that was fine with her, although she'd quickly found that he could annoy her. Like today, for instance. He was following her like a puppy and she wasn't used to having company wherever she went. She'd been alone a long time even before Noah's death and had learned to do things on her own. Because she had to.

Paige still had some business to complete in the city and Nate had agreed to stay on as well. After she was done she would fly to London with him for a few weeks.

To get to know one another.

"I don't need your help with this."

Paige checked her phone for messages as they walked down the crowded New York City street, the sun shining and the air warm. Just her kind of weather.

"As your new boyfriend it's my duty to help you pick out some new clothes. Afterwards we'll have some lunch. If you're a good girl, I'll buy you some ice cream."

Boyfriend. I may never get used to this. Damn.

She shot him a glare that only made him laugh in response. "I'm forty years old and I think I can pick out a few dresses by myself."

"Are you sure?"

Annoyed, she stopped in the middle of the sidewalk making the pedestrians go around them, muttering a few not so nice words under their breath. "I'm sure. Really, go back to the hotel and do whatever it is that famous movie stars do. Go to the gym. Read a script. Seduce a groupie. Just let me try on clothes in peace."

He shook his head, a smile playing on his lips. "Frankly, darling, I'm not sure I can leave you on your own. You might never make it back to the hotel."

That was an insult.

She placed her hand on her hip and gave him her best evil look. "Why do you think that?"

That smile became a shit-eating grin. "Because you passed our destination a block and a half ago. I was waiting to see if you'd notice."

Son of a bitch. The British bastard was right.

Blowing out a frustrated breath, she turned and without a word strode back the way they came, Nate easily keeping up with her short legs, chuckling softly to himself. Asshole.

To his credit he didn't say much as she introduced him to the stylist. Julie giggled and gushed but Paige would bet he was used to the female attention and took it as his due. He settled himself into a comfortable chair and pulled out his phone as she was swept back into a changing room to begin trying on a rack full of clothes.

Julie, however, had taken an instant shine to Nate and she wasn't going to leave him to play Angry Birds on his cell. As soon as Paige was in the first dress, Julie was dragging her out of the changing room so she could show off for Nate. Ugh. She didn't need his approval or opinion or whatever. But Julie was adamant. They needed a *man's* opinion.

He looked up from his phone and smiled warmly, his warm gaze taking her in head to toe. The dress was a dark purple with a halter top bodice and a flirty skirt that ended mid-thigh. Julie had shoved her feet into sky-high heels and Paige felt distinctly wobbly, as if she might topple over any moment.

"Now that, darling, is quite lovely. That color brings out your eyes."

What was it about his voice that made everything sound so fucking sexy?

"The dress is fine but these shoes are a hazard. I need something with a shorter heel, Julie."

The stylist's eyes went wide and her gaze darted to Nate and then back again. "It's just...he's so tall and you're..."

"So freaking short," Paige finished for her. "Yep, I'm a shrimp and even in high heels I'm not fooling anyone."

Nate was laughing and shaking his head. "I think Paige has a good point. We don't want any broken ankles."

Julie reluctantly relented and brought out a pair of gold sandals that Nate instantly approved of, which only made the stylist more enthusiastic to please him.

Him. Not me. You know, the person paying her.

The next two hours were excruciating as Julie and Nate turned Paige into a life-size dress up doll. The one saving grace of the morning was the admiring way he looked at her whenever she came out of the changing room. He liked what he was seeing and she'd become progressively weak-kneed as the appointment had gone on. It had been a long time since she'd seen that look in anyone's eyes and she hated to admit it but she missed it.

She was relieved when it was finally over and she was back in her own clothes - jeans and a cotton shirt. Nate tucked his phone in his pocket and handed Paige her handbag. The charmer had held her purse without complaint. "Julie, can you arrange for those clothes to be delivered?"

Paige had already done that and opened her mouth to tell him so but Julie beat her to it. "Of course, Nate. I'll have them packed up and shipped after the alterations are finished. It's been wonderful to meet you today and let's get together and talk about some outfits for that photo shoot you have coming up."

Julie gave Paige a big hug and wished her luck and then gave Nate a long, lingering look as they made their way to the door and down the stairs to the street.

Paige shook her head, amused at the play by play between her fake boyfriend and her stylist. It was as if he was walking, talking catnip and all the women were... felines.

"You conquered another one, Treetop. It's actually sort of fascinating watching you in action. You're good at it."

His brow quirked but he simply took her arm in his and led them down the street. "She was only being nice to me because she wants the work. Didn't you hear her at the end? She wants to dress me for a photo shoot. This didn't have anything to do with my manly attributes."

Of which he had many.

Paige snorted derisively. "Right. I beg to differ. She was looking at you like you were chocolate ice cream with fudge sauce."

He didn't take the bait.

"And what is this *Treetop*? Is that some sort of American endearment? How sweet, my sweet."

"It's a nickname because you're so damn tall. There's a whole world up there I don't even know about." He was laughing again as she jumped up and waved her hand as high as she could reach. "So glad I can make you laugh. At least one of us has had a fun morning."

But she planned to shake him for the afternoon. Being

this close to him made her...jittery, although she didn't know why. Maybe it was simply his proximity. He was one tall man and he towered over her.

"Darling, you have no idea just how amusing you are. Now let's have lunch. Are you hungry?"

They had a lot to learn about each other. Time to educate him.

"You have no idea, do you? If we're going to hang out, you need to learn a few things about me and one of the most important? I'm always hungry. In fact, if I start to get grouchy and bitchy just feed me. I'll be all smiles within minutes. I carry snacks in my purse just in case."

His brows shot up in surprise. "Good to know. I think we need to put a smile on that face right away."

———

For a tiny thing, Paige could really put away some food. Nate had taken her to his favorite Italian restaurant and so far she'd managed to eat every bite of her chicken parmesan plus three pieces of homemade bread dipped in olive oil and spices. Now she was eyeing the dessert menu.

She set the menu card down on the table. "You're looking at me like I'm an alien from outer space. Is it weird being with a female that actually...you know...eats?"

Paige had a lovely smile, dimples in both cheeks. She'd been quite adorable this morning trying on all those dresses like she was Cinderella getting ready for the ball

"Well, yes, as a matter of fact it is. Most women tell me they're not hungry."

Snickering, she took a sip of her iced tea. "Then they proceed to eat half of whatever you ordered, right?"

Not if he ate it first.

"Something like that."

Paige shrugged. "I like to eat and I like to cook. I watch too much of the food channel. When I get writer's block I like to try new recipes. About half of them turn out, and the other half is an inedible disaster."

He liked finding out things about her that he hadn't been able to dig up on his own.

"Feel free to try your experiments on me. I went to boarding school so I'll pretty much eat anything."

The waitress came and Paige ordered a slab of chocolate cake. Two forks. He'd just have to run a little farther tomorrow morning to work it off.

She was playing with the corner of the placemat and studiously avoiding his gaze. He was coming to know this was when she wanted to say something but she didn't know how to say it.

"Something on your mind, love?"

Raising her head, she nodded but still didn't speak, instead pressing her lips together for a long moment. "Why me?"

He let out a relieved breath. That was a question he was happy to answer.

"It all started during a visit to my mum's house. She was reading one of your books and raving about it. She's a big fan and is going to be excited to meet you. Anyway, I couldn't sleep that night so I picked it up and well...let's just say I didn't get any rest until I'd finished it. I couldn't put it down and I was intrigued with Flynn. I've read every book in that series and I want to play that character. I also want to try my hand at directing. Build a resume behind the camera. My management tells me that I'm aging too quickly."

They'd actually been much more brutal, telling him his window of opportunity for leading man roles was quickly closing. He needed to do something fast.

Her smile was lopsided. "This seems like you're going to an awful lot of trouble just for a role."

"I couldn't take any chances," he said simply.

She seemed to think about his answer before posing another question. "Is the role that important to you? You probably turn down jobs every day."

The conversation had taken an unexpected turn. Normally he wouldn't dream of telling her the truth, giving her that sort of power over him but there was something about her. Something trustworthy. She wasn't someone who was going to go for the jugular.

"Sadly since last year and... all that happened... the offers are slower in coming. Especially the bigger roles. The kind that change the direction of an actor's career." Their gazes met and he found himself admitting to her what he barely admitted to himself. "The fact is other than the *Thunder* commitments, I don't have anything else but a London play on the horizon."

Her mouth fell open and her eyes were soft with sympathy. "I'm sorry. You're too talented to have that happen to you. It's not fair."

Nate shook his head. He'd been over and over this in his brain and she was wrong. "Actually it's completely fair. I fucked up and Hollywood is punishing me, but they love a comeback story even more. That's why I need to make something happen for myself. A reinvention, if you will. I want to show Hollywood I can do more than ride a motorcycle and be the bad boy. Succinctly put, I need you and Flynn. I need this project to revive my career."

She blinked and sucked in a breath. "Jesus, no pressure there. Your whole entire career and livelihood are riding on some words I've written. Yep, no stress at all."

He smiled at her nervousness. He was used to people who were as self-absorbed as he was. Yet here he sat with a lovely woman who was taking the responsibility for his future onto her own shoulders.

He couldn't allow that.

"It's all going to be fine," he assured her, although he wasn't as confident as he sounded. He was an actor, after all. "If this doesn't work I'll find another way. I've made enough money that I don't have to work anymore. That is if I don't buy an island or something."

She smiled, one of the few genuine smiles he'd been gifted with since they'd met. It transformed her face from pretty to breathtakingly beautiful. "You do it because you love it. Because it's a calling."

It felt wonderful to be understood. She got him, at least this part of him. "You feel the same way, yes? Writing is more than a profession?"

"It's who I am," she said softly. "I can't not do it. It's as necessary as breathing."

They had more in common than he'd thought.

CHAPTER
Nine

PAIGE FINISHED TAPPING out a text to her son Jason to let him know she'd arrived safe and sound. While they'd always been close, after Noah's death that bond had been strengthened exponentially. They kept pretty close tabs on one another even now that he was attending college. She was so proud of the man he was becoming. A little like his father and a little like her, but mostly himself.

Tucking her phone back in her pocket, she craned her neck to see out of the taxi, all of nighttime London spread out before her with its purple sky and twinkling lights. While she was here she wanted to see it all. Already her mind was whirling with story ideas and characters that begged to be written.

"Have you never been here before, darling?"

There was incredulity in Nate's voice and she supposed there should be. He'd traveled the world, after all.

"I've been all over the United States but I've never been to Europe. But I've wanted to visit for a long time."

She dragged her gaze away from the skyline and back to her companion of the last three days. Three good days. They were taking those first shaky steps into friendship but it looked promising. Right now a wrinkled brow marred that gorgeous face she still wasn't used to. Frowning again? He better be careful or he was going to have to spend more time in the makeup chair.

"Why didn't you, love?"

She'd learned that Nate was a nice man but he also didn't have a clue how the average single mother lived in suburbia. Even a financially successful one. It wasn't his fault but he was truly sheltered.

"Because I was busy taking care of Noah and raising Jason when I wasn't writing my next book." She sighed heavily, remembering those years. She'd existed on massive amounts of caffeine, little sleep, lots of hugs from her son, plus a healthy dose of support from her friends. "There wasn't much opportunity to travel."

He winced and shook his head, his expression contrite. "I should have realized. Of course you would be busy caring for your husband. He was sick for a long time, yes?"

She turned back to the cityscape, not wanting to see the pity in her new friend's eyes nor let him see the tears that shined in her own. Every now and then the past caught up with her.

"Too long," she said softly. "But now I can travel and I'm glad to be here in London."

"I'm glad too."

That made Paige smile. "You weren't too glad back in New York. In fact, I think you were ready to strap me to the wing of the plane because I was getting on your nerves."

Approximately eight hours before on a British Airways flight...

Paige white-knuckled the hand rests and took several deep breaths, which seemed to capture Nate's attention. He paused in arranging his backpack under the seat and gave her a frown.

"Are you okay? You look tense."

"I don't like to fly," she confessed ruefully. "I took a sedative after we got through security so it should kick in any time now but until them I'm a little anxious, especially during takeoff and landing."

The perfect bastard had the nerve to frown even harder as if he didn't understand. "We're going to be doing an awful lot of flying in the next year or so, Paige. There's no real rational reason to be afraid, you know. It's safer than driving a car."

She knew that but it didn't make any difference. "I don't really like driving a car either to be honest. I have a lot to live for and I don't want to die."

He was still frowning. What was up with him?

"Perhaps you might want to see someone about your social anxiety and your fear of flying. Are there any other phobias I should know about?"

"I'm not too fond of heights or snakes," she replied testily. "But I don't have social anxiety. Being nervous about walking down a red carpet with reporters and photographers is a perfectly natural and human reaction. And I did see someone. They're the ones that gave me the pills."

"I mean see someone and talk to them. Try to get better, not just mask it with medication."

She'd closed her eyes as the engines revved and she opened just one to look at him. "I'll tell you what. If you go talk to a shrink about your commitment phobia, I'll go talk to one about my fear of flying and walking down a red carpet. Deal?"

He turned in his seat and faced forward. "On the other hand, I'm sure the drugs work just fine."

Asshole.

"Yep, that's what I thought," she laughed, closing her eyes again as the plane began to move. "You can dish it out but you can't take it."

He didn't reply but he did hold her hand as the plane took off, which she thought was pretty human of him when she'd been kind of short about the situation. The sedative's magic began to work and by the time the flight attendant came for their drink order she was in a great mood. The prescribed drug had a habit of lowering her inhibitions and also making her sleepy. She intended to take a nap while they were in the air.

The attractive attendant placed a flute of champagne and orange juice in front of each of them. She'd had to lean over to do it and damned if she didn't make sure Nate got an eyeful of her cleavage. Her shirt hadn't been unbuttoned that far a few minutes ago.

"Breakfast will be out in a few minutes. My name is Sherry." She leaned over again and gave Nate a come-hither smile. "Let me know if you need anything. Anything at all."

"Jesus," Paige giggled as Sherry sashayed down the aisle. "You're up to your elbows in fan-girl tail. Do want me to create a diversion while you and Sherry sneak off to the lavatory and join the mile-high club?"

Nate's brows shot up and looked around quickly to see if anyone had heard her.

"Will you keep your voice down? What are you even talking about?"

The cabin of the airplane spun for a moment and then righted itself. Yep, the pills had kicked right in. Excellent. Paige leaned in closer to Nate, his spicy scent tickling her nose. He always smelled so good. If some company could bottle his scent they'd make billions. Women would erect monuments in their honor.

"I'm talking about those two boobies our lovely and helpful Sherry shoved in your face, and don't pretend you didn't notice. You were eyeing her up and down like she was a steak and you were a starving dog. So much for not embarrassing your fake girlfriend." She poked him in the bicep and got a sore finger for her trouble. He was all muscle. "She thinks you're on the market and you're supposed to be devoted to me. Epic fail, Treetop. But if you want some strange, hey, don't let me get in your way. Go for it."

A muscle ticked in his jaw. She'd hit a nerve apparently but at the moment she was too relaxed to care. "I have no interest in that woman, I can assure you."

Paige giggled again, taking another gulp of her drink. "You're so fucking fake. Fake. Fake. Fake."

"I am not fake."

He sounded outraged. Whatever.

"You're fake. You probably want to smack me upside the head right now but you're all British gentleman instead, stiff upper lip and all that jazz. You never let down your guard around me. You are constantly Nate Mason, Prince Fucking Charming. When are you going to be just Nate?"

"I am just Nate," he said defensively. "This is how I really am."

Paige turned to him, their gazes colliding. "Bullshit."

"You think you know me?" he asked, eyes narrowing. "You think you have all the answers?"

"I took a couple of psychology courses in college and clearly you have issues, my fake boyfriend. You have a deep need for approval and you'll go to any lengths to get it, even subverting your own wants and needs. It's sad, really."

His face had turned a lovely shade of purple but surprisingly he was still in control. "A couple of classes? Well, why didn't you say so? You're practically an expert." He snatched the champagne flute out of her hand. "And don't drink that. I doubt it's good to mix your sedative with alcohol. You said you had a lot to live for, remember?"

"Good point, Treetop." Paige yawned, well into the second phase of the medication. "I'm going to sleep. Let me know if I snore. You and Sherry enjoy your shag. Say my name when you come. Cause you know...I'm your girlfriend."

Nate shook his head. "It's eight in the morning, you

can't go to sleep. You'll be all messed up when we get to London. It will be evening when we get there."

The vagaries of time zones were mostly lost on her when she was stone cold sober, so in this state she'd just have to take his word for it.

"I'm tired now," she pronounced. "You can eat my breakfast."

Paige's lids were heavy and she didn't fight them as sleep took over. In the distance she could still hear Nate trying to get her to wake up but she was just too sleepy to listen.

Back in the present...

"I don't want to strap you to a wing now," Nate laughed. "But it was touch and go back there."

Paige smirked. "If it doesn't work out with me, I'm sure Sherry would be glad to hear from you. I saw her give you her card as we left."

Nate smiled as well, pulling that card from his front shirt pocket where he'd tucked it and then holding it up for her inspection. Next he rolled down the window of the vehicle slightly, a cool wind blowing in the car and making Paige shiver. Last, he shoved the card in the opening and let it flutter away into the wind.

"Smooth, Mason. Very smooth. I'd be impressed but I know you'll get a whole new set tomorrow."

But at least he'd thrown that one away.

CHAPTER
Ten

A WAVE of happiness and contentment washed over Nate as he and Paige crossed the threshold to his home in London. He hadn't spent nearly enough time here in the last few years so it was precious when he could. Of course if he couldn't revive his career soon he might be spending quite a bit of time in London whether he wanted to or not. His agent was getting offers - lots of them - but they weren't the kind that were coming in only a year ago. Smaller pictures. Lower budgets. The one place that seemed to still embrace him was the stage and for that he was grateful. If it didn't work out with the Flynn role, perhaps his new play might revive his career. Being a serious actor and getting good reviews certainly couldn't hurt the situation.

No, he wouldn't allow himself to think negatively. It simply had to work out with Paige and her book. Hollywood wanted the project badly; the only thing holding up the deal was that she wanted quite a bit of creative control. One of her contractual demands was that she be allowed to approve the casting. That was where he came in.

He trusted her to fulfill her end of their bargain and he planned to do the same. He'd help raise her profile, sell some books, and hold her hand on the red carpet. He felt badly that she was going to get some nasty backlash from some of his crazier fans - and that was something he should warn her about - but he didn't regret the agreement. Flynn was his ticket to giving him a new start. It was a romantic and heroic leading man role, plus he'd get to direct as well. There was probably already a long list of actors that were salivating to be cast.

They'd be disappointed. For once he was ahead of the game.

"This is nice," Paige said as she walked around his living room, taking in the decor. He was rather proud of it actually as he'd picked everything out himself. "Startling white walls but otherwise very nice. You're probably too busy to paint."

Nate took in the room - clean lines, black leather furniture, and beige throw rugs on the gleaming wood floors. He had been busy but he hadn't ever planned to paint. What was wrong with white?

Then he realized she was just baiting him again and he inwardly rolled his eyes and kept his mouth shut. She wanted him to react but he was starting to see how she operated. She called him a fake? She wasn't any better than he was. This was how she kept him at arm's length, letting him into her life but not too close.

If he was being honest she was smart to do it. He wasn't a man that did "forever" with a woman. If she got too close she might get burned. He liked her and the last thing he wanted to do was break her heart.

"Exceedingly busy. Let me show you around."

She trailed after him as he showed her the kitchen and laundry room at the back of the house. His study was off of the living room next to the stairs and he ushered her to the second floor where there were three bedrooms - the master, the guest, and a spare. Paige would stay in the guest room that used the hall bathroom. She'd have it to herself. His bedroom had an ensuite.

She seemed most fascinated with the third bedroom that really wasn't a bedroom at all since there was no place to sleep. There was a long table that he used when he was packing for a trip but this space was mostly filled with his career memorabilia, including gifts his fans had sent him. Paige was currently studying a painting of Kai from the *Thunder* movies that he'd hung on the wall.

"This is amazing. A fan sent this to you?"

Nate was incredibly proud of his fans and the devotion they showed him. He'd lost a few after last year but most had stuck by him even when he didn't deserve it.

"Yes, I received that after the first *Thunder* movie. It's a good likeness, yes?"

She turned, an excited smile on her face. "It's almost a photograph. It really shows the complexity of the character too. Kai's playfulness but also his arrogance mixed with anger. You can see betrayal in his eyes but also hope."

"Hope?"

"Hope that someone will love him." She laughed and ran her fingertips over the edge of the frame. "Let's remember that I write romantic stories."

"Of course. You must have your happy ending."

"It's required. Why read a book otherwise?"

A myriad of reasons.

"Some stories don't end that way. In fact, most don't. *Romeo and Juliet* is a great love story but it doesn't end happily."

She snorted and made a face. "*Romeo and Juliet* is not a romance or even a great love story, Nate. It's two teenagers with a dramatic crush playing house. Six people die because of their antics, including themselves. That's not great love. That's stupidity. It might, however, make great theatre which is something Shakespeare was good at."

So *Romeo and Juliet* wasn't her favorite play. Noted.

"You like Shakespeare?"

He'd love to discuss it with her and lots of other books as well. Get a writer's perspective.

"He's okay," Paige shrugged. "I'm more of a Tennessee Williams kind of gal."

Nate had read several American writers as well and that was one he enjoyed immensely. It would be nice to have someone around that he could talk literature with. Most of his girlfriends called him a dork or a geek and changed the subject when he brought up books.

The doorbell pealed and Nate frowned, checking his watch. "It's eleven at night. Who could be at the door?"

"We'll never know until you answer it."

Cheeky woman. He liked her sarcastic and funny tone.

"Au contraire." Nate pulled his phone from his pocket and pulled up his security app before showing the screen to Paige. "There's a camera at the front door. I'll get your phone set up with this too in case you're ever here by yourself. I've had some close calls with some rather...passionate fans, you might say."

He loved his fans but sometimes they crossed a line or two.

"Stalkers. Got it. I read *Misery*, and that shit is not funny. At all." She squinted at the screen and looked more closely. "Is that Maxwell Hayes?"

He was and Nate had a feeling he knew why. Or at least he hoped so. Things were progressing exactly as planned.

"Just call him Max." Nate led them down stairs and opened the front door to his friend who he hadn't seen in months due to them filming on opposite ends of the world. They were good about texting and staying in touch but it wasn't the same. He'd make sure they had a couple of pints at the pub so they could catch up. Nate still owed Max a rematch at darts from last time.

"Nate, you're home. I hope you don't mind but I called your assistant to find out what time you'd be in."

So this wasn't a spur of the moment visit because the lights were on.

"I don't mind at all. Come in and meet Paige."

Max's brows went up and Nate realized his friend hadn't been expecting Paige to be there. He'd become quite protective of Nate since last year, constantly advising him about the press as if he hadn't had his own issues. Still, it was done out of care and concern so he appreciated it and didn't say anything except thanks.

Nodding stiffly, Max shook the hand Paige offered. "Nice to meet you, Paige. I'm Max."

No one could be formal and stuffy like Max and this moment was no exception. Paige darted a confused glance at Nate but smiled warmly despite the chilly reception. "It's nice to meet you too, Max. I must say that I am an admirer of your work."

What had crawled up Max's arse?

"Thank you." Max turned back to Nate, dismissing Paige rather rudely. "I hope I'm not interrupting anything."

Fishing for information, Mr. Hayes? Just what do you want to know?

"I was just showing Paige around and thinking we might order in a pizza before heading to bed. We're knackered after that long flight."

Well, he was anyway. Paige looked wide awake after her long nap. He'd warned her but she didn't listen.

He hoped that didn't become a habit.

Nate stole a glance at Paige and was surprised to see that far from being miffed or angry about Max's behavior, she seemed rather amused by it all. She was perched on the arm of his couch and watching the back and forth between him and his best friend with a smile playing on her lips.

Max looked at Paige and then back at Nate, sighing. "I actually need to speak with you, Nate. In private, if possible."

Nate was about to tell Max it would be impolite but Paige simply stood and waved them off. "Go right ahead.

I'll just avail myself of the facilities. I'll even fix my hair to give you extra time."

With her handbag slung over her shoulder, Paige disappeared into the powder room off of the kitchen which left Nate alone with Max. First things first.

"You were very rude to her, Max. I'd like you to apologize when she comes back. She didn't deserve that sort of treatment. She's a nice woman."

Max's eyes narrowed. "A woman who is spending the night apparently. How long is she here for? Is she moving in?"

Nate crossed his arms over his chest. "Max, why are you here?"

His friend exhaled noisily and pulled an iPad from his jacket pocket, touching the screen a few times before turning it so Nate could see. The photos were a tad blurry but anyone could see it was Nate and Paige boarding a plane at JFK. The caption was the usual crap.

Who is the mysterious blonde with Mason? Has he found a new love?

It was exactly what he'd been hoping for. He wanted a candid shot of them to make its way to the press so they could start slowly getting the public used to seeing them together. This was a solid beginning. Hopefully Garrett and Helen were already on top of things.

At the right time everyone would know he was involved with a smart, accomplished woman who liked to keep a low profile. And that was the plan. They would not be splashing photos of them kissing and holding hands on the front page of every tabloid. They'd go quietly about their business and let the press come to them. Mystery was the order of the day.

"So? Paige and I were at the airport. Is that why you came over here so late? To show me a picture in some gossip rag?"

"Nate, what in the hell are you doing?"

"I'm not sure what you're asking, mate. That's a photo of me and Paige boarding our flight back here."

Max flicked a gaze toward the kitchen but Paige was nowhere in sight. "Who is she and how did you meet? Jesus, how naive can you be? She probably had that pap at the airport waiting for you two. There are a lot of women that want to ride on your coattails after last year, Nate. Women who don't care if the publicity is good or bad."

Nate thought about stringing Max along a while longer but Paige would be returning soon and he was too exhausted anyway.

"It's a contract, Max." He held up his hand as his friend's face turned red. "Well, not an official contract but an agreement, really. All my idea. Believe me, Paige is about as innocent as you can get when it comes to publicity and PR relationships. It took three of us to convince her to do it and honestly I'm not sure she even likes me all that much, although I'm working on that and making progress."

Eyes wide, Max shook his head. "Then why did you do it, mate? What can this Paige do for you? Is she an actress?"

Nate shuddered at the thought. He was done dating actresses and models. No more.

He pointed to the doorway where she'd disappeared.

"That intelligent and lovely woman is none other than Paige Mitchell, the bestselling author. I'm going to play Flynn and also direct. In return, I'm helping her raise her profile so she'll have more leverage with the studios plus giving her a hand with the personal appearances. So please try and be nice when she joins us. She can be a pain in the arse but as of a few days ago, she's *my* pain in the arse."

CHAPTER
Eleven

SHE'S *my pain in the arse.*

Paige kind of liked the possessive nature of Nate's statement. She couldn't deny she was a handful of trouble with her smart mouth and snarky attitude. So far he'd done well dealing with her and even at this moment he could have denied her spot in his life but he hadn't.

Maybe the fucker isn't as annoying as I thought.

"I realize she's not my usual type, Max, but don't you see that's the beauty of this arrangement? There's no chance I'll fall in love with her so there's no way I can get hurt. Unlike last time, I'm in complete control of the situation. Because she's so new at this I call the shots."

Or he's even a bigger bastard than I'd ever imagined.

No chance? Ouch. That fucking hurt. She'd known it already, of course, but hearing it out loud still hurt. More than she'd expected. She pressed a hand to her chest where he'd shoved the imaginary dagger as if they were in some

Shakespearian tragedy. This was why she wrote happy endings. Shit.

There was also the little issue of him thinking he was calling all the shots in this showmance. Another cute little factoid about herself? She was a fucking control freak and this didn't sit well with her at all. She wasn't a pawn to be moved around a chess board and if he thought that was how this was going to work he was in for a huge shock.

Time to let them know I'm standing here.

"Gentleman." She entered the living room to see two tense men glowering at one another. "Have you finished your business or do I need to go upstairs and unpack to give you more time?"

Nate turned and smiled, although it didn't reach his eyes. "You're fine. We're done here. Max, do you want to stay for pizza?"

Max didn't answer immediately, his gaze running from Paige's head to her feet and then back up again. He was probably agreeing with Nate about how unlovable she was. Fan-fucking-tastic. So far this trip to London had been memorable.

That friendship with Nate wasn't looking too good either. She didn't like the people in her life to have hidden agendas about her.

Struggling to smile, Max shook his head. "I'm afraid I can't. I have an early meeting. Paige, it was lovely to meet you. I hope you enjoy your stay in London. I'm sure we will meet again."

"I look forward to it. So far this trip has been so very *educational*."

Brows pulled together, Max was at a loss but Nate

interjected smoothly. "It's always good to learn new things. Thanks for stopping by, mate. Let's get together for a pint this week."

"Yes, let's. Goodnight."

When Nate closed the door behind his friend, he turned to Paige with a big smile. "So, what do you want on your pizza?"

———

The pizza was inhaled, only bits of crust left in the box. Paige had consumed three glasses of wine which was one more than she usually allowed herself. She shouldn't have let the earlier conversation bug her but the longer she sat there the more her anger grew. Now she was on full blast and pissed the hell off. Who the fuck did he think he was? Was she getting played? Had she put herself into an untenable position?

Nate patted his stomach and folded up the pizza box. "That hit the spot. I'm exhausted. I think I'll head to bed. You should get some rest as well."

"I'm wide awake," she dead-panned. "I think we need to talk, my new friend."

"Maybe in the morn–"

"This won't wait. I think we need to talk about how you perceive this relationship working because if you think you're going to control everything you are sadly mistaken."

Venom dripped from her voice and Nate, despite his fatigue instantly went stiff, his spine straight as a board.

He wasn't completely stupid because he had the good sense to look a little afraid.

"Darling–"

Paige hopped to her feet and cut him off. "Don't even try and use that British bullshit charm on me, Nate Mason. I heard what you said to Max and I almost couldn't believe my ears. Am I just some dumb American pawn to you?"

Nate levered to his feet and reached out for Paige's arm but she knocked his hand away. His expression turned wounded but she wouldn't be swayed by the puppy dog eyes. She'd come too far to let some guy take her for an idiot.

"Of course not. But might I say that eavesdroppers never hear good of themselves. If you had come in a few minutes earlier, you would have heard me telling him how wonderful you are."

"Don't you dare try and turn this around on me. I wasn't listening in. I was coming back out here and you two were talking loudly. I'd have to be deaf not to have heard you."

Nate sighed and rubbed the back of his neck. "I'm sure it was hurtful to hear me say those things and for that I unreservedly apologize."

How sweet. He didn't regret saying it, but he regretted getting caught.

Paige rolled her eyes. "And I *unreservedly* don't give a shit. I'm not upset that you said I wasn't a woman you could ever fall in love with, asshole. That was something I already knew and that's why I told you that no one would ever believe this. No, what I'm upset about - make that livid - is that you're trying to control me. I've come too far to let some B-list actor with more than his share of self-esteem try to manipulate me. I'm in charge of my career, Nate, and I sure as hell won't be turning that over to you."

His mouth opened and closed a few times, his face a bright red. Finally he shut his mouth, his expression fierce with his lips a tight line and his brow furrowed. She thought he was about to speak when he whirled on his heel and stomped up the stairs. She heard the slam of a door a moment later.

Okay, that was interesting. She remembered reading somewhere that he didn't like conflict or confrontation or something stupid like that. No wonder he'd never had a relationship last. Getting mad was part of the deal and working it out was mandatory. Her suitcase was still by the door and she grabbed her laptop from her carryon before settling into the soft leather couch.

If she couldn't sleep, she'd work. It was the one thing that had been there for her all these years whenever things turned to shit. Her characters and their worlds. They never let her down and they never hurt her feelings. In that, she was always in control.

She wouldn't bother to unpack either. She had a feeling she wouldn't be staying. He'd throw her out in the morning.

CHAPTER
Twelve

THE NEXT MORNING Nate pulled on a pair of sweats and a t-shirt before padding barefoot out into the hallway. He hadn't slept well at all, tossing and turning most of the night. He was deeply ashamed of his behavior and embarrassed that he'd acted like a three-year-old having a tantrum. When he'd stomped up those stairs last night, his one thought was to keep from saying something he knew he would regret later. Because there was a secret he was keeping from almost everyone in his life, except very close friends and family.

He had a nasty temper.

When he was angry he tended to lash out at the nearest - usually quite innocent - person targeting whatever weakness he was aware of. With surgical precision he'd go after their deepest fears and insecurities, never thinking about the damage he was inflicting until the anger had passed and he had calmed down.

When Paige had called him fake she hadn't been far from the truth.

He also had to admit that he kind of hoped that Paige would follow him, come after him and make him talk. Because he had a temper he avoided conflict and confrontation like the plague but when forced he would eventually deal with the underlying issue.

A soft knock on the spare room door didn't get a response so he cracked it open slightly only to see that the bed hadn't been slept in.

Shit, had she left? Called a taxi and fled?

He wouldn't blame her if she had but he'd hoped to apologize this morning and clear the air. He liked Paige, and not in just a superficial way. She was smart, funny, slightly cynical, and always good for fun and a laugh. She was charmingly down to earth while somehow being highly creative. It was a fascinating combination and he'd be lying if he said he wasn't attracted to her, not that he was planning on doing anything about it. They were friends now and business partners. By the end of this coming year she'd know the real him whether he liked it or not, and when she did, it wouldn't matter if he was attracted to her.

Coffee. He needed coffee.

He was at the bottom of the stairs when he saw her, scrunched into some sort of pretzel shape on the couch, still dressed in the clothes she'd worn all day. Instead of being stretched out long ways she was balled into a corner, her laptop on her thighs and her head lolling to the left. She was going to be in a world of pain when she woke up.

Why hadn't she gone upstairs to sleep? Had she been contemplating her options when exhaustion overcame her?

Whatever she'd been planning to do he now had a chance to apologize and talk her out of it. Carefully, so as not to wake her, he lifted the laptop and placed it on the coffee table. His fingers had brushed her arm and her skin was chilled from the cool night air. Feeling even guiltier that she'd been cold and miserable all night, he grabbed the wool throw from the armchair and tucked it around her body. She stirred slightly and he froze but she settled herself again, snoring softly in her awkward position. He wanted to move her but he was afraid if he did she would wake up for sure.

Letting her sleep, he headed into the kitchen and started the coffee pot before digging out a couple of eggs. He normally ate eggs and toast for breakfast when he was home, and they hadn't discussed what she'd like to have in the morning. He'd be happy to fix her whatever she wanted when she woke up or take her out if she preferred to not eat his cooking. At this point he'd do just about anything to get back in her good graces.

He'd finished his breakfast and was pouring his third cup of coffee when she entered the kitchen. Looking incredibly adorable, her clothes and hair rumpled and her eyes slightly unfocused, she didn't say anything. She simply stood there in the middle of the room rubbing her sore neck, her gaze darting from the coffee pot, to the table, then to him.

"Hi," he finally said, not able to stand the silence any longer. "Coffee?"

She nodded and he poured her a cup but she didn't

drink it, sort of staring at it like she'd never seen a novelty mug before. This one said, "Have a Thunderous day."

Blinking a few times, she scrubbed at her eyes and yawned. "Cream. Sugar. Where...?"

He drank his black so he hadn't even thought of it. Great host he was. He didn't have any cream but he did have milk courtesy of his assistant who had stocked the refrigerator. He set the sugar on the counter and retrieved the milk from the door of the refrigerator.

"Is milk okay? I don't have any cream. I need to do some shop–"

"It's fine." She reached for the milk. "Just as good."

After stirring her coffee she sat down at the table, sipping her beverage and not saying a word. Clearly she was waiting for him to apologize and he intended to do just that. The sooner he got it over with the better.

"Paige, I'd like to apologize for my behavior last night."

Whatever response he was expecting, the one he received wasn't it.

"Thank you. I'd like to apologize too."

Now that he hadn't expected. What exactly was she apologizing for?

He sat across from her at the table, his hands clutching the mug. "That's very sweet of you but I'm not sure that you have anything to apologize for. Me, on the other hand..."

The corners of her lips turned up and she gave a tiny snort. "Yeah, because I'm such a sweet and innocent little lady in all this. Butter wouldn't melt in my mouth. That argument last night took two of us, Nate. So let me say it again...I'm sorry. I hit you below the belt and it wasn't a nice thing to do."

His mouth was hanging open. He knew it was and yet he was having a hard time closing it so he could form words. She'd apologized. A real, live, sincere apology. He hadn't been on the receiving end of those very often in any of his relationships. She was truly sorry and regretful. She'd admitted her mistake.

What the ever-loving hell? It was beyond his comprehension almost.

"I–I–I don't even know how to respond. Of course you are forgiven. That goes without saying."

Her eyes narrowed and her smile grew wider. "Okay, here's where the rubber meets the road, my new friend. It's time to drop the Prince Charming shit. I pissed you off last night and probably hurt your feelings too. Don't let me off the hook here because I'm not going to let you off when my turn comes. Hold yourself and people accountable. It's the only way to have an honest relationship."

"You get very preachy sometimes."

The words were out of his mouth before he could stop them and he waited in horror for her to light into him but she laughed instead, nodding in agreement. "Honey, you have no idea. You better hope I didn't pack my soapbox. Now...I meant what I said. Talk to me. Honestly this time."

He was far too used to pushing down any honest emotions, his public persona had taken precedence for far too long. Frankly, how he felt wasn't important much these days. Paige had been right on the nose when she'd called him fake. It was hard to allow himself to feel the hurt and anger he'd bottled up last night and he wasn't sure he wanted to let it run wild.

"I have a temper," he admitted to buy some time. "I hit out at people where they're the weakest. Then I've hurt them and I can't take it back."

She took another sip of her coffee, contemplating his words. "Then you would be exactly like most people in the world. I did it last night too. Now, is there anything you want to say to me?"

His gut churned and he gripped the handle of his coffee mug tightly until the knuckles were white. What she was asking of him was something he wasn't sure he was even capable of. He'd played a part for years now to the point where it was second nature. Controlling himself and giving the fans what they wanted was paramount. Their love and approval hinged on him being what they wanted him to be.

"It hurt me when you called me fake," he suddenly blurted, not sure where that came from but now that the pump was primed he couldn't seem to shut up. "It hurt when you called me a B-list actor even though that is actually what I am. I want to be so much more, you know. I take pride in my work and the way you said it made it sound like I was some no-talent hack that got lucky."

If he thought she was going to be upset, he was wrong. Her expression was perfectly serious and she waited for him to continue, content to let him have his say without interruption.

"I'm sorry about trying to control you, Paige, but frankly I'm not sure what to do with you. You keep coming at me with your honesty and your no-nonsense attitude and after years in Hollywood I don't know how to deal with someone I'm not supposed to screw over. You've called me out on my behavior more in the last three days than all the women I've dated in the last five years combined. And it rubbed me the wrong way because you're right. There's a part of me that does think that I'm entitled to be a prick. That if I work hard I should get whatever I want even though I know intellectually that's crazy. I feed off of the approval and attention and I'm not proud of that either. There's a part of me that takes the applause and adulation as my due and I'm ashamed of that. And yes, that includes women too."

Dear God, he'd gone too far, revealed too much. How could she even begin to like or respect him now knowing he was such a loser? As soon as she finished her coffee she'd be sprinting for the front door and never look back.

Which was sad because he was really starting to like her. Like-like. Deep down and for real. She was the most genuine person he'd met in years and he'd probably just scared her off.

"Apology accepted. Now let's move on."

Confused, he shook his head. "But what about the hubris I admitted to? Doesn't that make you hate me? Think less of me?"

She smiled and calmly sipped her coffee. "Nate, everyone likes approval. Do you think I don't care about the reviews I get on my books or whether they sell? Hell, I love it when people tell me they enjoyed my stories. It's okay to like approval. It's not okay to do anything to get it. There's a difference. As for women, well, look at you. It's the butt crack of dawn and you look like you stepped out of the pages of fucking *GQ* while I look like something the cat threw up on the carpet. I can see why you expect female attention. And your career..."

She paused and seemed to be looking for the right words. "I get that your ambitious because I'm ambitious too, Nate. Do you think I would have agreed to the schedule of social engagements this next year if I weren't? Think about that. Think about how brutally ambitious I have to be to go so far out of my comfort zone that I agree to a PR contract with you. Just sit on that thought for a while and let it ruminate. You'll see that I understand what you did last year. I get it. You've worked hard and by God, you want your reward. You played the Hollywood game and lost but you could have just as easily won. It was a roll of the dice. I'm not judging you, handsome. You're judging yourself."

He sat in his chair, stunned, not knowing what to say but he should have known Paige would come to his rescue. "As I said I accept your apology. But I have to be honest—I was upset as well last night."

He opened his mouth to apologize again but she held up her hand. "Let me get this part out because this is not going to be easy. I don't like being angry with people."

Having her mad at him wasn't high on his list of favorite things. He might have only known her a short time but he found he wanted her friendship and approval.

"You don't have to do this."

She smiled and took a deep breath. "Yes, I do, but it's not easy. You see, I'm kind of fake too. Isn't that a slap on the ass? I accused you of being something I am as well. Most of the time I'm me, but sometimes I'm just a scared little girl. I've been alone a long time, even before Noah died, really. I had to be strong and in charge, always in control because who else was going to take care of my family? There was no one to take care of me though. I always came last and I got used to it but that doesn't mean I enjoyed it. Every now and then I simply get terrified when I see all the things I need to do and be. My readers expect one person, my son another, my agent, my assistant, and now you. You, Nate, expect me to save your career and goddammit, I want to do that for you but I'm scared. I'm terrified that I'm going to fuck this up and you're going to end up hating me for it and that's something I don't think I could take because I really like you when you're not being a jerk."

Tears were falling down her face now and Nate rushed to the other side of the table, kneeling in front of her to brush at her cheeks. He was a complete and total asshole and he'd do whatever it took to make it up to her.

"That's why what you said hurt, Nate. I think you're a good person and then I hear last night that you want to control all of this and me. I can see that you are a kind man most of the time, and you aspire to be better and so do I, although we sometimes fall short. So when you said you were calling all the shots, it hurt. It hurt a fucking lot that you thought I was just some dumb female without a brain in her head, and that's one of my fears. Maybe I'm just not good enough and eventually everyone is going to figure that out."

Imposter syndrome. He knew it well.

His chest was tight with an unfamiliar emotion and he pulled her from the chair, crushing her body to his only to hear her squeak with pain. He instantly released her and couldn't stop the smile as she rubbed at her neck and shoulders.

"I think I slept wrong or something."

Moisture had gathered in his own eyes and he wiped at it with the back of his hand. "Look at the pair of us. We're a mess."

"We are. Someone call in Dr. Phil."

Laughing, he pulled her into his arms, carefully this time before dropping a kiss on the top of her head. "I'm so sorry I hurt you. I didn't really mean it and the moment I said it I regretted it. I don't think you're dumb or a pawn or anything even remotely like that. You're a smart and beautiful woman and I'm lucky that you're my partner in crime."

She scrubbed at her cheeks and smiled. "What do we do now? I think we just became close friends."

He couldn't agree more. She was okay with him. All of him. The good, the bad, the even worse. She'd accepted it and it was...

Not going to be easy. They had a rough if not impossible road ahead of them and he was who he was. Relationships - even platonic ones - in the spotlight were fraught with potholes and she was new to all of this.

"I think I should make you something to eat. Then I plan to give you a neck rub since it's all my fault that you slept in a ball on the couch."

He'd been holding her for the last few minutes but finally her hands slid around his middle too. They were in each other's arms and it shouldn't feel this good. Red alert. He dropped his arms and stepped back to catch his breath and get a little perspective. If she thought his behavior was strange she didn't say anything.

"You know that eating makes me happy so cook away," she giggled. "While you're doing that I'll take a shower."

He started breakfast as he heard the water turn on upstairs. They'd weathered their first real argument and their bond was stronger for it. He'd showed her a side of himself that he rarely let people see and she hadn't run away in horror.

It would be a challenge to strip away the veneer he'd so carefully put in place one brick at a time until there was hardly anything left of his true self. Did he even want to do it? It felt safer behind this wall, much more secure. Paige said she wanted to see the real him, but then they all said that.

And then they left.

CHAPTER

Thirteen

PAIGE DIDN'T GET her neck rub. She had a phone interview with a magazine and Nate had a business meeting with his agent and then one with Garrett right after. He'd promised her a raincheck but she would probably let him off the hook. It had been her own stupidity and stubborn nature that led her to fall asleep on the couch. With the way she liked to write at night after everyone else was in bed, the chances were good it was going to happen again.

Nate did promise that he was all hers for the evening, so once her interview was done she headed out to the shops to pick up some supplies for dinner. She loved to cook and Nate had said he'd pretty much eat anything.

Time to put that statement to the test.

He'd sent her a text saying he was spending the afternoon with his trainer so she expected him to be tired and hungry when he came home. She planned a hearty meal of pot roast, garlic mashed potatoes, baby carrots, and homemade dinner rolls with honey butter. It was a quin-tessential comfort meal and after what they'd been through the night before and then this morning she felt they deserved it. The weather in London was also much cooler than she was used to in Florida and there was something about chilly weather that made her think of home cooked meals with simple ingredients.

Remembering his sweet tooth, she also made chocolate lava cakes to serve with the vanilla ice cream she'd picked up. Her stomach was growling with anticipation and the kitchen smelled divine when he walked through the door just a little after five, sweaty and disheveled but smiling.

"What is that heavenly smell?" he breathed, following his nose to where Paige stood behind the kitchen counter buttering the tops of the risen dinner rolls. She didn't want to put them into the oven until the last minute. He sniffed the air again. "I smell garlic and beef."

"Honey, you're home," she giggled, waving the fork in the air. "I thought I'd cook dinner. It's pot roast, mashed potatoes and something chocolate for dessert. Do you want something to drink? Water? Beer?"

He had his nose practically in the pan of mashed potatoes.

"Darling, I'm awash in an ocean of my own sweat and I smell like an old pair of shoes. I'll take you up on that offer as soon as I've scrubbed up. But everything you said sounds wonderful, especially the pudding."

"Dessert," she shot back with a grin.

"Pudding," he corrected with a stern tone. "You're in London now. I'll turn you into a Brit yet."

"Good luck. I'm red, white and blue, baby."

He pulled his clinging t-shirt away from his well-muscled torso. It was easy to see why women loved him. "Technically our flag is also the same colors. How long do I have before dinner?"

"We can eat pretty much whenever you're ready to. These rolls only take about twelve minutes."

Nate grinned and headed for the stairs. "Perfect. I'll be down in ten to set the table and open the wine."

She watched as he bounded up the stairs two at a time, his strong thighs easily propelling him forward. If she'd tried to do that she would have ended up in a broken heap at the bottom of the stairs. Her knees at forty weren't what they were at thirty. Or twenty. Add in that she could barely walk and chew gum at the same time and it was a recipe for disaster.

It was nine minutes later when he joined her, smelling better than the dinner. His cocky grin as he opened the wine told her in no uncertain terms that he knew exactly how he smelled. The man appeared to be a master at gaining a female's attention.

What always struck her so vividly when she was with Nate was his zest for life. He was enthusiastic about everything, whether it was good weather or melt in your mouth pot roast. Tonight it was the latter and he kept making yummy noises with every bite, joyfully helping himself to seconds.

"Leave room for dessert, handsome. You don't want to miss out on chocolate lava cake with ice cream."

He sniffed the air again and smiled. "Don't worry, I wouldn't miss it. Everything is just so delicious. I love a home cooked meal that I didn't have to make. I can't thank you enough for this, love. I usually just bake a piece of fish or chicken. I never go to this much trouble."

"I told you I liked to eat and cook. Besides, it totally makes it worth it to see you enjoy your dinner this much."

Nate shoved a mouthful of mashed potatoes into his mouth. "Enjoy it? I love it. This is the best meal I've had in ages."

Now that she didn't believe.

"You eat in five-star restaurants all the time and I'm supposed to believe that this meal is better? I'm afraid I don't but thank you for trying."

Looking affronted, he placed his fork on the plate. "I mean what I say, darling. I get tired of eating out no matter how well prepared the food is. I miss sitting at a table and eating at home with someone I can talk to. That's you, by the way."

"I was hoping, unless you'd invited Max over to finish what we didn't eat."

Nate's face fell at the mention of his friend. "He still owes you an apology."

She would not come between two old friends even if one was kind of a prick.

"That's between me and Max. I don't want you to give him shit about it. You said you'd grab a pint and you should."

Nate picked up his fork and resumed eating. "He shouldn't have treated you that way."

"You're absolutely right and I'll deal with that next time I see him. You know, he has an absolute right not to like me. It would be nice if we became friends but it might not happen."

"It's fine if you don't become friends but he was quite rude to you. That I won't stand for."

"He's kind of a pompous ass from what I saw."

"He's really not. He's lots of fun and a good person but he has trust issues with people he's just met."

She hadn't seen any sign of that but she'd take Nate's word for it.

"Except to female fame whores."

She needed to change the damn subject.

"He has his reasons, I assure you. He's had some bad experiences with women. Been burned badly. I don't know for sure but it's my opinion that his wife married him for his Hollywood connections."

That was horrid but it still wasn't an excuse to be an asshole. She'd met crappy people in her life but that didn't mean all of them were shit.

"So I was thinking about something we could do while we eat our dessert."

"Pudding."

He was persistent, she'd give him that. He had that in common with Flynn.

"Whatever. Anyway, it feels like you and I have had a rough day and I thought it would be nice to turn that around. I was thinking maybe we could get to know one another by sharing some good memories. You know, things that make us happy. I can't see how that would start another argument and if we're going to pull off this fake romance deal I think we should know more than that we both like pot roast."

Stroking his chin, Nate nodded. "I think that's an excellent idea. There's so much about you that I don't know yet."

She'd been dying to ask him a question. "When you were thinking about this...did you have me checked out? Investigated?"

His cheeks took on a reddish tone. *Bingo.*

"I did. I had to be careful that there wasn't anything in your past that could come back and bite us both in the ass."

She stood and took their empty plates to the sink before pulling the chocolate cakes out of the oven. "That makes sense. I'm not upset or anything. Mostly I'm curious. What did you already know before you met me?"

"I knew that you'd been married and lost your husband to cancer. I knew that you had a teenage son who was starting an Ivy League school. I knew that you were active on social media and close to your fans. You like dogs and chocolate. You don't like the cold, which is something that baffles me because I love it. You watch old movies and spend a lot of your time reading. You enjoy the beach and Disney. You have a few close friends but tend to keep others at arm's length. You're a workaholic just as I am and you've produced an amazing amount of stories in the last ten years. You have no arrests, no speeding tickets, and you've never bounced a check. You were an excellent student in school and played on your high school tennis team. I think that's about it."

That was enough.

"Wow, all of that information is floating out there? I guess if you studied my Facebook account you could get a lot of that." She placed the plates of cake and ice cream on the table and handed Nate a fresh fork. "I have veneers on my front teeth and I birthed Jason by C-section. Looks like your guy missed a few things."

"Duly noted." Nate took a big bite, closing his eyes in ecstasy. "This is poetry on a plate. I'm never letting you go even if I have to tie you to a pipe in the basement to keep you here."

He looked like he was kidding. Maybe.

"That wasn't creepy and disturbing at all. Just so you know, if I don't call Carrie in the morning she'll send out Scotland Yard."

Carrie had flown back to Florida from New York and was taking care of a few marketing items for Paige.

"Tell Carrie you are in good hands."

They agreed to wait on the getting to know one another until they'd finished eating. Nate was done first, of course, and began loading the dishes into the dishwasher. When Paige finished she tried to help him but he shooed her out to the living room. She settled in front of the fireplace where it was toasty warm. She was having trouble getting used to these temperatures.

"Are you still cold, love? We can wrap you in that wool throw."

Nate handed her a glass of wine and sat across from her on the rug, their knees brushing momentarily.

"I'm fine but I will admit this cooler weather is really different. Carrie said it's about ninety degrees at home. I'd be in the pool right now if I was there."

Nate leaned forward, his expression earnest. "I'm glad you're here."

Swallowing the lump that had taken up residence in

her throat, she took a sip of her wine to give herself time to get herself together. He could shake her up all too easily and she couldn't allow that to happen. But it wasn't about him per se. She'd simply been without a man too long, that's all. She'd have this reaction with any guy that paid her as much attention.

Keep telling yourself that.

"So how about we start with a simple one. Happiest Christmas memory."

Nate's smile widened and his blue eyes lit up with happiness. "That's easy. I was seven and I wanted a new bicycle. A blue one with silver stripes. My mum and dad spent the entire autumn telling me I wasn't going to get it."

"But you did, right?"

"I woke up before dawn Christmas morning and ran downstairs to find it next to the tree, a red bow on top. I think I was the happiest boy in England that day. Even though it was terrible weather, I put my coat and boots on over my pajamas and rode that bicycle outside until my parents dragged me back in."

She loved watching him tell that story. "That's lovely."

"What about you, love? What's your best Christmas memory?"

"I don't have one." She held up her hand when his smile fell. "No, wait. It's not bad. I don't have one specific story. I have many memories each year of my whole extended family getting together on Christmas Eve. We eat, sing carols, play games, and open a few presents. No one year sticks out in my mind but every year is something I look forward to. For one evening we all stop our busy lives and spend time as a family. That's what I'll always remember."

The smile was back. "That sounds wonderful, although I have to admit I was hoping you'd spend Christmas here with my family in England."

For some reason Paige didn't want to talk about meeting his family and spending a holiday with them. That denoted something...serious. They didn't have that type of relationship. It wasn't for real and meeting family made it seem that way. At least to her.

Did he even realize what he was saying?

"I don't know where I'll spend Christmas but I do know one thing. My son will be there. We're never apart on that day."

Nate set his wine glass on the hearth and then reached for her hands. In the past three days she'd learned that her new friend was touchy-feely. He liked to hug, put his arm around her, hold her hands. It wasn't a bad thing but it was something she wasn't used to. Noah hadn't been someone given to outward displays of affection. "Your son is always welcome, darling. I hope that Jason and I can become friends too."

That was an interesting thought. How would these two men get on?

"There's time for that. Maybe you can talk when I Skype with him? Introduce yourself. He knows that I'm here with you."

"I'd like that," Nate said quietly. "Okay, next question. Let's go for the ultimate happiest memory. You first."

This didn't take any thought at all.

"The day Jason was born. Hands down. You go through

this incredibly painful process but you get this perfectly beautiful little human at the end."

Nate smiled at her answer and continued. "Best career day."

"You didn't answer the ultimate question yet," Paige chided him with a giggle. "You can't ask another question before you do."

"Just answer this one and then I'll answer both of them. Go on."

This one took a little more thought. She'd worked hard and been fortunate.

"I guess the first time I made the New York Times Best-seller list. I didn't expect it but it happened. It was the beginning of so many good things for me. I hope I never take it for granted and not get excited. I don't want to be jaded. Any book could go out into the world and flop."

"You're talented, Paige. I doubt that would happen but I agree about not being jaded. I want to keep my enthusiasm."

She nudged him with her sock-covered foot. "Your turn. Best career day."

His entire demeanor changed in that moment. His spine straightened, his gaze narrowed, his smile became less playful and more...evil? Sexy? All of a sudden Nate was gone and replaced by...

"When I reached my true potential and became an outlaw turned bounty hunter." Even his voice had gone deeper to portray his famous character Kai and it sent a shiver up Paige's spine. Although she had reservations about Kai as a person, he was sexy as hell, and he was hitting all her buttons. If he'd been in the black leather costume she would have fallen at his feet. Luckily for her, he quickly slipped back into Nate mode and laughed at his own antics like it was a big joke. All the while she was sitting there barely able to breathe. She made a mental note.

Don't let Nate do Kai. Too dangerous.

"Well, that's certainly one of my favorite roles you've done."

Understatement of the year.

"I'm arrogant enough to ask if there were any more. Have you seen anything else?"

"*Ice Blue Lovers.* I really liked Alex."

"That melancholy sculptor. I should have known. You would have tried to nurture him back to happiness. Don't deny it. You like to care for people, I can tell."

Maybe. Sometimes.

"You didn't answer the ultimate happy question. What's your absolute happiest memory?"

He frowned, his lips pursed in thought. "I'm not sure about that one. Can I take a raincheck and think about it?"

"Yes, but I hope it's because there are too many to choose from and not because you can't think of even one."

Laughing, he raised one of her hands to his lips, kissing the knuckles. He was such a ham, always onstage acting for an audience. Even if she was an audience of one.

"I have many to choose from and I want to do so wisely. I promise I will answer. Now I have another question for you."

"Shoot. I'm all ears."

He leaned forward, still holding her hand, his gaze

intent. "Are you ready to do this? Are you ready to give it your all?"

Her heart stuttering, she had to stop and think about what "this" was because for a moment it sounded like something else. Something far more sweaty and carnal, but then she realized he was just talking about the showmance. It was a good question though. They'd been living in their own little cocoon for the last few days and that couldn't last. She'd committed to this and for a damn good reason.

"Go big or go home, handsome. I'm all in."

Let the games begin.

CHAPTER
Fourteen

PAIGE WANTED to see London but Nate's idea of important landmarks was interesting. She'd made a list that she thought was normal for a first time tourist. Buckingham Palace. London Tower. The Eye. The London Dungeons. St. Paul's Cathedral. The Tower Bridge. Big Ben. Madame Tussaud's Wax Museum. His list was slightly different.

Funky bookshops off the beaten path that she'd never be able to find again on her own. Lively pubs. The Globe Theatre. Plays at the West End. A visit to Shakespeare's tree on Primrose Hill. Out of the way cafes on narrow, winding streets. This was Nate Mason's London and she couldn't wait for him to share it with her. She felt privileged that he was showing her his favorite places, and she had a strong feeling that he didn't do this often, if ever. It was like getting a glimpse into his soul.

Today they'd visited his favorite bookstore in Hampstead and now she was laden down with books, her arms aching. Nate had offered to help her carry them but his own hands were overflowing, so she'd thanked him graciously but refused. His lips had tightened slightly but he'd simply nodded in return. She was beginning to get the idea that he liked to help. In the last three days she'd lost count of the cups of tea he'd made for her. She wasn't a huge fan of hot tea but she didn't want to hurt his feelings. He was sweet to do it and she'd drink every damn cup even if it killed her.

"It's just up the street here," Nate said. "Best fish and chips in the area. I hope you're hungry." She gave him a look and an eye roll that had him laughing. "What am I saying? Of course you're hungry, and tired too, I would expect."

The time zone had hit her hard in the last few days, her sleep cycles completely topsy-turvy with the five hour time difference. Her nap on the flight here hadn't helped but the sedative always made her tired. Nate had subtly suggested taking another one to help her sleep but she was adamant that she'd get on London time naturally. Unfortunately, that was taking longer than she'd expected. Yawning was becoming her most frequent mode of communication.

"My arms hurt. My feet hurt. And my stomach is empty," Paige declared with a grin. "I want food and then I want to curl up in a chair with all my lovely new books."

He opened the pub door for her and found them a booth near the back. "Then you're not upset that we spent the afternoon in a bookstore instead of seeing Big Ben or the Tower Bridge? I promise we'll go to those soon."

She slid into the booth and gratefully dropped her

books onto the seat next to her. "Are you kidding? I could spend many hours in a bookstore and never get bored. Besides, we did the Tower of London this morning and that was cool. I think this was a good plan. My list in the morning and your list in the afternoon. I really liked that cafe you took me to yesterday and I'm excited about the play we're going to see tomorrow night."

"Don't forget Shakespeare's tree tomorrow. If the weather is nice maybe we can have a picnic in the park."

The waitress came and took their order. Fish and chips, of course. When it came to her drink, Nate urged Paige to try the cider while he had a pint. She wasn't a big beer drinker, especially the dark ones that he favored but a refreshing cider sounded perfect. The waitress hurried away, leaving them alone.

"So have you thought of an answer for the question yet?" she asked, shrugging off her jacket that was still damp from the light rain they'd walked in earlier. She'd quickly learned that it rained in London. A lot.

His brows pinched together. "I don't know what you mean. What question?"

"Absolute happiest memory? You said you needed to think about it. It's been three days."

"I'm still thinking."

He was obfuscating and delaying and just generally being a shit. "Just how many memories are on the list, handsome? Is it two, ten, a million?"

That grin she was becoming so fond of spread across his face. Not quite like his character Kai, definitely less evil but certainly as mischievous. "I'd say it's a few less than a million. This might take quite some time. Are you in a hurry?"

"I answered, I just think you should too. You can always change your mind later. I'm not planning on chiseling it in a stone tablet."

His expression turned to mock horror. "You're not? How disappointing. I was so looking forward to having my thoughts immortalized for all mankind for generations to come."

The waitress brought their drinks and Paige sipped the cider, the flavor exploding on her tongue. This would do quite nicely. Yes, indeed.

"You've got a healthy ego, I'll give you that," she taunted. "I, personally, would never assume that the future would be interested in the least in my thoughts."

Those blue eyes twinkled in challenge. "And yet you've written many books that you've had the audacity to publish. Are you sure you don't think that, darling?"

Okay, she'd give him this one.

"Touché, Mr. British Smart Ass. Now are you going to answer or not?"

"Not," he replied cheekily, his tongue peeking out of the corner of his mouth. "But I will when I decide. Now how do you like the cider? Did I guess right?"

She'd managed to drink down about a third of the large glass. "It's excellent. Great choice. I could drink this all evening."

"Steady on. That has alcohol in it, love."

A pleasantly warm feeling had invaded her bones. "I damn sure hope so. That rain made me cold. Now talk to me about Flynn."

His face lit up at the mention of her favorite character. "Have you written the script yet?"

"I have a rough draft but I thought you might want to read it and let me know if you had any ideas of your own."

His mouth fell open in shock. "You'd be open to that?"

"Sure, you're going to play him and direct the film. Sometimes it's good to get other people's ideas about my characters. They see things that I can't because I'm too close."

He straightened and took a drink of his beer. "Well then, I think that Flynn needs to be heroic but I also think we need to show his flaws to the audience. I don't want Sara to fall for him in spite of his flaws, I want her to want him because of them."

Paige nodded, already on the same wavelength. "Because she wouldn't want a perfect man. That would be boring as all hell. She'd want someone to fit her like a puzzle piece. Where she's deficient, he fills the void and vice versa."

Nate's face was red with excitement. Or alcohol. She wasn't sure and it didn't matter anyway. He slapped the table and practically bounced up and down in his seat. "Exactly. If she's high-strung, he's more laidback. If he's disorganized, she helps keep him on time."

"If he has trouble loving himself, she teaches him how easy it is to do by openly showing her love for him in as many ways as possible."

That statement seemed to throw him. The smile was gone and his brow was furrowed in thought. "How would she do something like that?"

Shrugging, Paige's brain whirled with the possibilities.

"There are lots of ways. Big gestures like romantic dinners and surprise weekend getaways. Little everyday things to show someone you care like giving them a foot rub. Or even something as stupid as watching a movie that you don't want to see but they do, so you do it anyway without a fuss. What have women done for you to show how much they love you?"

He didn't get a chance to answer. Their meals were placed in front of them and she embarrassed him by asking for ketchup for the fries, knowing full well they called them chips over here. He'd shuddered and hidden his face when she'd made the request so she'd lightly kicked him under the table letting him know she didn't appreciate the dramatics. She was American, dammit. The look on the waitress' face was enough, thank you very much. The woman had practically turned up her nose at the very thought but had dutifully brought the offending condiment.

It was just ketchup, not a nuclear warhead. Paige ordered a second cider at the same time.

They both dug into their meal with gusto, the food disappearing at a rapid rate along with her second cider, which had absolutely warmed her up from the inside. She was in a terrific mood, laughing and joking with Nate who was being silly and doing impressions of famous people. He was amazing with the different accents and expressions. He had so much more talent than just some guy who played a villain and rode a motorcycle.

Popping the last of her fries into her mouth, Paige reached across the table to pilfer one of Nate's but he caught her in the act and she got a playful slap on the knuckles for her effort.

"Keep your hands on your side of the table," he said with mock seriousness. "Eat your own food."

She stuck out her lower lip in a pout. "I can't believe you won't share your fries with me. I'm starving here."

"You might have had more chance if you'd called them chips."

Paige blew him a raspberry. "Boo on you. I'm an American and that means fries. They're damn good ones though. I'll just order more if you won't share."

"There's a bakery a few blocks down. I'll buy you a cupcake instead. Chocolate. Fudge. How does that sound? In fact, I'll buy you as many as you want."

Chocolate was one of Paige's major food groups.

"Deal, handsome. I'm holding you to it. As much chocolate as I want."

He looked worried. "I just want to make sure you don't overdo it and end up sick to your stomach. Then you'll blame me and London and want to go back home to Florida."

She waved away his concerns. "I never overdo anything. I'm a boring single mother that used to drive in carpools and volunteered for the PTA. The most exciting thing I've done in the last several years is..."

"What?" he prompted when she didn't finish her sentence.

Pathetic and sad. That's what she was. "I can't think of anything exciting that I've done."

"You must have done something."

Rubbing her chin, she had to think hard before it came

to her. She must be tired because her brain was all fuzzy and muddled. "I know. Meeting you and being in this fake relationship. That's the most exciting thing that's happened to me by far."

It was the truth.

"Things are going to get much more exciting when we start to go to parties and premieres together. I think you'll enjoy it."

A shuffle of feet and some girlish giggles drew their attention. Four young women, maybe in their early twenties—Paige was terrible at guessing ages—stood by their table with starry eyes and hopeful smiles.

The tall and pretty blonde standing in the front of the group appeared to be in charge.

"Hi...um...I'm Crystal, and these are my friends Dahlia, Fiona, and Gwen. You're Nate Mason, aren't you?"

Paige had vague memories of being that young but it had been a long time ago and another world away. By the time she was twenty-two she'd been a wife and a mother. She hadn't had a cell phone with a camera either and apparently these ladies wanted selfies with Nate.

"I'd be happy to." Nate grinned and stood, his arms outstretched. "Who's first?"

Crystal was first, her arms going around Nate's waist and her cheek pressed to his. Just when the photo was taken and he was pulling away, she quickly turned her head to give him a kiss on the cheek. Good for her. Paige never would have had the courage, although poor Crystal was beet red after her brazen action. Each girl took her turn, gushing about his character Kai. Then the questions began flowing. When was the next movie out? How many more times would he play Kai? Did he get to keep the black leather costume? Did he do his own stunts?

That last one had Paige stifling her laughter behind her hand. Nate had preened as he'd replied proudly that he did almost all his own stunts on the motorcycle and off. *Almost all* being the important words there. Then he told a story about laying the bike down during a scene and ending up at the emergency room getting a few stitches in his leg, even name dropping other stars while he spoke. The girls listened in rapt attention, their mouths open in awe at his bravery.

What in the ever loving hell was he doing?

Now that the young women had their photos, hugs, stories from the set, and even kisses on the cheek, Paige assumed they'd leave. No such luck. Somehow they'd crowded the booth so that she was pressed against the wall and they were front and center with Nate, who by the way hadn't even glanced in her direction for a good twenty minutes.

He liked his adoration.

Signaling the waitress again, she ordered another cider and settled in for the long haul while texting Carrie back in Florida. Even hero worship had to get old after awhile. She'd still be here when he was done.

CHAPTER
Fifteen

NATE HADN'T MEANT for his fans to hang around that long but it always seemed to get awkward at the end when they needed to go back to their life and he had to get back to his. Most of them were fine once they had their selfies but a few - like these young women - found multiple reasons to stay. Until it crossed the line into rude territory.

They'd monopolized him so thoroughly he'd completely ignored his charming and beautiful dinner companion and that was something he'd have to apologize for. He doubted she was used to anything like this and he hoped she wasn't too upset.

The girls finally drifted away rather reluctantly, leaving him alone with Paige. Her cheeks were quite red and his gut tightened with fear. Obviously she was livid with anger at his behavior and he needed to smooth this over right away. Things had been going so well and he didn't want to ruin the new friendship they were forging. She'd become important to him in a short period of time.

"I'm so sorry, love. I didn't mean for that to go on so long and I apologize profusely. Please forgive me."

She blinked a few times and then nodded. "Okay."

It couldn't be that easy.

"Okay?" he queried cautiously. "You're not...angry?"

"Does that happen a lot?"

She'd been with him for several days now so she should know the answer but he replied anyway. "Not often but sometimes. Once again I apologize for how long that went on. It's usually not like that. They get their pictures and that's it."

Staring at the door where the young women had exited, Paige turned back to him. "They didn't want to leave you. It looked like you were enjoying yourself though. It's always nice to meet fans as long as they're not creepy stalker types. Those girls looked pretty harmless."

Her words had come out slightly slurred and that's when Nate realized there were three empty cider glasses in front of her. When had she ordered and drank the third? It must have been while he chatted with the females.

That's why her face was red. She wasn't mad, she was drunk.

Inwardly berating himself for not paying enough attention to what she was doing, he waved the waitress down and asked for the bill. He had to get her home before she passed out right here in the pub. From what he could tell, Paige wasn't much of a drinker but even if she had been, three hard ciders would put anyone her size under the table.

"Love," he said, trying to get her wandering attention back to him. Her gaze was all over the place and she appeared to be having trouble focusing. "We need to get you home."

Smiling, she easily nodded in agreement. She was rather sweet when she was in her cups.

"That sounds like a good idea. Let's go home. I'm sort of tired."

"We've had a big day. Do you want me to carry your books, darling?"

She'd already slid to the end of the bench and slapped a hand over her mouth, giggling like a schoolgirl. "I forgot all about them. I would have just left them here."

Way too much to drink. Now that she was giggling she couldn't seem to stop. She really was adorable when she was like this but she probably wouldn't appreciate him saying so. He reached over the table and snagged her heavy bag. There was no way she'd be able to carry them in her inebriated condition. Holding a bag in each arm, he stood and nodded toward the door.

"Are you ready to go, love?"

Giving him a big smile, she stood for only a moment before going straight down and hitting the floor, smack on her delightful bottom.

Bloody hell.

She was giggling again as he raced to set the bags down and see if she was alright. A cursory inspection showed nothing broken but her rear end was probably going to be sore tomorrow.

How in the hell was he going to carry her and the books too? Fuck, this was all his fault. If he hadn't been strutting for those fans, she wouldn't have had a chance to drink that third cider. Son of a bitch. He needed her to get on her feet before they attracted any attention. All he needed today was for someone to take their picture and have it end up on Instagram or Snapchat with the words "Nate Mason with his drunk date." Paige would be mortified.

Still giggling so hard she could barely speak, she let him lift her to her feet and hold her there, leaning her up against the side of the booth.

"Stay right there and don't move," he commanded through gritted teeth but she wasn't really listening, instead chattering to herself about topics that didn't seem to go together. At one point while he was rearranging the books in the bags she mentioned Flynn and a knight in shining armor. Always Flynn, never him.

"Okay, we're going to try this again, love," he said, the two bags hoisted under his one arm so he could half carry her home. He was glad he was in excellent shape because otherwise he might have to abandon either her or the books. And he loved his books. But he liked Paige more.

"Are we leaving?" she asked in a breathy voice. "We were having so much fun. Is there dancing here?"

Jesus, she wanted to dance? Who was this Paige Mitchell? He might have to give her too much to drink more often. He was going to love reminding her of this tomorrow.

"Sorry, love, no dancing. Now you can take my arm and lean on me while we walk home. Can you do that for me? Take my arm."

Her head whipped around, taking in the surroundings as if this was the first time she'd seen it. "Can we go somewhere to dance? I want to dance, Nate."

Think fast.

"We can dance at home, darling. You and me. Now take my arm like a good girl."

She was looking at him as if she didn't believe him. "You promise?"

"I promise."

Now take my fucking arm before the other one falls off with all these fucking books.

Instead of taking his arm, she pressed close and wrapped her arm around his waist, which actually was even better. It might slow him down slightly walking but he was sure she'd stay upright, which at the moment was a major concern. He couldn't have her falling to the pavement on the way home.

It took damn near forever to get back to his house.

First, Paige had to wave and say hello to everyone they passed, luckily getting hellos and indulgent smiles back from the amused onlookers. As far as he could tell, no one took their picture. Second, she was rather unsteady on her feet and the tuneless song she insisted on singing didn't help as she also seemed to want to dance to it as well. By the time they reached his gate, he was ready to leave her on a bench and come back for her when she sobered up.

No more alcohol for Paige Mitchell. Ever.

It was with immense relief that he dumped the books on the floor next to the door and then helped Paige to the sofa where she landed with glee, laughing and bouncing up and down. At that moment she didn't look like a serious writer or the mother of a teenager. She looked like a sweet, happy child without a care in the world. She looked...beautiful...and innocent, and his heart ached as he took in the sheer delight in her expression. He'd had fun with her today. More fun than he'd had on any date in recent memory. Maybe longer.

No, no, no. This is not the moment for a casual shag. It might be fun while I'm doing it but tomorrow it would be a whole other story. She wasn't the type to have sex and have it not mean anything. Not like me.

"Thank you, Nate," she said shyly, looking up at him from under her lashes. Dear God, was she flirting with him? How much was he supposed to endure today?

"You're welcome. Maybe we should get you some black coffee."

Anything to get her to sober up faster but she was already shaking her head.

"I don't drink it black. But I am tired. I think I need to lie down."

"Excellent idea. You should lie down."

Holding out her arms to him, her lower lip pushed out, she gave him a hopeful look.

"Will you help me? I'm not very steady on my feet. I may have had a bit too much to drink."

A bit?

"You had three hard ciders, love. You should have stopped at one."

Throwing her arms apart, she grinned. "Too late."

"Yes, it is. Now let's get you upstairs."

He helped her to a standing position and she walked fairly well to the stairs but that's when things went awry. She couldn't seem to navigate the up and down motion that she needed to climb and between the stumbling and the giggling, he lost his patience. Swinging her up in his arms bridal style, he carried her the rest of the way, setting her gently on the bed in the guest room.

"Do you need help taking your shoes off?"

Falling backward onto the mattress, she shook her head. "I'm good. I'm just going to rest my eyes for a little while."

She was going to pass out and he needed to check her regularly to make sure she didn't choke on her own vomit. Cider paired with fish and chips might make another appearance this evening.

"You do that. I'll come back in a few minutes and check on you. I'll also put a water bottle next to the bed. You'll be thirsty when you wake up."

He was almost to the door when he heard her struggle to sit up. "Nate? Can you come back for a minute?"

No good deed goes unpunished.

Turning back, he sat on the edge of the bed next to her, but far enough away that they weren't touching. "Is there something you need? Do you feel sick?"

Reaching up, she placed her soft hands on either side of his face and pressed a chaste kiss to his chin, which was as far as she could reach as tiny and drunk as she was. "Thank you for taking care of me."

His throat tightened and his heart sped up at her nearness. Breathing in, his lungs filled with her scent - vanilla, rain, and something unique to Paige that made his head spin slightly as if he also had had too much to drink. His jeans were suddenly far too tight for comfort and if he wanted to keep his sanity he needed to get out of this room as soon as humanly possible.

"You're welcome." His voice sounded like a shovel

scraped over gravel and he had to clear his throat to continue. "You should get some rest now."

He helped her arrange herself on the bed, her head on the pillow and a light blanket thrown over her legs. Her eyes fluttered shut and her breathing evened out as he stood in the doorway watching her for a long moment before padding downstairs. A cup of tea would set things to rights. It was only a momentary attraction, nothing to be concerned about. He was a man and she was a woman. An attractive one. This wasn't unusual. But anything more than what they'd agreed to would be a supremely bad idea. Paige wasn't the friends with benefits kind of woman. She'd want a *relationship* and he knew how that turned out.

Out of habit his hands made tea while his mind was a million miles away thinking over the time they'd spent together so far. He'd had fun and frankly he hadn't expected to. Not that much fun anyway. He'd thought they'd be friendly but he hadn't expected the connection that was building between them. He liked her, he was attracted to her, and every day that he spent with her only made him want to do it again and again.

After the encounter with fans this afternoon, he was reminded of how he was wanted for one thing. Kai. They wanted to believe he was somehow like that character. They wanted Kai to date them, romance them, fuck them.

Paige didn't expect any of that. She simply accepted him as he was. Sometimes she laughed at him and it was probably deserved. She didn't have much use for the movie star lifestyle. She'd asked him tonight at dinner what women had done to show him their love and he hadn't answered. Hadn't known how to. He'd been in love a few times back before he'd become famous and those girls had done the usual things. Sex being the big one. Affection. Gifts. But if he really thought about it...

He couldn't think of one woman who had watched a particular movie just because he wanted to and hadn't made a big deal about it. Not one.

CHAPTER
Sixteen

GROANING IN PAIN, Paige buried her face in the pillow, trying to keep out the light that filtered through the curtains. Her head pounded, her mouth was as dry as cottonwool, and her stomach was doing Cirque du Soleil in her abdomen.

Where was sweet death when she needed it?

A quick inventory told her she still had all her limbs, although she wouldn't have been surprised if she'd woken up without a kidney considering there was a huge swath of last night she couldn't remember. Poor Nate. Paige had a tendency to get clingy when she was on the wrong side of alcohol. She'd been told that she liked to give hugs, kisses, and tell everyone how much she loved them. Some people were mean drunks; Paige was a walking Hallmark card.

Slowly - very slowly - she climbed out of bed, only noticing then that she was still dressed in the clothes she'd been wearing last night, including her shoes. Stripping down to her birthday suit, she crawled into the shower and let the steaming hot water run over her aching body.

My butt hurts. What the hell?

How she'd managed to bruise her tailbone was a mystery, one she wasn't altogether sure she wanted to solve. Had she pissed Nate off so much he'd had to spank her to get her to behave? Had she backed into a wall? Repeatedly and with force? Luckily nothing else seemed to be damaged.

Except her dignity, of course. That definitely had some door dings in it.

Once she'd scrubbed her hair, skin, and teeth, she wrapped herself in a robe and tiptoed downstairs, her hair still wet but at least combed into submission.

"There you are. I heard the shower so I made a fresh pot of coffee."

Pressing her fingers to her temple, she didn't even bother to look at him, heading straight for the coffee pot. He smelled freshly showered and probably looked like a damn...well...movie star. Shit, it so wasn't fair.

No eye contact for awhile.

"Thank you." She poured herself a brimming mug and then added cream and sugar. Even now she couldn't drink it black. "Um, listen, I'm really sorry about last night. I don't usually drink so much."

She heard coughing behind her but he wasn't sick, the Brit bastard. He was trying to cover up his laughing.

"Just which part are you sorry about, love? Was it when I practically had to carry you home along with all the books we bought? When you wanted to go dancing? Or could it have been when you kissed me? Is that what you're sorry about?"

Fuck and hell. In her inebriated state, had she given in to the physical attraction she'd been feeling? Nothing good could come from him knowing she thought he was handsome or sexy. Whirling around, she was forced to look Nate in the eyes. Those blue fucking eyes with the crinkles at the corner. He appeared to be amused by the entire situation and if she didn't think she might throw up she'd kick him in the balls.

"I kissed you?" she squeaked, clearing her throat and trying again. "I mean, I kissed you? That doesn't sound like me."

He stood and refilled his own coffee cup before answering, leaning his hip against the counter. When he was this close it reminded her of just how much taller he was. He dwarfed her by a foot, making her feel tiny and delicate. Two things she hadn't felt in a long time. "It doesn't, does it? You're always so prickly with me but I must say when you're drunk you're such a sweet thing. So nice and friendly. You kissed me...just here."

He pointed to the dimple in his chin and she exhaled slowly in relief. She hadn't laid one on his lips and propositioned him. Thank you, baby Jesus. She never would have lived that one down. A sloppy kiss on the chin wasn't exactly fantastic but it was much better than some of the alternatives.

"I tend to get that way when I drink. I am sorry, and I'm sorry that you had to drag me back here like that. Truly, truly sorry."

He reached into a cabinet and brought down a bottle of

painkillers. She almost kissed him again in gratitude. "You'll probably want a couple of these. Take them with a full bottle of water. That's an order."

She wasn't sure he believed her. "I swear as God as my witness I don't often drink like that and I am so very sorry."

He was looking at her with what appeared to be sympathy. "One cider would have done it. What made you drink three?"

Good question and one she'd thought about in the shower. "The first I drank because I was thirsty. The second I drank because the first was so good and warmed me up. The third I drank because the first and second were yummy and I was bored."

He bowed his head for a moment. "And for that I'm sorry. It was my fault."

She popped two of the ibuprofen and chased them with the scalding hot coffee, burning her esophagus and not giving a shit. "How is my stupidity your fault? Although if you want to take the blame I wouldn't object."

"Those fans," he reminded her. "If I hadn't spent so much time with them, you wouldn't have drunk the third cider."

Maybe, although this wasn't the first dumb thing she'd done in her life. Sadly, it wouldn't be the last. "We don't know that for sure. I really liked it and I might have convinced you and myself that I needed another one. As for those girls, I thought it was cute the way they were gushing about you and when that blonde got up the courage to kiss you. I wished I had had the guts to do that to my crush when I was her age."

He popped two pieces of bread into the toaster. "Who was your crush?"

"George Clooney, but then he was everybody's crush so I guess I'm not all that original."

Picking up her coffee cup, he placed it on the table and motioned for her to sit.

"Still, I am sorry about that. Most fans get their selfie and go but some do sort of outstay their welcome."

Wrapping her hands around the warm mug, she took in his worried expression. He thought she'd been so upset she'd drank herself stupid. "Seriously, I wasn't bothered. You seemed to really get off on it but I figured it would get old after awhile. I drank too much because I'm an idiot, not because I was upset with you. You're a fucking movie star. This goes with the territory. Now if you'd gone off and just left me there, well, that would piss me off."

"I would never do that," he said in that upper crust British accent she loved and hated so much. This morning she was in love with it again because it wasn't too grating on her already oversensitive hearing. "And thank you for being so understanding about my fans. Not many in my life have been so welcoming."

"I believe you. Now do you accept my apology?"

He placed the toasted bread on a plate in front of her. "I do. Eat your breakfast."

"No butter?" she said, wrinkling her nose.

"Dry toast will settle your stomach. Now do you accept *my* apology?"

"I do. Wow, we're getting this relationship stuff down. We should be in the couples Olympics or something. If we keep this up, the next year is going to be smooth sailing, my friend."

Shaking his head, he pulled a bottle of water from the refrigerator, twisted off the cap and handed it to her. "Let's not jinx ourselves. Now drink your water. We have a big day ahead of us."

She almost choked on her toast. He wanted her to leave the house?

"Big day?"

"The Shakespeare tree," he replied, rubbing his hands together with glee. He'd been talking about this goddamn tree for three days. "I'll pack us a lunch and we'll go later this afternoon. You'll love it."

He'd carried her drunk carcass over a mile from the pub with about fifty pounds of books too. The least she could do was go to the park and see this amazing, stupendous tree.

She'd smile about it too because he'd made her coffee this morning and given her painkillers. There was nothing in their agreement that said he had to take care of her when she did stupid shit.

He'd just been that sweet.

She only had one question for him.

"Nate, can you tell me how I hurt my ass?"

———

It was just a tree. A plain, ordinary oak tree on Primrose Hill. It wasn't even the original tree that had been planted in 1864 to celebrate the three-hundredth anniversary of William Shakespeare's birth. They'd replanted a replacement tree in 1964. She'd heard the entire story from Nate. Twice.

But the sun was warm and the picnic was good. Nate had packed some bread, crackers, and an assortment of cheeses. There was no wine and Paige heartily thanked whatever deity might be listening for that, but he'd packed two large bottles of water which she drank thirstily, still slightly dehydrated from last night's antics.

"This was a better idea than I thought it would be," she confessed after popping another piece of cheese in her mouth. "Thanks for bringing me."

His lips quirked up. "Don't pretend you were thrilled with the tree. Yes, even I know it's just a tree but it's what it represents that's important. But I am glad you're having a good time."

Sighing, she spotted Maxwell Hayes striding up the hill, looking right at them. "I was having a good time. I think that's about to go out the window."

Nate followed her gaze and grinned. "If he doesn't apologize, I'll punch him right in his pretty face just for you."

That made Paige laugh. "His pretty face? What about your pretty face? Don't you have a play or something coming up?"

"I have a photoshoot tomorrow so perhaps you have a point," Nate smirked. "You'll have to punch him yourself."

"Whatever happened to chivalry?"

Nate didn't get a chance to answer as Max was right up on them by then. Leaping to his feet, Nate greeted his friend cautiously, his jaw tense. Paige had meant it when she said she didn't want to cause trouble between these two but it looked like it was unavoidable. She was going to have to be the adult today.

"Hello, Max," she said, looking up and shielding her eyes from the sun. "Would you care to join us?"

Lips twisting, he glanced at Nate. "Do you mind, mate? I'd like to speak with Paige alone just for a moment."

Paige nodded her consent and Nate gathered up some of the paper plates and napkins. "I'll take these to the rubbish bin but then I'll be right back."

Max settled on the blanket next to Paige. "Thank you for speaking with me. Nate mentioned that you two were going to be here today and I thought it might be a good venue for an apology. I'd like to say how sorry I am for how rude I was that first night. It was unforgivable and I hope you can give me another chance. I'm told I'm not a bad chap when you get to know me."

She'd had time to think about that night. "You did it because you were worried about your friend. It's not a perfect excuse but it's a decent explanation."

"I really am sorry. I can see now how happy Nate is. You two seem good for each other."

She was shaking her head before he finished his sentence. "We're not together like that. We're friends, that's all."

Rubbing his chin, Max contemplated her words. "That's all good, of course, but Nate does like you. A great deal. He talks about you constantly. He's very proud of you."

"I'm proud of him too," she said defensively. "Doesn't mean that there's a romance brewing here. We're helping each other, nothing else."

Nothing else. Nada. Zip.

"If you say so. Nate is happy though, which bodes well for the next year. Looks like he chose well."

It had slipped her mind that out of all the women Nate could have fake-dated he'd chosen her. It was a weird kind of honor.

"So far, so good. I do accept your apology, Max. I'm sure you're a nice person and that we just got off on the wrong foot. Well, maybe."

His grin was lopsided. "Maybe?"

Smiling, she spied Nate jogging up the hill. "Or maybe we'll hate each other's guts when we get to know each other better. At this point anything could happen. I think the most important thing is that you and Nate stay friends no matter what. I vow right now that even if you and I can't get along that I will never stand between you and your friend."

Coming to a stop right in front of them, Nate's gaze darted from Max to her. "Kiss and make up?"

Laughing, Max stood and brushed off his jeans. "We made up. We thought we might save the kiss for when we're alone. Thank you for giving us a moment. I need to be off. See you at the photoshoot tomorrow."

Without a look backward he was off, leaving Nate and Paige by themselves. Crouching down, Nate began packing up their food.

"He's in the photoshoot as well?" she asked, watching his retreating figure disappear in the distance.

"He is," Nate confirmed, closing the basket with a flourish. "It's a fashion shoot for a designer who I cannot name but you'll be able to see tomorrow."

A grin spread across her face. "Are you going to wear a suit?"

Damn, he looked fine in a suit.

"I don't know. It's up to them. Why?"

She stood so they could fold up the blanket. "No reason. What do you have planned for us tonight?"

They'd decided to see the play another time when she was feeling better. He'd given the tickets to his neighbors who had almost cried with gratitude. Apparently they were hard to get seats.

"I thought we could watch a movie or something. Even order pizza later if you're hungry. Do you like *Jurassic Park*?"

Not at all. It scared the shit out of her. There were dinosaurs in a kitchen.

Creepy velociraptors. In. A. Kitchen.

"We can watch that," she said, not voicing her fears. He was smiling like a little kid, excited about the prospect of dinosaurs and a pizza. She couldn't harsh that buzz.

"Really?" His blue eyes lit up with joy. "Are you sure?"

"I'm positive, handsome. Dinos and pepperoni."

For a movie star he was easy to please.

CHAPTER
Seventeen

THAT SENTIMENT APPEARED to be patently false the next day as Paige watched Nate being fussed over by a stylist, a hair dresser, a makeup artist, a photographer, and two photographer assistants, in addition to Nate's own publicist, Garrett.

Nate was in his element, all eyes focused on him. The females flirted and he flirted right back in that smooth as silk tone that made panties dissolve. The women wanted him and the men wanted to be him and two hours into the shoot, Paige wanted to vomit. He wasn't acting like himself. He was acting like...?

Kai.

Jesus, it hit her like a freight train going a hundred miles an hour, knocking the breath from her body. Arrogant, evil, cocky, sexy, flirty, and smolderingly hot. That summed up the Kai character and as much as Paige might love to watch the films, it was hard to watch him be that person when she knew that he wasn't anything like that.

Probably. He was an actor and he could have been fooling her all along but she didn't think so. Being Kai at times was necessary, she was sure. But this was a simple photoshoot. He'd played other parts, although they weren't as well known. Was being in character so important?

She didn't know and she couldn't watch any longer. The sweet man she'd spent time with was long gone and she missed him. Watching this was like slowing down and rubber-necking a car accident on the side of the road. She shouldn't watch but she couldn't stop either. Better to go back to the house and pretend this never happened.

Standing and tugging her purse strap over her shoulder, she marched over to Nate, who was in deep conversation with Garrett. She hated to interrupt but just leaving without a word would be rude.

"Um, excuse me. Nate? I think I'm going to go on home."

Brows pulled together, he looked unhappy with her declaration. "Leave? But why?"

She glanced at Garrett, who was watching the exchange with great interest. "This has been really interesting to see but I've thought of a great idea for a book and I absolutely must write it down immediately. You understand, right?"

He couldn't argue with that, although it was looking like he was going to try. "It's just a few more hours, love, then I'll take you anywhere you want to go."

"I need to get it down right away before I lose the idea," she pressed on. "I need to go now. I'll just take a taxi."

One of the female assistants appeared at Nate's elbow. "Nate, the lighting's fixed and we're ready for you."

He gave her that smile. The Kai smile that made a woman feel like she was the only one in the room. Which made Paige feel like she didn't exist at that moment. She didn't have any right to be jealous of a girl Nate was only smiling at but she couldn't help how she felt. She was indeed jealous and sitting here for two or three more hours sounded like cruel and unusual punishment.

"Darling, I need to get back to work. Are you sure you can get a taxi? I can call a car service."

She didn't want to wait. "I'm positive. I'll be fine. Have fun and I'll see you at home."

Leaning down, he brushed his lips over her cheek, sending a rush of heat through her body all the way to her fingertips.

It doesn't mean a thing. He did it because there were people watching.

"Please be careful and text me when you get home."

She promised and hurried toward the exit just as Max was coming back in from making a phone call. "Leaving already? Is Nate's part done?"

"I'm going to head back to the house while he finishes. I have some things I need to do."

Max frowned and looked over her shoulder where Nate was posing in an industrial setting, complete with pipes and tools.

"Does Nate know you're going?"

These British gentleman weren't going to let her go without a fight. "He does and it's fine. Have fun."

Darting past him, she didn't dare look back. This was her issue. Hers and hers alone to deal with. She was being petty, jealous, and she didn't like it at all.

She was falling for Nate Mason, and her feelings definitely were not returned.

————

Nate let himself into the house quietly in case Paige was taking a nap. She'd been agitated when she'd left the photoshoot and he'd been worried and distracted all afternoon wondering if she was alright. She'd been checking her mobile, so perhaps she'd received bad news? He didn't buy her story about a book idea that simply had to be written down at once. He'd seen her talk into her phone, making a recording when something for her latest novel came to mind.

The familiar tap-tap of her fingers on the keys of her laptop echoed through the house and he followed the sound up to her room where she was lying on the bed in her favorite pajamas, the computer balanced on her thighs. She didn't hear him at first and that gave him a chance to study her when she wasn't aware.

Fully engrossed. Total concentration.

That's how he would describe Paige when she worked. Even in a room with the television on and him talking on his phone, she managed to drift off somewhere where the world simply melted away and time didn't matter. Eventually she would shake herself out of the flow and look up at the clock in surprise but still seem rather proud of herself.

Right now there was a little wrinkle between her brows as she frowned at her screen. Her fingers flew over the keys and every now and then the corners of her lips would curl up into an almost smile. Writing was not a serene activity for Paige. She was right in there with the characters, feeling their emotions and fighting their battles. Joy, anger, frustration, and sadness all flitted across her expressive features one after the other and he couldn't tear his eyes away. When she looked like this she was more beautiful than any supermodel or famous actress. Her brain was as much a part of her charms as her exterior and she had smarts in spades.

When she paused he cleared his throat. "Hello, love. I'm home."

Looking up from her keyboard, a smile spread across her face and it felt like he'd been punched straight in the abdomen. The effect she had on him without even trying was humbling. "Hey, I didn't even hear you. Did it go well?"

He entered the room and sat down on the chair next to the bed. "It did, although some of the clothes were a little out there."

An unladylike snort escaped from her lips. "They were hideous but you looked good. All the fan girls will be swooning."

The outfits were pretty awful. It was part and parcel of his life that sometimes he was dressed in clothes he thought were ugly and today was one of those times, but he'd stayed professional and tried to do his best.

"Is that why you left? You hated the clothes?"

Her gaze skittered away before coming back to rest on him. "I'm sorry about that. I know I was rude."

Leaning forward, he rested his elbows on his thighs. "That's fine. I was concerned though. Is everything okay?"

"I'm fine," she assured him with a little smile. "I just needed to get out of there."

"Because?" he prompted, holding her gaze with his own. "What happened today, love?"

Sliding the laptop onto the bed, she turned to face him, her legs crossed on the mattress.

"It was you."

Him? What the hell had he done? They'd been getting along great.

"Can you explain, please?" he asked cautiously, looking for any signs of disgust or anger. She appeared normal and happy.

She sighed heavily and nodded. "I'm not used to this movie star stuff, Nate. It's going to take me some time. It's just today...you weren't acting like the guy I've been getting to know. You were acting like..."

"Kai," he finished for her. "That's true."

If her expression was anything to go by, she was surprised he'd admitted it. "May I ask why?"

Easiest question ever. "Because, darling, that's what they want. Nate Mason, the man, is just a boring Englishman who likes Shakespeare and quiet evenings at home. Nate Mason, movie star, is much more exciting. He's like Kai, dangerous and sexy. I learned the hard way last year that he's what they really want. If I want to move my career forward I have to play the game."

"I like you better."

The words were said so softly he almost didn't hear them. So straightforward and to the point, just like her, and he felt that pain in his heart that he was becoming accustomed to. It was the overwhelming need to reach out but the even bigger fear of what that might lead to. So he didn't do it. Always the coward.

"Thank you," he replied soberly, deeply cherishing the compliment but not allowing his expression to give any of his swirling emotions away.

She plucked at the comforter, her gaze riveted by her toes. "You're welcome. Can I ask you a question?"

"You can ask me anything you like."

As long as it's not something about how I'm beginning to feel about you.

"Will you tell me your side of it? You know, what happened last year. All I know is what I've read."

The Incident. He hated to even think about it but it would always be there. It was time.

"I will but I need you to let me tell the whole thing before you ask me any questions. Can you do that?"

CHAPTER
Eighteen

ONE YEAR AGO...

Nate sipped his whiskey and relaxed back into the leather seat, watching the other partygoers. This was his first real night off in over three months and it felt glorious to be free. He could feel the beat of the music under his feet as the crush of bodies gyrated under the colored lights. He could smell the sweat and sex and booze. He'd been a good boy for too long. He wanted to cut loose and have some fun tonight. Dance too much, drink too much. Maybe even have too much sex. Celibacy was definitely not enjoyable.

Max drained his own glass and slapped it down on the table before leaning forward to speak. The music was so loud he had to either be close or shout. "I'm heading out. I told Alana I wouldn't be late."

Nate's brow raised and he chuckled at Max's worried countenance. "Is the old ball and chain cracking the whip, mate? The night is young and those two young ladies across the way have been eyeing us since we walked in."

One blonde and one brunette. Both curvy and buxom just like he liked them. They'd been smiling and playing with their straws, running their painted nails up and down as if giving him a preview of what they might do to his cock.

"I'm a married man," Max groaned. "A man desperately trying to save his marriage and you're not being much help. I came for a drink but now I'm leaving. I don't think you'll need my help anyway. They look like a sure thing."

Nate hated the way his friend was begging for scraps at his wife's table. He needed to have some bloody dignity. "She cheated on you, mate. I don't know why you didn't kick her out and get a divorce. She's not worth your time."

Scraping his hand down his face, Max shook his head in despair. "You don't get it. I took vows, Nate. Vows. Until death do us part and all that. Plus, I actually love her."

Nate slammed down his glass. "How can you still love that cow after what she's done? I can't believe she has the nerve to look you in the eye."

Max sighed as if speaking to a child. "You don't stop loving someone just because they've hurt you."

"I'll have that embroidered on a pillow," Nate sneered, taking another gulp and enjoying the burn in his belly. "Just stay and have another drink."

Max shook his head and stood, throwing a few bills down on the table. "That's for my share. Have a good evening." He glanced at the two girls still watching from across the room. "And wear a fucking condom for bloody's sake. You can't be too careful."

Nate had been careful for the past six months. Desperate to raise his profile, he'd been in a PR relationship with Stella Riley, America's latest romantic comedy sensation, and it had turned into an unmitigated disaster. The character Kai was well-known but Nate himself much less so. Add in to the mix a couple of bad box office movies, one right after the other, and he'd been terrified. His PR team told him he had to do something so he'd agreed to the contract. It seemed simple enough. Go places with her, be seen, get his picture taken. He had to pretend he cared about her, which at the beginning hadn't been all that difficult. He was an actor, after all.

The whole thing had been a non-starter from day one as few people ever believed in the coupling to begin with. Looking back, it was clearer. They'd had little in common. She hated Shakespeare and reading in general. She wasn't close to her family nor did she understand why Nate was. She liked bands he'd never heard of but mostly she liked drama that kept her name in the papers. She liked being seen and having her picture taken as often as possible. She always seemed to be embroiled in some mess, which was why she'd contracted with him in the first place. He was supposed to be a diversion and he'd served his purpose well. No one had been talking about her issues when they were talking about how pussy-whipped he appeared to be.

Whipped. That was ironic. He hadn't gotten anywhere near her private parts. Sure, he'd been smitten when they first met. She was charming and cute and she'd flattered him shamelessly. He'd enjoyed their first evening and he liked that she wasn't afraid to make the first move. But that's where it all ended. Before long he realized it was bait and switch. She'd never had any feelings for him and his hurt and disappointment meant little, if anything to her. This was all about business.

So he'd carried on the business and played his role to the best of his ability. He'd even sworn off sexual liaisons while the showmance was in progress. He didn't have to do it as long as he was discreet but while he'd been on a movie set it hadn't been that difficult.

But now he was free. He'd met with her yesterday and they'd come to a somewhat amicable end. Their PR agents would release statements tomorrow about how they couldn't make their schedules work but they remained close friends. Or some shit like that.

He was single once again.

It was in that spirit that he picked up his highball glass and walked across the room to meet those females. He was ready to cut loose tonight. The only question was whether to go with the blonde or the brunette.

"Ladies," he said with his most charming smile. He'd had the gap in his teeth fixed a few years before *Thunder* at the behest of his agent. "May I buy you a drink?"

The women glanced at each other and giggled. The brunette nodded and waved to the seat next to her. "That would be lovely, thank you. Would you like to join us?"

"Don't mind if I do. My name's Nate, what's yours?"

The blonde giggled again and did a little hair flip. "I'm Bridget and this is Lisa. We know who you are."

Of course. They wanted Nate Mason.

Lisa blushed red under the hot lights. "I'm such a big fan. I love Kai."

Scratch that, they wanted the leather clad bad boy.

The blonde leaned forward, her breasts pushed together for his perusal. "Kai is so much better than Haden. And that leather outfit is so cool. When he talks I just melt."

Nate picked up Lisa's hand and threaded their fingers together. "I'm broken and battered," he said in his best Kai voice. "But I'll protect you with my life."

Bridget and Lisa swooned. This was going to be easier than he'd thought. Since playing Kai, picking up women wasn't much of a challenge anymore. A few Kai lines and they were throwing their panties at him. Funny how before he was just a regular guy who got shot down like everyone else. He'd had good luck with the ladies but he'd never been any kind of Casanova. Now he could pick and choose.

Correction. Nate Mason could do that, not regular old Nate.

He ran his hand up Lisa's thigh and giving it a squeeze. "How about we go out and dance? Work up a thirst."

He planned to get very thirsty indeed.

———

"Christ, Nate!," Edward, Nate's publicist, was yelling and throwing his hands in the air. "You couldn't keep it in your pants? Do you have any idea what a shitstorm you've created here? You're getting crucified in every publication except the Farmer's Almanac and they might be next. Jesus, what were you thinking?"

Nate sat on the edge of the sofa cushion, his head in his hands, staring down at the polished wood floors of his home. A home that had become a prison. He couldn't leave his house without a phalanx of reporters and paps following him, shouting questions about being a cheater and a liar. Or better yet, they asked him about being a kinky bastard. Stella Riley was playing the victim and using this to keep her name in the papers. Along with his, and none of it positive. What should have been an evening that was nobody's business, she'd turned into a three-ring circus.

He looked up, defeat in his tone. "I was thinking I was going to get laid."

Nate's agent, Josh, sat across from him, watching the proceedings but saying very little. Something that Nate was concerned about. Usually Josh would chat and have a laugh or two but he'd been quiet, almost as if he didn't want to speak.

"Laid?" Edward paced the floor. "If you wanted sex we could get you an escort or something. Why didn't you come to us?"

"Because," Nate spoke more loudly this time. "I don't usually discuss my sex life with you or Josh. It's personal."

"Not anymore," Edward said grimly. "Everyone on this planet now knows you had a kinky threesome with a couple of girls you picked up in a bar. There are photos of you leaving the bar with them and going into a hotel. It's ruined your perfect gentleman image. An image I worked hard to craft, Nate. It's blown to pieces now."

Launching to his feet, Nate got into his friend and publicist's face. "Now wait a minute. I worked at that too. It's not easy to act like a goddamn Prince Charming every fucking minute of every fucking day. I can't even be in a bad mood, for fuck's sake. How I feel or what I want doesn't matter. So don't tell me that you're the only one who's worked here, mate. I'm the one that actually does the work around here. I'm the one that brings in the money, remember?"

"Knock it off," Josh finally interjected. "This isn't getting us anywhere. Nate, please sit back down and explain what happened."

Nate fell back into the sofa and shrugged. "It was just like any other night. I met a couple of girls. We drank and danced. Then we went back to their hotel room. I hope I don't need to describe what happened in detail."

"You're dating someone," Edward growled but Josh shook his head in warning.

"I am not," Nate replied succinctly. "She and I ended it the day before. Her people were supposed to get with you to write up one of those breakup press releases about how we'll always care about each other. Why didn't you do that?"

"Because I didn't know," Edward said defensively. "No one called me. And no one from their side released anything either. As far as the world is concerned you cheated on her. You cheated on America's fucking sweetheart. And not for true love, which they might have forgiven. You did it with a couple of girls because you wanted to have kinky sex."

"She's not the victim here," Nate said heatedly. "Why is she acting heartbroken to the paps? She doesn't give a shit about me."

Josh finally stood, effectively silencing both Edward and Nate. "I've made some phone calls this morning and I think I've been able to piece together what's happened. Let me explain."

Nate threw up his hands in surrender. "I would love someone to explain this because I have no idea why this is a big deal. I'm a grown man who had sex. Not front page news."

Walking over to the window, Josh looked out to the front yard where dozens of paps were camped out across the street. "Nate, I believe you. I believe that she told you she was ready to end it and that she would contact her PR team."

"Thank you," Nate breathed, giving Edward a scowl. "I'm glad someone does."

"But here's where it goes off the rails." Josh came to stand right in front of Nate. "She set you up so she would be the victim and garner all the sympathy. That's how she works. Those two girls were planted in that nightclub. She paid them to take you back to their hotel room and then give their sordid story to the tabloids the next day. Every dirty detail and there were plenty. The paps were tipped off and waiting for you to leave so they could get a photo of the three of you going to the hotel and then in the morning when you left. This was all a game to her, Nate. You were the pawn."

Anger warred with disbelief. She'd been cold but this was beyond the pale.

"No, that can't be right," he said faintly, the bitter taste of betrayal turning his world on its axis. "What evidence do you have?"

"I know some people who were willing to talk. Shit, Nate. Look what she did to the last one. He got caught with his pants down too. There's a pattern here." Josh turned to Edward. "It's your job to make sure that people see it. They need to know that Nate didn't set out to hurt her. That he was just blowing off steam after working for months. Everybody was an adult and it was all consensual. His relationship had already ended, not that many people believed it was real in the first place. Then for God's sake, change the fucking narrative to his work. His hair. His next play. Anything but his cock which has now been described in excruciating detail on Tumblr. Jesus, he's a serious actor who has played Hamlet."

Edward grabbed his phone and strode outside to start making calls, leaving Josh and Nate alone.

"You know you're going to have to fire Edward," Josh said gently. "He's bungled this from beginning to end and is in way over his head. He won't be able to dig you out of this but I know someone who can, if you're interested."

Nate's head lolled back onto the cushion, tears burning the back of his eyes. His life had gone to shit in less than twenty-four hours. All because he'd trusted someone in Hollywood.

"I can't fire Edward. He's not just my publicist, he's my friend."

Josh sat next to Nate on the couch. "Listen to me. You're my friend too and I need you to know that you're not going to have a career to publicize if you don't get ahead of this story and spin it. Hollywood isn't pissed off that you had a threesome. Frankly, that's pretty tame in their world. What they are angry about is your showmance wasn't believable and you exposed the PR games they play to the public. They don't like people to see what goes on behind the curtain. Already I've had several meetings and calls cancelled. You're losing jobs, Nate, and it's only been a day."

Nate shook his head, still deep in denial. "That can't be right. I'm up for the big franchise. It's what we've all been working for."

"It's history," Josh said bluntly, the news hitting Nate directly in the gut and sucking the air from his lungs. "It's over. Time to find the next big thing because you're not getting that job."

"Tell them I'll do an audition." Nate grasped at straws, anything. He wanted that part. He'd been counting on it and had been so close. "I can do it. Tell them I'll take a cut in pay."

Rubbing the back of his neck, Josh sighed. "There are other issues as well."

Nate sat up. This was the first he was hearing of this. "What other issues?"

"You're aging too fast. If you look at the first *Thunder* five years ago and now the third one, you look ten years older."

"Playing that last part was hard on me," Nate replied wearily. "But I'm in the best shape of my life. You know that."

"You've worked hard but you need a month of intensive skin therapy and a career makeover. You need to be looking at playing mature roles that match your skills and challenge you. You can't play a pretty boy biker or Romeo forever. You need to start thinking about going out and finding projects instead of waiting for them to find you. Take control of your career."

His stomach knotted and his chest tight, Nate tried to swallow the feeling of pure hopelessness that had taken hold of him. He had to right the ship. There was no choice in the matter. He was an actor and this was what he did. People depended on him for their livelihood and it wasn't like he was prepared to do anything else for a living. This was all he knew.

"Call your friend," Nate said simply. "I want to talk to him about his ideas for fixing this fucking mess."

Josh was already dialing his cell phone. "I can talk to Edward for you if you want."

Nate shook his head sadly. "I'll do it. It's my responsibility."

Josh clapped his hand on Nate's shoulder. "You're doing the right thing. We have to act now before you lose everything you've worked for."

Scraping a hand through his hair, Nate laughed but not with happiness. "You know, I just wanted to have some fun. I just wanted to celebrate my freedom. Now I'm more imprisoned than ever. I trusted those girls and why? Because they stroked my ego and told me how wonderful I was, something I sorely needed to hear. I trusted Stella too and she turned on me. Isn't that rich? I trusted the facade even knowing it wasn't any more real than my own. I'm a bloody idiot. I deserve this."

"You were just naive, and you weren't the only one it happened to. You're not alone."

That would be cold comfort as he repaired his damaged career. But he'd learned so much from this. It had been a painful and costly lesson.

He couldn't trust someone to give a shit about him. Not

really. Not Josh, not Edward, not her. Everything and everyone was fake and phony and the sooner he dealt with that fact the better. No one wanted Nate, the regular guy. They wanted Nate Mason, the movie star.

That's exactly what he would give them.

———

Six months later...

Josh pointed to two spots on the contracts in front of Nate. "Just sign here and here. Then it will be official. You'll be at the Donmar starring in *The Taming of the Shrew* early next year. This is going to be huge for your career, Nate. They think the tickets will sell out in minutes."

They were sitting in Josh's office, a posh building that overlooked the Thames. Nate scrawled his signature with a sense of relief and more than a little excitement. It would be good to get back on the stage again and out of the Hollywood spotlight. He'd tried to lay low these last months but working on a *Thunder* film and being invisible didn't exactly go together. Luckily his new PR guy, Garrett, had worked hard to rehabilitate Nate's image from a kinky philanderer to one of a serious actor who got caught in a situation he couldn't control. The best part was he was no longer referred to as *her* ex-boyfriend anymore. She'd moved on and so had the press. For the most part, they were only interested in Kai.

The public had also been forgiving and he'd found that most of his fans had stuck by him despite the lurid headlines. He'd lost a few but had picked up new ones who had never heard of him before and had watched his movies after seeing him dragged through the mud by Stella Riley. Garrett assured Nate that as long as he kept doing good work the public wouldn't care about his personal life.

As for Hollywood, they were slower to forgive. Punishment had to be meted out and his career was suffering. Josh was right. He needed to search for his own roles, but where to start?

Nate handed the contracts back to Josh, who tucked them into a folder. "Have you heard from Edward?"

Nate shook his head. Out of all the things that had happened, he felt the worst about that.

"Not since the day I told him I had to fire him. He said he understood but he hasn't answered any of my calls. I was hoping we could still be friends."

Josh sat down in his leather chair. "Edward knows enough about this business to know that someone had to fall on the ax. You had to make a public statement that you took this situation seriously. It had to be him, Nate. He got you into an untenable position and he couldn't get you out. If he's not talking to you I think it has more to do with his feeling that he failed you than any actual anger." Steepling his fingers, he seemed to weight his next words. "How are things with your family?"

Rolling his eyes, Nate groaned. "That is another complicated situation. Mum now knows all the dirty, naughty things her baby boy likes to do to girls in the sack, courtesy of the tabloids. It makes for a tense family Christmas. I've apologized a million times and they say they forgive me but I can't go back in time. Everything has changed."

"They love you, Nate. Of course they forgive you."

Nate laughed and palmed the car keys in his pocket. He needed to get out of here. Talking about this wasn't helping his mood.

"You know what Max said to me that night? He said that just because someone hurts you it doesn't mean you stop loving them. Do you think that's true, Josh?"

"I do. It sounds like you don't believe it, though."

He wanted it to be true more than anything.

———

The present...

"That's pretty much it," Nate said, barely able to look Paige in the eyes after the whole sordid tale. The mere thought that she might have seen some of those detailed articles about his sexual proclivities made him sick to his stomach. Most women wouldn't care or would think it was arousing to know so much about him. He doubted Paige was in either of those categories. She was a mother and how could she approve of his behavior? He was a kinky bastard.

"Lots of people have done worse than you did." She placed a hand on his knee and his skin burned through the thick denim of his jeans. "It wasn't like you were caught in a cheap roadside motel with a pound of blow, a bottle of tequila, and a couple of underage cheerleaders. Like you said, you were all adults."

"Hollywood wasn't mad about the sex. They were mad

that I didn't make the showmance with Stella look real. People didn't believe us as a couple."

Laughter bubbled up from Paige's full pink lips. "No shit. When I saw those first photos of you two I think I rolled my eyes so hard I sprained my eyelids. As a couple you made no sense whatsoever."

In his naïveté, he'd thought he could sell anything but now he realized they'd never looked right together. The party girl and the serious actor.

"You don't like her?" Nate questioned. "I thought all of America liked her."

"There is no way three hundred million people like her. Maybe some do, but I never bought that innocent as the driven snow act she likes to sell. Somehow she always seems to be in the middle of some mess and eventually you have to say to yourself, maybe it's her."

It was Nate's turn to laugh. "It is her. She loves that. But the whole thing taught me so much and now I know to give them what they want. Nate is just an ordinary guy, not exciting. They want bigger than life."

Rubbing her chin, she grimaced, her expression full of sympathy.

"I don't know how to tell you this, handsome, but you learned the wrong lesson."

CHAPTER
Nineteen

PAIGE STUCK her tongue out at her reflection in the mirror. Slim black jeans topped with a cream colored sweater. Simple jewelry and makeup. She was wearing her hair down tonight and she'd blown it into glossy waves that just brushed her shoulders. In deference to Nate's height she was wearing a pair of black boots that lifted her about three inches, which wasn't nearly enough, but it was all she could handle. Sober or drunk.

It was a mini-reveal tonight. A party with Nate's friends. It wasn't the public at large but in many ways this was more important. These opinions might actually be important to him and she wanted to make a good impression even if the relationship wasn't real. If they were his friends, she hoped they'd become hers too. A year was a long time for a guy's friends to not like a person.

"You look absolutely gorgeous, love. How will I keep the men away from you?"

That smooth accent never ceased to send shivers down

her spine and tonight was no exception. She was becoming addicted to listening to him speak and she'd be concerned about that if she didn't enjoy it so damn much.

"I'm wearing jeans and a sweater, handsome. Nothing special."

She'd been told the party was "casual, come as you are". He better not have been mistaken, although he too was wearing jeans and a button down shirt along with a black vest that made the outfit more than everyday but not too dressy. He'd gelled his curls slightly and hadn't shaved since this morning, leaving a lovely stubble that begged to be touched.

"You make nothing special look spectacular, darling. Everyone will know I'm the luckiest man on the planet."

She paused in applying her blush, the huge makeup brush resting against her cheek.

"Yes, you are."

He threw back his head and laughed. "I'm glad we agree. Now, are you ready to dance the night away with me?"

"Like it's 1999," she assured him with a laugh. "I've warned you though. What I lack in actual talent I make up for with enthusiasm."

Nate quirked an eyebrow. "It's going to be an interesting night."

"That's one way to put it. Might I say that you look very handsome this evening. Love the vest. Very British."

He touched the hem and grinned. "Waistcoat."

"Vest."

"Waistcoat."

Paige shrugged and reached for her lip gloss. "Either way you look like the movie star you are."

"Darling, what a sweet thing to say." He glanced down at his clothes. "Maybe I should wear the black button down?"

He was worse than she was, always worried about his outfit.

"That won't go with the vest and believe me, it's the vest that makes that outfit. Besides, we don't have time. We're already late."

"We'll make a grand entrance."

She rolled her eyes and took one last look at her hair. "And we all know how much I love that. I'm already nervous as it is. I'm meeting your friends tonight. I want to make a good impression."

"They'll love you. You don't need to worry about a thing."

"Who all is going to be there again? I know you told me once but I was a little out of it working."

"Not everyone can make it but the core group will be there. Mike and Amy, of course. It's their party. Max said he'd be there. Plus several people we've worked with at the BBC. Maybe a few more."

She turned toward him and took a deep breath. She could do this as long as Nate didn't stray too far away.

"Let's do this."

The evening was going quite well. Paige had met most of Nate's friends and they had been enthusiastic and nice. His friends didn't know their relationship was a showmance though. Except for Max, that is. Nate had assured Paige it was better the fewer people that knew the truth.

Speaking of Max... The British bastard was beginning to grow on her. She even danced a few times with him and found that he was pretty good. Everything was awesome.

"Another drink, love?"

They'd finished a slow dance that Nate had capped off with a twirl, making her a little dizzy. She'd learned her lesson from the night at the pub, however. "Thank you, handsome, but just soda. I'm going to freshen up in the powder room. I'll meet you by the food."

Nate chuckled as he headed to the bar. "Of course. Food. I should have known."

It didn't take long to take care of business in the powder room and she headed for the kitchen where the table was piled with food. Paige picked up a plate and began to fill it, wondering if she should try to make small talk but Amy, the hostess of the party, made it easy for her.

"Hey, we're really glad you could make it tonight. We've been anxious to meet you. Mike says Nate talks about you constantly on their morning runs."

That was news. Just what had he been saying?

"Really? Wow, I had no idea." Paige decided to keep it simple and true. She'd get all mixed up if she started lying to people. "Nate's a sweetheart and your husband seems like a terrific guy."

"Nate is a sweetheart," Amy agreed, helping herself to a cheese ball. "He deserves to find someone that makes him happy. Mike says that Nate is so proud of you. He brags about what a great writer you are. I have the first book in your Flynn series and as soon as I finish the one I'm reading I'm moving on to that one. I'm looking forward to it."

Nate was proud of her. *Proud.* It had been so long since she'd inspired that emotion in someone that wasn't either on her payroll or related to her.

"I hope you enjoy the book," she said sincerely. "Flynn is one of my favorite characters that I've ever written. Nate reminds me of him."

Funny how he hadn't until she'd spent time with him. Now she could see all the things they had in common.

"Then I really look forward to reading it." Amy popped a pretzel in her mouth. "I talked to Nate about this but he says he needed to speak with you before he committed. Once a month we have a movie night here at the house. Invite a bunch of people over, watch a couple of movies, eat food, and generally have a good time. It's next Wednesday night. Do you think you and Nate would like to come?"

Overwhelmed by Amy's warmth and welcome, Paige nodded in agreement. "I think that sounds fantastic. How do you pick the movies?"

Giggling, Amy rolled her eyes. "We do themes. One month it's monster movies like *Godzilla* and *King Kong.* Another month it's slapstick comedy or maybe teenage angst films. This month is classic black and white. Do you have any suggestions?"

"More than you probably want to hear. How about *The Thin Man* movies?"

"Dick Powell and Myrna Loy." Amy bounced up and down with excitement. "That's a wonderful idea. I love those but haven't seen them in ages. You have great taste in movies. Does Nate let you pick out what you're going to watch at home?"

"I'm happy to let him watch whatever he wants, although he's partial to *Jurassic Park* movies and they scare me a little. Those dinosaurs in the kitchen give me the willies."

"Me too, but I'm fine as long as I have Mike to grab onto in the dark."

Paige didn't think Nate would welcome her grabbing him anywhere at any time.

———

"She's a keeper and much too good for you."

Max's words weren't much of a surprise to Nate. His friend loved Paige's writing as much as he did, so admiring the woman behind the words wasn't a stretch. They'd had a rocky start but Max had apologized and Paige had accepted it, so things were looking up.

"Thank you for those kind sentiments," Nate growled. "It's not even real."

Max chuckled and ordered a beer from the bartender. "That's why you're an idiot."

"You don't know any more about love and relationships than I do," Nate said defensively, shoving his hands into his pockets.

"I won't argue that point except I do know one thing. Love is a good thing to have if you can find it. Sadly, I think marriage for me is not in the cards. I don't seem to have the best taste in women."

That was true. Everyone had warned him about Alana but Max had fallen head over heels and couldn't think straight.

"Stop thinking with your dick," Nate said bluntly. "That's your problem."

"That's every man's problem," Max shot back.

"Until they find the right woman."

"Is Paige the right woman, my friend? Women like her don't come around very often. Don't let your pride and stupidity get in the way of something that might be good."

Not that Nate would admit it out loud, but he'd been thinking along those lines. Wondering what a real relationship with her would be like.

"I'll take it under advisement," Nate said, not wanting to get into it tonight. The thoughts were still too new and personal. Like tiny buds in the soil, they needed to be nurtured to grow and blossom.

"Do that. My fans think I'm a very wise man."

Nate needed a cigarette. He'd quit a few years ago, only smoking for movie roles now, but he had a real craving tonight for some reason. He could get one from Mike who quit about every other month.

"Wise? That's a laugh. I should think about getting new friends. I'm going out for a smoke. I'll be right back."

After bumming a cigarette from Mike, Nate stepped out of the back door of the house, the cool night air hitting him right in the face. Leaning against the porch railing, he didn't turn around when the door opened again, too intent on finishing his cigarette.

"Can I get a light?"

Nate reached into his pocket and turned toward the voice. "Of course—"

Bethany.

He should have known she'd be here. She worked for the BBC and was a casual friend of Mike and Amy. She and Nate had dated a few years ago but it had ended when he had to be out of the country for months on end. She wasn't the type to wait around.

She looked the same. Long dark hair pulled into some side ponytail. Red dress that clung to her figure and showed off her long legs. Her lips painted crimson.

That mouth was smiling as she held up her cigarette, a well-shaped eyebrow raised in question.

"Hello, Nate. Can I have a light?"

He fumbled with the lighter but managed to light her cigarette without causing an incendiary accident. Bethany reminded him of Stella Riley. They both liked to play games and cause drama.

She inhaled and then blew out a puff of blue-gray smoke. "You look good. Haven't seen you around lately."

For good reason. He'd been avoiding her.

"Hello, Bethany. I've been working."

She smiled, leaning closer. He could smell the cloying sweetness of her perfume and instead of arousing him, it turned his stomach a little. What had he ever seen in her? Looking back, he barely recognized himself.

"We've missed you around here," she purred. "When are you going to do another project for us?"

He shrugged, taking a drag on his cigarette. "I don't know. I'll be tied up most of this year with a play. Maybe next."

Her fingers trailed down his arm and he had to steel himself not to snatch it back. "It was too bad about how we ended things. But it looks like we have another chance. How about we both get out of here and head to my place? We can order Chinese and reminisce about old times. I miss you, Nathan."

God, he hated being called that and Bethany had never listened when he'd complained.

He brushed her hand away and stepped back, throwing down his cigarette and grinding it with his heel. "I don't think so. I'm with someone."

It didn't take a genius to figure out what she was offering. That trip down memory lane included getting naked.

Instead of going inside as he'd expected, Bethany threw her head back and laughed, her cheeks going red. "Right. Nathan has a girlfriend. So what? Since when has that ever stopped you from having a little side fun? I know you couldn't have forgotten all the things we used to do together. Things I bet that little vanilla won't do. I saw you come in with her, baby, but you don't have to leave that way."

His fake relationship with Paige was better than the real thing with Bethany. Far better. With Bethany he constantly felt like he had to pretend to be something he wasn't, with Paige he could simply be himself.

"I'm not that guy anymore."

Maybe it would be more accurate to say he wasn't sure if he *wanted* to be that guy anymore.

"I find that hard to believe. Nathan, you will always be that guy. It's in your nature so don't fight it. Being tied down to one woman would only bore you. You may not sleep with me tonight but eventually you will. And if not with me, with someone. You love the excitement, the thrill. You're not the come home after a long day, dinner at six, and sex on a Saturday night kind of man. Leopards don't change their spots. Why are you trying to fight who you are?"

Sweat had pooled at the back of Nate's neck despite the chilly temperature. "That's not who I am. I've changed."

Snorting, she shook her head. "People don't change that much. You might think that it's all good now but what happens when you go on location and she's not with you? You think you can keep it in your pants for months? I always knew you couldn't and I understood when you needed to let off a little steam. I don't think she will. She'll hate you and then dump you."

His greatest fear. Being left alone. But Bethany only thought she knew who he was. She thought he was Kai when inside he was just boring old Nate. Wasn't he? After all this time pretending to be someone else had he turned into a character? Was there anything left of the man he used to be?

"You don't know what you're talking about. You know nothing about me."

Bethany stepped back, her brows almost to her hairline. "What are you going to do, Nathan? Get married and have a couple of kids and a dog? Is that what you want out of life? I don't think you do. It will only make you unhappy. You aren't the marrying type."

"You don't have a very high opinion of me, Bethany." Nate moved closer to the door, not wanting this encounter to go on any longer. "I can assure you that I'm not who you think I am. In fact, I'm rather boring and stuffy."

At least I think I am.

If his old girlfriend wanted to say more, she didn't. Instead she smiled and tossed her own cigarette away. "Then I wish you all the luck in the world. I sure as hell think you're going to need it."

Brushing by him, she went back into the party, leaving Nate standing in the cold all by himself lost in his thoughts and wondering if this was the opinion of all of his friends. Did they all think he was a philandering cheat?

Turning on his heel, he headed back into the party and grabbed a drink for Paige on the way. She was probably wondering if he'd abandoned her despite the fact he hadn't been gone for that long. He entered the kitchen and saw Paige and Amy talking animatedly. As he got closer, he could hear them more clearly. They were talking about movie night. He'd promised to speak to Paige about it but it had slipped his mind.

"Dick Powell and Myrna Loy," Amy said. "That's a wonderful idea. I love those but haven't seen them in ages. You have great taste in movies. Does Nate let you pick out what you're going to watch at home?"

Paige spooned some dip onto her plate. "I'm happy to let him watch whatever he wants, although he's partial to *Jurassic Park* movies and they scare me a little. Those dinosaurs in the kitchen give me the willies."

Nate's heart fell to his feet and then shot back up into his throat.

She'd said it herself. Little signs of love. She'd watched

a movie that he liked and she didn't. And hadn't once complained.

Did he dare take a chance? He was tired of being a coward.

He was tired of being alone.

His feet moved forward of their own volition and before he could take a full breath he was standing in front of Paige, stripped bare of the veneer he wore like an armor. He had hope but little else.

Her smile could have lit up all of London and he felt a warm glow flow through him. Only this woman made him feel this way. "Nate, we were just talking about movie night."

He didn't want to talk about movie night.

"I think we should go."

It barely even sounded like his voice but Paige must have understood his urgency because she didn't argue, simply placing her plate on the table and making a polite excuse to Amy. Tomorrow he'd apologize to his friends, but he needed to get this woman alone as soon as humanly possible. He'd told Bethany he'd changed. He didn't have to be someone he wasn't to make Paige care about him. He could be himself and not be so obsessed with his career. Tonight he would tuck his ambition away and bring out the romance.

CHAPTER
Twenty

PAIGE HAD no idea what was going on. One minute they'd been having a lovely time at the party and the next Nate was practically dragging her out of there as if they were being chased by demon dogs. Since she'd become chilled during the walk home, he'd tenderly placed her in front of the fireplace, tucked a wool throw over her legs, and made hot chocolate. He was at his best when he was caring for someone.

Tension between them built as they sat on the floor, facing one another and sipping at the smooth cocoa. He didn't say much, simply watching her closely, his gaze, soft as a caress following her every move. Unsure as to what was happening, she was beginning to feel self-conscious and when she was nervous she babbled.

"So the party was great, huh?"

Awkward.

He placed his mug on the coffee table. "It was alright."

Help me here, Nate. I don't know what to say or do.

"Is that why you were in a hurry to leave? You weren't having fun?"

He took the cup from her nerveless fingers and set it aside while his large hands wrapped around her knees, his touch sending electric sparks flying through her veins. He pulled her toward him until their faces were inches apart, his warm breath teasing her flesh. She could smell the fresh tang of his skin and feel the heat from his body. His blue eyes were dark and his pupils blown wide.

He was looking at her like she was something special. Her heart shifted into high gear and her breath became shallow, her emotions a tangle of hope and fear. This couldn't actually be happening. Could it?

Please.

"I brought you home because I finally have the answer to your question."

She could barely move her lips to form words. They'd gone numb. "Question?"

"My happiest memory?" he prompted with a gentle smile, his fingers tightening on her knees. "I told you I needed to think about it."

Swallowing hard, she nodded, baffled by the turn the conversation had taken. "I remember."

"My happiest memory is the first time we kissed. It was magical."

Wait. What? It was there.

In his eyes. What I hadn't even dared to hope for.

Her lips curved into a smile and butterflies began to take wing in her middle. This was no time for fear or doubt. They'd been leading up to this since the moment they'd met.

"We haven't kissed."

Yet.

"I can fix that right now."

Yes. A million times yes.

Paige didn't know how she'd waited this long. She had assumed kissing Nate would be exciting and wonderful. That he would be skillful and ardent, a master of technique with all the women that threw themselves at him.

And he was. But...

It was so much more. It started out tender, sweet, and almost tentative, as if he was waiting for her to end it, push him away. One of his hands cupped the back of her head, holding her gently in place while the other traveled down her torso to her hip, leaving a trail of heat in its wake.

When his tongue swept her bottom lip she opened to his explorations eagerly. He tasted like chocolate and wine and Nate and she couldn't get enough. His kiss deepened and became more passionate and demanding as they slid to the rug, she on her back and his body hovering above hers. His shirt had come untucked and somehow her hands had slid under it to the smooth skin of his back, drawing a ragged groan from his lips as he nibbled at her earlobe, sending a shock of arousal to her toes.

He kissed a wet trail down her neck to her collarbone, his nose nudging her sweater aside so just the curve of her breast was exposed. He nuzzled and nipped, then ran his tongue into the sensitive valley before tracing the lace top of her bra, leaving her trembling with the power of sensation that he'd evoked.

Her hips lifted and she ground herself against him, his

hard length rubbing against her and she gasped at the currents that threatened to drag her under. The room spun as his lips found the spot where her pulse beat madly and he chuckled as she dug her fingers into his muscled shoulders. She was hot and ready for him and they'd barely even begun. If a kiss was this good, the lovemaking was going to be out of this world.

But as amazing as it would be, she wasn't quite ready to do that with him. Not yet.

He must have felt her momentary withdrawal, maybe a slight stiffening of her body, and he lifted his head to look down at her. His eyes were heavy-lidded with desire, surveying all he had conquered so easily. His hand came up and his finger traced her lips slowly as a smile bloomed on his handsome face.

"See? I told you. Best first kiss ever."

He wanted her to speak? She'd try. "It was. Amazing."

His expression softened as he ran his fingers through her hair, tugging lightly on the ends.

"Don't overthink this. I'm not pushing for anything more tonight. I want to do this right. Woo you, court you the way you deserve. Romance for a romance writer." He pressed his erection into her hip. "But don't think that I don't want you, because I do. This isn't about desire or attraction—this is about wanting more than a shag. For once I want to do the right thing."

Slowly she exhaled, partly in relief and partly in disappointment. She wasn't ready to sleep with him tonight but if he'd pushed a little she would have given in. Without a doubt it would have been spectacular.

He rolled them onto their sides, his hand taking up a

stroking motion from just below her breast to her knee, sending bolts of pleasure straight to her extremities.

"I want to," Paige admitted through the knot in her throat. "It's just that..."

Jesus, this was hard. Honestly, she'd thought this part of her life had ended. When she was widowed she assumed that she was done with sex and romance.

Nate seemed to know what she was going to say. "You haven't since...?"

She nodded, relief flooding her body. He got her trepidation. This wasn't about him. He was wonderful.

"And even before. He was sick a long time so it's been years."

She hoped she didn't sound pathetic.

He pressed his lips to hers briefly but with a mountain of emotion that he didn't bother to mask. "I can't tell you how it makes me feel that you trust me like this. When the time comes I promise we'll take it as slow as you need to."

She quirked up an eyebrow and smiled, her insides jangling with excitement. The thought of being with him as close as two people could get was heady. "What if I don't want slow?"

She could feel his chuckle rumble in his chest, masculine and deep. "Then we'll go as fast as you like."

Like it? She was going to love it. Then hopefully do it again. Nice and slow.

CHAPTER
Twenty-One

THINGS WERE GOING SURPRISINGLY WELL. On the day after the first kiss, Nate brought Paige flowers. The next day he came home after his run with cinnamon buns from a local bakery. Each passing day brought another sweet and thoughtful gesture. Every night they had dinner together and talked about their childhoods, books, movies, and even politics. They agreed on many things and vehemently disagreed on some others but were able to respect each other's opinions.

Nate was intelligent, charming, and incredibly nurturing. Nothing made him happier than for her to need him to do something, whether it was to bring coffee to her in the morning or rub her shoulders after she'd written all day. He liked to run a bubble bath for her and pour her a glass of wine. He was even working on rearranging his office so they could both have their own workspace.

He was making room for her in his life.

So of course when the relationship was moving

forward rather smoothly it was time to test it. Paige had been invited to do a Q&A and a signing afterward at a book convention and Nate was going along. The press would be in attendance and it would be their first "official" outing together, although they'd been photographed several times since the airport. The idea was to introduce them as a couple at a low-key event that didn't involve paparazzi and a red carpet.

Garrett and Helen also thought it would be more fun to keep her identity a secret for a little while so she was currently being referred to as "the mystery blonde" which always made her laugh. She was about as far away from mysterious as a human being could get. After the book convention, she would be a mystery no more.

"Darling, I need to discuss something with you."

His usually smooth as melted chocolate voice didn't sound as calm as usual. Agitated. But what did he have to be upset about? She was the one sitting in a chair having her hair and makeup done by a professional. The only thing that would have made the day worse was high heels, which she had immediately vetoed when Helen suggested it. Instead she'd chosen Prada red leather boots paired with a winter white wool dress that she'd fallen in love with when Julie pulled it off the rack.

"Shoot, handsome. I'm listening even if I don't look like it."

The makeup artist was currently lining Paige's eyes, requiring her to stay absolutely still.

"It's Max, actually."

"How is Max?"

Nate's words came out in a rush. "Funny you should

ask that. What is the saying you Americans have? Up shit creek without a paddle? He needs our help - well, really your help, love. I told him I would speak with you about it."

She couldn't imagine what Max needed from her but she had to admit her curiosity was piqued.

"I'm still listening."

The makeup artist had moved on to mascara and that was plain scary to have someone wielding a wand covered in black gunk right next to her eyeball.

"It turns out Max's mother is a huge fan of yours. When he mentioned that he had met you she went into a fangirl tizzy. Max said the last time he saw her that excited was when he got his first big part. So he just couldn't say no and that's the problem he needs your help with."

That was sweet. Paige made a mental note to sign some books for Max's mother and give them to Nate to send over.

"A man who can't say no. That's not usually an issue. How can I help?"

Stalling. Hemming. Hawing. "It's just...well...Max found himself promising to get his mother a ticket to the book convention today. She wants to see your Q&A and meet you."

She wasn't sure why this was a problem. Paige had been given a welcomed reprieve. She was supposed to meet Nate's mother today but Elaine was sick. It wasn't that she didn't want to meet Elaine Mason...she did. She just didn't think it needed to be so soon.

"Nate, it's fine. Your mother was going to join us and

now she can't because she has that nasty cold. We have an extra VIP pass. Problem solved."

Maybe Nate had an issue with math.

More silence. Jebus on a cracker.

Paige held up her hand to the makeup artist who was selecting a shade of lip gloss. "Can you stop for just a minute? Give me one minute." She turned to Nate, rapidly losing patience. Public appearances were extremely nerve-wracking for her and here she was dealing with this shit when she should be deep breathing and meditating. "Spill it, handsome. What's going on here?"

Nate's cheeks were pink and he was staring at his shoes. Not the ugly gray ones he'd originally had on. She'd taken one look at them and sent him back upstairs to change. These were a lovely black leather and looked perfect with the blue suit he was wearing.

"We need three VIP passes," he finally blurted. "One for Max's mother, one for his father..."

"And?" Paige prompted.

"One for Max. His parents want him to go as well."

Fuck. Shit.

"It's not nice to tease a woman who is nervous as hell, Nate. I'm on the edge of hysteria here and I still have two hours to go before my Q&A."

"I'm not kidding. Love, I am so sorry. Max is sorry too. I swear."

Rubbing her temples, Paige pointed to her phone on the coffee table. "Please hand that to me and I'll see what I can do. That little SOB is going to owe me one if I can pull this off. What was he thinking?"

It only took two calls but Paige managed to secure the

extra passes. Nate was practically on his knees in gratitude and she couldn't stay angry when he looked that cute and grateful. He was promising back rubs and chocolate and weekend getaways to Paris.

"You don't owe me anything. Max owes me a trip to Paris so let him know. I expect a five-star hotel."

Nate leaned in, his lips next to her ear. "You're amazing. I'd kiss you but I think your makeup lady would punch me."

Paige tapped him on the chin where a goatee was taking shape. She'd made an offhand remark about how much she loved his facial hair in *Ice Blue Lovers*. "As soon as I'm done today I want lots of kisses."

With that business out of the way and her hair and makeup done, they climbed into the limo. Nate was trying to be helpful and relax her but his constant talking was beginning to take its toll on her nerves. Normally she had Carrie here to deal with all the extraneous people and noise around her but the assistant was stuck in the States with her fiancé who had broken his leg.

Paige was on her own.

"I find when I'm nervous that imaging helps," Nate went on, although she hadn't heard the first part. "Picture yourself doing it perfectly, no issues. Picture yourself being calm and in control and—"

"Nate," she broke in, placing her hand on his and squeezing his fingers. "I appreciate all you're trying to do for me today. But honest to God, if you don't shut up I'm going to kick you from the car and it's going pretty fast so I think you might get seriously injured. I'm just getting more tense hearing from you about how not to be tense, if you know what I mean."

He looked a little shamefaced. "Of course, love. I'm sorry. I think I might be as nervous as you are. This is our debut and I want the whole day to go well."

"It will. Have faith."

Traffic wasn't too bad and soon they found themselves at the back door of the venue being ushered to the green room by two burly security guards. Once safely behind closed doors, Paige knew what she had to do.

"Nate, I'll be fine."

He looked a little startled, his brow wrinkled. "Of course you will, darling. Perfectly fine."

"What I mean is you can go to your seat. The Q&A starts in fifteen minutes and I need some quiet time to get psyched up. Besides, you should check that Max and his parents found their way. Their seats are supposed to be right next to yours."

Nate opened his mouth as if to protest but then seemed to think better of it. "Good luck, darling. I know you'll be wonderful. We'll celebrate tonight."

"In Paris. Max's treat."

One of the guards escorted Nate from the room and Paige walked over to a small couch and sat down, concentrating on her breathing. In. Out. In. Out. Eyes closed. Images of fluffy bunnies and cute puppies running through her head. Everything was rainbows and freakin' unicorns.

———

"I've never been so nervous in my life. I think I've sweated straight through this Armani suit. Is it hot in here or is it just me?"

Nate fanned himself with the paper program he'd been given when they'd seated him. It was like a sauna in here.

"It's just you," Max intoned. "In fact, it's rather drafty. Are you nervous about being photographed today?"

Max didn't understand at all. "I'm nervous for Paige. She hates being the center of attention and being in front of a crowd. I feel so terribly for her—this much be the worst torture imaginable for her."

Max's features softened and a smile came to his face. "You're quite smitten, aren't you, mate? I take it everything is going well."

"It's bloody fantastic," Nate declared, thinking about the last week. "Paige is the most amazing woman I've ever met. That reminds me, you owe her a trip to Paris for getting these tickets. I offered to take her but she said you should foot the bill, old chap. Can't say that I disagree."

Barking with laughter, Max nodded. "She's saved my arse today so she can demand whatever she likes."

Max's mother Karen waved toward the ushers who were closing the doors. "It's starting. I'm so excited."

"You'll get to meet her after," Nate said. "She's a real sweetheart and loves talking to her readers."

He didn't have time to say anymore as the announcer came out to introduce Paige. The crowd went wild as she stepped onto the stage looking every inch the gorgeous and successful woman she was.

She owned that stage.

The woman up there was another facet of Paige he

hadn't yet seen. Confident. Sexy. Completely in her element as she fielded question after question, some of them easy, some difficult, and some rather nasty. She didn't falter or blink an eye. She smiled, joked, and remained humble when fans gushed, never apologized for what she wrote, and staunchly refused to give away any secrets regarding future character storylines. She'd charmed the crowd.

Clearly she'd never really needed Nate's help today.

"She's fucking brilliant," Max whispered in Nate's ear. "She's got these people eating out of the palm of her hand."

A flush of pride ran through Nate and he beamed as Paige handled another prickly question from the crowd. "Now you know what I was talking about. She's different, special."

Max nodded. "She is. Don't mess this up, mate."

As she was taking a sip for her water glass, she caught Nate's eye and smiled. A smile intended just for him alone. Even in the midst of all this, she'd remember him.

"I'm the luckiest man alive."

Don't fuck this up.

CHAPTER
Twenty~Two

"DON'T LOOK AT THE PAPS," Nate warned Paige as they slipped out of the venue and headed for the limousine. "Just smile and look at me. Act like they're not there."

They were supposed to meet Max and his parents for dinner but first they had to navigate a labyrinth of photographers who had apparently realized she was here with Nate. They were like sharks smelling blood.

Nate's arm was around her shoulders protectively as they strode through the gauntlet, flashbulbs making a strobe effect that almost blinded her. She leaned more heavily on Nate as he was taller and could see through the throngs of people.

"I was so proud of you today, love," he whispered in her ear as they climbed into the vehicle, reporters yelling questions that they had no intention of answering. She'd answered more than her share this morning. "You didn't really need me but I'm glad I was here."

The door closed and the limo sped off, leaving the

crowd behind. Every tense muscle in her body began to relax and she went limp on the seat, her head lolling back and her eyes closed. "I'm fucking exhausted. If I never say another word to anyone ever again it would be perfect. I am completely talked out. You're going to have to do the heavy lifting at dinner with Max and his parents. I've talked more today than I have in the entire last thirty days combined. This extrovert shit is for the birds."

His silence had her opening her eyes. Normally Nate was a chatterbox. He looked confused.

"You seemed like you were having fun today. You were magnificent during the Q&A and your fans were in heaven during the signing. You laughed and chatted with them, took selfies. Are you saying you didn't have a good time? You did so well."

It wasn't unusual for an extrovert to not understand what being an introvert really meant, but there was no better time than now to educate him. If they were going to be in any kind of relationship, he needed to get this.

"I like people just fine. In small doses and small crowds. I can absolutely be Paige Mitchell and be onstage and performing when I need to be. I can take a million selfies with my readers and answer all their questions. But you need to know that sucks out every bit of energy that I have. I don't recharge with people. I can only recharge in solitude."

Stunned, he simply nodded and digested her words. "I have to tell you no one would have ever known that you weren't one hundred percent comfortable up there. You had me fooled."

She didn't say what came immediately to her tongue -

that he was so used to being in superficial situations that he was in the habit of not bothering to look any deeper. But that was a cheap shot and she didn't really know if it was the truth. He'd certainly looked past the veneer with her.

"I'd like to thank the Academy," she teased. "Seriously, I can do it. I told Helen that. I just don't enjoy it like you do. I will say it's nice to have you hold my hand through this. I can't even imagine doing this on my own."

He leaned down to rub their noses together. "Glad you gave us a chance?"

"For more reasons than one."

Pure, unadulterated exhaustion wasn't going to get her out of dinner though. After meeting Karen and Timothy, Max's parents, she'd agreed to this meal and she would see it through. They were lovely people and sharing the next few hours with them wasn't going to be that bad. She only had to keep herself together a little longer. Then she could crawl away to the bubble bath, a book, and a cup of hot chocolate.

It might not be a bad idea to skip the appetizer and dessert courses.

———

"So you don't base your characters on real people?" Karen asked with a laugh. "That's kind of disappointing. I was hoping to be written into your next book."

Dinner with Max's parents was going well. "I make it a point never to base a character on anything more than a physical resemblance to real people. Their personality quirks are all their own."

The plates were cleared and Paige took the opportunity to excuse herself and visit the ladies room. She was fixing her lipstick when the door swung open and Nate strode in like he owned the joint. The bathroom. Tossing her lipstick back into her purse, she gave him her best mean look which had put Jason back in line more than a few times. What in the hell was Nate doing in here? Had Max pissed him off again?

"Can't you read? This is the ladies' room. You can tell by the picture of a stick figure in a skirt on the door."

His blue eyes had darkened dangerously and instead of replying he dragged her into one of the stalls, clicking the lock behind them and then pressing her up against the door. His body seemed to take up all the space in the small cubicle and her own body roared to life immediately, responding in its now predictable manner. Stiff nipples. Heat between her thighs. Racing heart and a little sweaty. Their kisses had grown increasingly urgent since that first one, and they'd found themselves making out like teenagers on more than one occasion. But they had yet to make love, something Paige was anxious to rectify.

"What are you doing?"

"If it's not obvious I'm doing it wrong," Nate growled in her ear, right before he bit down on the lobe, sending a shiver down her spine.

Her knees went weak and she was grateful for his arm supporting her waist as his lips nibbled at the cord of her neck and down to the collar of her dress. She mewled in protest when he lifted his head but he didn't relent, his gaze hot and full of lust.

"I had to sit there all day and watch you. So sexy and confident. So fucking gorgeous. Then even tonight I've had to play the sweet suitor when all I've really wanted to do is bend you over the nearest flat surface and fuck you until you're screaming my name. You're mine and I'm yours and I want everyone in the world to know that."

The breath was knocked from her lungs and she was glad she didn't have to reply because forming actual, real words at the moment would have been impossible. Instead she let her kiss say everything she couldn't. His hand slid under her dress and up the quivering flesh of her thigh, his fingers discovering her naughty secret that was only going to throw gasoline on this raging fire.

"You little minx," he groaned, his voice like ground glass. "You've been walking around all day with no knickers. If I had known..."

"I couldn't wear any," Paige confessed. "They would have ruined the line of the dress."

"That's got you in big trouble, baby girl. You have no idea."

She might not but it was becoming clear fast. Those long, skillful fingers had found her wet and ready, stroking her clit as one digit slid easily inside of her, quickly joined by a second. She couldn't keep down the gasp that escaped from her lips nor the gush of honey that drenched his hand.

"That's a good girl. Can you come on my hand? Come for me, sweets. Can you, love?"

Her brain was becoming increasingly muddled as her

arousal went into overdrive. The tension in her lower abdomen kept building until it was almost unbearable. He held her there on the brink, her fingers digging into his biceps, a sheen of sweat covering her skin.

She cried out his name when she tumbled over the precipice, something inside of her snapping free. Riding his fingers to the end of her climax, she reached up and pulled his head down, fusing their lips together until the last moment. When it was over Nate pulled his hand from her sensitive core, lifting his fingers to his lips and slowly licking them clean as he gazed into her eyes.

"Sweet. I can't wait for more."

It was so good she wanted to cry. But she wouldn't. She had no doubt she was already a mess, her makeup ruined. She could barely stand and speak and this man had been the entire reason. He was smiling triumphantly now, male pride evident in every line of his too gorgeous face.

She reached up and straightened his crooked tie. "How fast can you eat dessert?"

He leaned down so their mouths were mere millimeters apart.

"Darling, I'm going to take great delight in having every inch of you for dessert. Tell them you have a headache and let's get out of here."

CHAPTER
Twenty~Three

IT FELT like Nate had waited years but it was only two hours later when he threw open his front door, sending it sailing into the wall with a bang. Practically carrying Paige over the threshold, he impatiently pushed her up against the wall as the door swung shut with a resounding click. While one hand slid up her thigh and under her dress, the other reached out and flicked the lock on the door, effectively shutting out the rest of the world. Finally it would be just the two of them.

"I can't wait to get you stripped naked and under me," he growled into her ear. Her hands slid down his spine and gripped his ass cheeks, fingers digging into the muscles. His cock hardened painfully and he knew without a doubt their first time together was going to be fast and hard.

A seductive giggle escaped from her swollen lips, courtesy of his kisses in the limo on the way back and she gazed up at him, her expression promising sin and heaven all at the same time. Her pupils were blown wide and when her tongue snaked out to wet her lips he couldn't hold back the groan that tore from his throat as he captured that mouth with his own. The kiss rocked him inside and out, his knees turning to jelly as their tongue tangled and played.

Her deft fingers worked on the buttons of his shirt, sliding against his bare flesh and he simply couldn't take it anymore. Bending at the waist, he hauled her over his shoulder in a fireman carry and sprinted up the stairs as she shrieked and laughed at his impatient antics.

"Have you lost your mind?" she asked as he dumped her on the bed before tugging at his own clothes that were most definitely in the way. She was kicking off her boots and tossing them aside. "You could have dropped me on my head."

"You're as light as a feather." Nate tore at the rest of the buttons, a few of them flying across the room and hitting the walls and floor. Throwing the useless fabric down, he went to work on his belt.

"Easy there, big guy. You're going to take out an eye at this rate." Paige dropped to her knees in front of him, her smaller fingers covering his own. "Let me take care of this."

Her voice had dropped to a husky tone and the blood surged through his veins, creating a roaring sound in his ears that drown out all extraneous noise. His lids grew heavy as she unzipped his trousers and pulled them down, his cock springing free. He hadn't bothered with undergarments today either. Her hand wrapped round the base and her head dipped to lick at the head. Not able to stop himself, his fingers curled into her silky hair, tugging at the strands and holding himself steady, otherwise he might have collapsed from the sweet pleasure that was running through him. Her mouth worked its magic, the heat finally forcing his eyes shut as he surrendered to her skillful ministrations. He'd never had it this good.

When the pressure in his lower back became too much he moaned her name and reluctantly pulled away, immediately missing the warm cavern of her mouth. He stood there for a moment, overcome and disoriented. He wanted to rip her clothes off and give it to her hard and the other part wanted to take his time and savor the moment.

Fuck it. Fast was going to win. His cock was in charge. Later his brain might get a vote too but right now he'd deprived that organ of any blood flow.

Paige seemed to be reading his mind. She'd moved to sit on the edge of the bed and was sliding her dress over her head, a smile playing on her lips. "I've been thinking about this all day too."

"Really?" Nate dropped to his knees and reached up to help her pull the dress over her head, leaving her in a lacy beige bra that pushed up her breasts in a tempting manner. "You naughty little girl. So randy when you were supposed to be working. Tsk, tsk."

Her hand went to her back but his fingers were already there, pinching the hooks and tossing her bra aside, his gaze feasting on the gorgeous body he'd bared. Her skin was a pale gold, perhaps from the Florida sun, and her curves were perfectly formed for his touch. She was petite but not too delicate. Slim but not skinny. Her breasts were round and full and topped with dusky pink nipples that begged to be tasted. Her firm thighs were pressed together but he could see a hint of moisture on the skin, glistening and beckoning. Letting him know in no uncertain terms that she wanted this as much as he did.

"Like what you see?" she asked, her tone a little shy. He could see the uncertainty there in her eyes and he wanted to take it away now and forever. She was perfect, and right now she was everything. "It's been a long time since anyone has seen me, you know, naked and all."

He pushed her legs apart and took up residence between them. "Love, if I liked what I saw any more this would all be over and I would have disgraced myself quite embarrassingly. You are the most beautiful woman I have ever seen in my life, and I'm a lucky man."

He punctuated each of the last words with a kiss to her quivering thighs, his shoulders pushing them even farther apart. She lifted up from the mattress and looked down at where he was perched between her legs, her eyes wide with surprise.

"What are you doing?"

He gave her a wicked grin. "You ask me that quite a lot, love, and I'll give you the same answer. If you don't know then I must be doing something wrong."

———

Nate was doing every single, solitary thing exactly right.

Nibbling a path up the flesh of her inner thigh, his nose nuzzled her clit and the sensation almost sent her flying off the mattress. It had been a very long time since she had felt a man's breath that close to the most sensitive part of her.

Her heart pounded against her ribs and she had to take a few breaths before she could speak.

"You don't have to do that just because I did."

She didn't expect him to and she sure as hell didn't want him doing anything out of obligation. That was the worst feeling in the world.

He lifted his head, his eyes narrowed as his gaze stroked up and down her body. "I know that."

Shifting on the bed, she tried to press her legs together but he was firmly lodged between them. "So, you know, you don't...have to."

"I know." He rubbed his chin, still regarding her closely. "But I want to. Is that okay? Do you not like this? If I do something you don't enjoy just tell me to stop, love."

He'd completely misunderstood and it was all her fault. "No, I like it, it's just I don't want you to feel like you have to."

His finger ran up her drenched folds and then circled her swollen clit, dragging a tortured groan from her lips. A coil of arousal tightened in her belly and her fingers fisted the bedclothes. "When was the last time a man had his mouth on this sweet spot, love?"

That finger was drawing patterns through her folds, sliding over and around the one place she needed him the most, making it extremely hard to concentrate on his question. What did he say again?

"A long time," she finally rasped. "Years. Noah didn't like..."

She didn't bother to go into any detail, sure Nate could figure it out for himself. If anything his grin became more evil, far more diabolical and for a moment she wondered if she should grab her clothes and make a run for it. Luckily it was far too late.

Two long digits were pressed into her, finding the sensitive spot on the inside as his mouth began to work on her clit on the outside. He lapped at her with the flat of his tongue until the room spun and the world tilted on its axis. White heat swept through her veins as she fell over the cliff, calling his name over and over and riding his mouth until he'd wrung every ounce of pleasure she had to give him in tribute.

She lay there in a sweaty heap, still buzzing from the havoc he'd wrought as he fumbled in the bedroom drawer. She heard the crinkle of plastic and the snap of a condom before he came down on top of her, his body so much larger than her own. It made her feel feminine, delicate, and rather protected as well, although the thought was silly. She was well capable of taking care of herself but at this moment she was happy to give into his dominance.

His cock, long and thick and steel-hard, nudged at her entrance and she braced her hands on his shoulders, closed her eyes, and waited for his invasion.

It didn't come.

She opened her eyes to find him looking down at her, straining to hold back. The cords of his neck stood out in stark relief and a muscle ticked in his jaw. He was being patient. For her.

"Are you sure, love?"

Her chest tightened with an emotion she wasn't sure she should allow herself to feel. This man...this gentle and sweet man who sometimes made her crazy with frustration...he was holding himself in check. At times he was the

most self-centered asshole she'd ever met but at an intimate moment when he could have taken almost anything
he wanted...he did this. A lump rose in her throat and her
answer came out choked.

"I'm sure. I want you, Nate."

They may have been the truest words she'd ever
spoken.

He entered her slowly, giving her ample time to get
used to being filled after such a long dry spell. Her walls
stretched to accommodate his size and for a moment she
wasn't sure she could take all of him but he paused, letting
her catch her breath before pushing in to the hilt. With
every delicious inch inside of her, she began to move her
hips in a slow sway as he pulled out and then thrust back
in. Over and over, they found their rhythm. Slowly at first,
but then building up speed until he was riding her hard
and fast, each stroke running over that spot inside of her
that sent her closer to the edge.

The coil in her abdomen tightened painfully and she
clawed at his shoulders, the pleasure more intense than
anything she'd known before. Nate was caught up in the
moment as well, his eyes squeezed shut, his head thrown
back. A fine sheen of sweat covered their bodies and her
breathing grew ragged and labored as they raced toward
the finish line.

"Are you close, baby?" Nate's voice sounded tortured
and hoarse and he reached between them to rub her
already swollen clit. "Can you come on my cock like a
good girl? Come for me."

That little bit of dirty talk was all she needed to go
rocketing into space. Everything around her seemed to

shatter into a million pieces of light, spinning around the room before settling into the sky as twinkling stars. Nate groaned her name as he reached his own peak, collapsing on top of her, sucking air into his lungs. His full weight felt lovely and she reveled in the closeness, even knowing they couldn't stay like this forever. She'd suffocate and there was nothing romantic or sexy about air deprivation.

Nate nuzzled her temple. "I swear I'm going to move in a minute but my limbs don't seem to be functioning at the moment."

She giggled and ran her hand down his muscled back, the skin damp under her fingers.

"It's only oxygen. Don't worry about little old me down here."

This time he did lever up slightly and roll onto his back, his arm around her waist, tucking her into his side. She didn't even think about objecting or making a fuss. This was where she wanted to be.

"That was bloody fantastic. We need to do that several more times, darling. In fact, let's make a habit of it."

Laughing, she pressed chaste kisses to his chest, his scant chest hair tickling her nose.

"I think that's a bloody good idea, mate," she said in her best British accent. "Smashing idea. Just brilliant."

That bit of a tease earned her a smart smack on the ass. "Minx. Are you making fun of me? Naughty girls get punished, you know."

She sure as hell hoped so.

"I'm kind of counting on that."

She heard his indrawn breath and the way his muscles jerked under her palm. His fingers slid into her hair, twisting and pulling her head back. "Are you sure you know what you're asking for? Because I'm just the man to give it to you."

"I'm counting on that too."

He bent his head and ran his tongue over her nipple, watching it tighten in response.

"Then I think it's time for round two, love. I hope you don't have any appointments in the morning. I don't think you'll be getting out of this bed any time soon. In fact, if you can walk tomorrow I won't have done my job properly."

A hard man is good to find. Or whatever that saying was.

CHAPTER
Twenty~Four

SITING DOWN CAREFULLY on her sore lady parts, Paige answered the Skype call from her business manager Carrie. She'd been monitoring social media since Paige and Nate's debut yesterday and was ready to give a full report about how it was going.

Paige had vowed to stay away from her laptop no matter how much she wanted to see what was going on but that hadn't been a problem. Nate had kept her busy pretty much all night and into the morning. That was why she couldn't sit or walk comfortably.

Lucky me.

She couldn't say he hadn't warned her.

After they'd rolled out of bed at the crack of noon, the smirking, cocky bastard had gone for a run, promising to bring back food she didn't have to prepare.

Carrie's smiling face appeared on the laptop screen.

"Talk to me. Tell me what's happening. Good or bad?"

"Mostly good. Some bad, but you know, we expected

that. Helen and Garrett are all over any negative stuff. I just got off a conference call with them."

Paige wanted to rip the Band-aid off fast. "Tell me the bad first."

Carrie laughed and shook her head. "How about I tell you some of the great stuff? Most of his fans really like you. They think you look cute together and that his dating a writer totally makes sense. The press coverage has been quite positive overall now that your mystery identity has been solved. I think you'll find that you'll see more paps following you from now on, though. Those pictures of Nate being protective of you as you walked to the limo are all over the place. That really moved things in your favor."

The bad must be really terrible if Carrie was avoiding it.

"And the bad?"

"I haven't even told you yet about your fans. Their response is overwhelmingly positive, and they're already calling for him to play Flynn, so that's all good."

"And the bad?" Paige repeated, her stomach dropping to her feet. It was going to be ugly, she could feel it.

Carrie's smile fell and she sighed heavily. "Some of his fans aren't taking it well. They've flooded your Twitter and Facebook but don't worry. Helen and Garrett have some people working on cleaning that up."

There was more. Something Carrie didn't want to tell her. Paige could see it in her body language even over Skype. She was fidgeting in her seat, her gaze darting away every few seconds.

"And?" Paige prompted. "Jesus, just spill it."

"His fans have been one-star reviewing your books all

over the place - Amazon, Goodreads, Barnes and Noble, iBooks, Kobo. The reviews are open that they haven't read your books but that they hate you because you took their Nate."

Their Nate. Like he was a thing, not a person. Like he really was Kai.

Acid rose in the back of her throat and she had to swallow hard to keep from hurling what little was left in her churning stomach. It was one thing to call her names, flood her social media with venom, but to play with her career? That was something completely different.

"I want you to promise me that you will not under any circumstances go read your reviews. Promise me, Paige. Cross your heart and hope to die and all that jazz. I am as serious as a heart attack here."

She'd stopped reading her reviews a long time ago but at this moment it was all she could do not to open up her Amazon page and take a look. Just how much did these fangirls hate her?

"You're not promising me. Promise," Carrie commanded.

"I promise," Paige finally agreed. Carrie was right in that nothing good would come from reading them. She'd only feel shitty and depressed and she hated feeling that way. "Is Helen working on them with the book vendors?"

Carrie nodded. "Absolutely. They'll try and get them cleaned up as best as they can. Personal attacks are against the Terms of Service. It just might take some time. But you'll be happy to know that your fans have seen what's happening and they're out there writing reviews on the books they love to try and mitigate the damage."

Blinking back tears, Paige's throat tightened with emotion. It was those readers that had put her on the best-seller list and now they were coming to her defense. She truly was a blessed woman, but she wasn't sure it was a good idea to drag them into the middle of this. The less attention they gave these fangirls the sooner all of this would die down.

"We're not asking them to do that, are we? Because I don't want to do that. It's not something I want to ask my readers."

Carrie shook her head. "Absolutely not. We've been clear on Twitter and Facebook that we don't want them engaging with anyone that comes there to bash you. It's just something they've done on their own."

Overcome, Paige didn't even know what to say. She'd never imagined that she'd be in this position to begin with and now that she was, she was out of her depth.

"There's no training class or book about how to handle this, is there?" Paige asked to no one in particular. "Nothing really prepares you for people that hate your guts but don't even know you."

"You've been preparing for this your whole life, Paige. Back when you were in the corporate world and now dealing with all kinds of people. It's all grace under pressure and you have it. This isn't even about you. There is no woman in the world that would make those fans happy. Not one."

Intellectually she knew that, but it still kind of hurt. She was a good person or at least tried to be, yet there was a faction of the population who would as soon see her fall off the planet.

The front door opened and Nate burst through, humming a song, a huge grin on his face. He ought to be fucking smiling after all the sex last night.

"Nate's home with food so I'm going to let you go. Keep me in the loop with everything, okay?"

Carrie promised to do that and then signed off, leaving Paige feeling rather deflated and sad. Her mood was in sharp contrast to Nate's enthusiasm but so far he hadn't seemed to notice.

He came in to the living room and nuzzled her neck, pressing a kiss to the pulse point.

"I'll head upstairs and take a shower and then we can eat. How was your afternoon?"

"It was great. Good. It was good."

She was a lousy liar apparently because Nate came around the sofa and sat down on the coffee table in front of her, moving her laptop aside.

"Don't ever take up professional poker, darling. Your expression tells a completely different story than your words. What's wrong?"

She pulled her knees up to her chest and wrapped her arms around them, giving herself a much needed hug. "I just talked to Carrie."

He nodded, understanding in his eyes. "Yes, I spoke with Garrett about an hour ago. They're working on cleaning that all up, love. I'm just so sorry that happened to you."

His tone was regretful and she believed that he was sorry but he shouldn't have been in the situation in the first place. The fangirls had put him there though and for that she was kind of angry. He was convinced that he needed to be something he wasn't to keep his fans happy. To have a career.

"It's not your fault. Your fans are rather...passionate, shall we say? You get anywhere near a vagina and they lose their minds."

Nate laughed and took her hands in his, pulling her into his arms, and she took comfort and strength from his closeness. "That's one way of putting it. Listen, it doesn't matter what anyone thinks. We belong to each other and that's the way it is. Once they see how happy I am and that this is for real and isn't going anywhere, they'll get used to it. It will all blow over. Let's take solace in the fact that the reaction was overwhelmingly positive. I told you they were going to ship us and they do." He hung his head for a moment. "I feel badly because I should have warned you. I wish I could protect you from all of this but responding just fuels the fire."

Paige shook her head. "No, I absolutely don't want you to respond to them. You're right, the less said about any of this the sooner it will fall into oblivion." She sniffed his shirt and wrinkled her nose. "Boy, you are ripe. Go take a shower and I'll set the table."

He hesitated, his expression unsure.

"I'm fine," Paige assured Nate, nudging his shoulder. "I've had much worse reviews and I've developed a thick skin. I just had a moment, that's all. By dessert I will have forgotten all about this."

His hands slid up her thighs, his fingers brushing a particularly sensitive area. "Perhaps there are a few things I can do to take your mind off of all of it."

He had to be joking. She could barely move and he wanted to fool around?

"I can't believe you're serious." Paige slapped at his hands and tried to wriggle away toward the other end of the couch. "Do you know how sore I am? I can hardly move or walk."

A grin magically appeared on his handsome face. Asshole. "That was my goal. I'm a little sore too but I'm willing to play through the pain."

Her brows shot up and her mouth fell open. "You're sore? You've got nerve, Mason. Nerve. I have delicate parts down here that need tender loving care. You treated them like toys last night."

Standing, Nate bounded toward the staircase, chuckling the whole way. "They were more fun than the bicycle I got for Christmas. Seriously though, after dinner we'll soak in a hot tub. I do want to take exquisite care of my girl."

That was quite a compliment. Better than a bike from Santa.

"We'll see. Feed me first."

No sense making things too easy for him. He already knew she was going to give in but he needed to work for it, if only a little. He wouldn't appreciate it otherwise.

CHAPTER
Twenty-Five

ANOTHER PARTY, another red carpet. In the last month Paige and Nate had attended no less than four charity events, two movie premieres, and the opening of a bookstore. Tonight was an event to raise money for the homeless and so far it had gone off with military precision. She had the process down. First, there was hair and makeup. Then dressing, which usually involved keeping Nate out of her lingerie drawer long enough to find whatever bra and knickers she needed. It wasn't that he wanted to wear her lingerie. Oh no, that would have been easier to deal with, actually. The problem was he had an opinion about what she should - or shouldn't - wear. He was quite the proponent of her going commando so they could shag in the bathroom wherever they were. He also liked lacy black bras and he wanted her to wear them with everything even if it showed through, something she simply wouldn't allow.

After they were finally dressed, they'd pile into a limo

and head for whatever fancy venue was hosting the party. They walked the red carpet, holding hands and posing for pictures. And smiling. Always smiling. Nate would sign some autographs and give a few interviews. Sometimes she'd join in and other times she'd hang back, depending on her mood and how much Nate begged. They'd dance, drink, and eat tiny food, then leave, grabbing some Chinese or a pizza on the way home where they'd eat and make love in front of the fire before heading to bed to do it again.

All in all, life was good. But tonight was the biggest event yet.

Paige watched as Nate buttoned the crisp white shirt he would wear with a dark blue suit. A new one the stylist had chosen for him. He'd lost a few pounds of muscle in the past few months and his other suits didn't fit quite right. He was such a clotheshorse, fussing with his cufflinks and tie as the makeup and hair artist had worked on Paige. This was an important night for Nate and he wanted it to go well and so did she. It was the end of an era and the cast and crew were sending it off in style.

Tonight they were in Los Angeles for the *Thunder* party to celebrate the end of shooting, although Nate had finished his scenes the week before he'd met Paige. His character Kai had been killed off with a hero's death that galvanized the remaining characters to vanquish their opponent.

It was also the last movie for a good chunk of the actors and actresses, Nate included. The last few weeks he'd appeared tense and a little moody. At first, she'd put it down to his suddenly having a live-in girlfriend, but it soon became clear what the issue was.

He was going to miss Kai.

The makeup artist finished and wished them luck before leaving Nate and Paige alone. Paige had chosen to wear a white chiffon dress with a halter neckline and a handkerchief hem. Her accessories were gold, right down to the Christian Louboutin high-heeled sandals.

"You look so damn sexy I may have to have you right there in the limo," Paige giggled, running her fingers down his arm. "I don't think I'll be able to control myself."

Nate smirked and pulled on his jacket, smoothing the lapels. "I don't intend to, so why should you, love? I'm all yours."

Paige gave him a smile of pure delight. "Yes, you are. I'm a lucky girl."

"I'm a lucky man." He turned to the mirror, frowning at his reflection. "What do you think?"

"You look gorgeous." She reached up to smooth the frown lines on his forehead. "Stop making that face. You're giving yourself wrinkles."

Snorting, Nate leaned down to rummage in the closet for his shoes. "I doubt anyone would notice when their eyes are immediately drawn to my receding hairline. Jesus, I saw a comparison of me in the first *Thunder* movie and now. Fuck, I've lost at least an inch or more of hair."

And he was still the sexiest man she'd ever seen. Who would notice his hairline when he had that long, lean body to ogle?

"You could see a doctor about that."

She didn't really want him to, hating the look, but Nate was an actor and he had to worry about these things.

He straightened and shook his head. "Not unless I absolutely have to. I really don't want to do any medical intervention. The facials that you give me are fine but I don't think I'd ever have a face lift." He shuddered. "I hate hospitals."

He'd bitched about those treatments but they had improved his skin a great deal and had easily taken off five years.

"I think you're wise to grow old gracefully. Now are you ready to go? We have a red carpet to walk."

Checking his tie in the mirror, he looked at her reflection. "Just one more question. I don't suppose you know where my gray shoes are? I'm sure I packed them."

Shit, she was hoping he wouldn't notice.

"Your gray shoes?" Shrugging, she played innocent. "Are you sure you brought them?"

He looked down at the black leather shoes on his feet. "I'm positive, yet somehow they walked out of my suitcase all on their own, like magic. Do you know anything about that, love?"

Clearly she was busted by the smirk on his handsome face. "I might have seen them on the floor by the bed at home."

"They were in my suitcase."

"And now they're not."

Throwing up his hands, Nate tucked his phone and the room key into his jacket pocket.

"What do you have against those shoes? It's like a

vendetta with you. They're comfortable shoes that look good, and they were expensive too."

"They're ugly," she said bluntly. "I'm sorry I took them out of your bag but you're so good-looking and then you wear those shoes. They make your feet look long and skinny."

"My feet are long and skinny," Nate laughed, holding up her wrap. "Thank you for the apology though. I do appreciate it but I don't want to encourage this going forward. I think you need some form of punishment for this behavior."

Ohhh. That sounded...kinky and dirty. Just the way she liked it.

"I have been a bad girl," she nodded, her pulses leaping at all the possibilities. "Very bad. Clearly I haven't learned my lesson."

"I think you'll spend the limo ride to the party on your knees." Nate leaned forward to whisper in her ear, his breath hot. "With my cock in that pretty mouth of yours."

Paige gave an exaggerated sigh even as her legs began to quiver. He was going to mess up her makeup. "If that's what it takes to make this up to you, then I guess I have to."

She needed to be bad more often.

———

Paige was reasonably put back together when they stepped out of the limo. What had started out as purely an oral exercise had quickly turned to something else. She'd spent the entire drive in L.A. traffic bouncing up and down on Nate's very hard length. At first, he hadn't wanted to let her come - part of her punishment and all - but a few raunchy suggestions in his ear won him over. She'd come in a glorious waterfall of technicolor pleasure. Then they'd had the task of freshening up, using almost the entire tiny box of tissues in the back of the vehicle. She'd swiped on a fresh coat of lipstick just as they'd pulled up to the curb.

Nate stepped out first, offering her his hand before leaning down to whisper in her ear. "I'm going to hold you to those suggestions, you naughty minx. When we get back to the hotel, you're in for quite a night."

Smiling broadly as she stepped out, she waved to a crush of fans behind a barricade.

"That's the plan, handsome. When you say night, you better mean *all night*."

His deeply satisfied laugh could be heard all the way up the red carpet and heads swiveled at the sound. "It's a promise, my love."

Just as they had a dozen times or more, they worked the red carpet slowly and methodically. Posing for pictures and signing autographs. It didn't bother her as much anymore, especially with Nate at her side. She wasn't blasé about it either but this was something she could handle. Loving it was out of the question. Nate, on the other hand, was in his element, laughing and joking with reporters and fans alike. He was energized by the attention and sometimes she simply wanted to stop and watch him work. He loved them as much as they loved him.

By the time they reached the end of the carpet and the entrance to the venue, Paige was ready for a strong drink. This evening was supposed to be a chance to have fun and let loose. She wasn't much of a party girl but this night was important to Nate. It was his final goodbye, although he'd see all of his friends when it came time to promote the film. This chapter of his life was coming to a close and she hoped he was in the right frame of mind to move on. With her and Flynn.

The minute they walked inside the venue they were greeted by a grim-faced Max.

"Max, smile. It's a party," she teased him, giving him a hug and getting kisses on the cheeks in return. "Loosen up. Have some fun."

Not even a little smile from him. He grabbed Nate's arm and dragged him aside, whispering fiercely into his ear. Paige stood there trying to figure out what was going on or read Max's lips. Nate, for his part looked just as agitated, his cheeks turning red and his fingers scraping through his perfectly gelled hair.

Something was definitely up. Nate straightened his tie and strode back to her, placing an arm around her waist. "Love, we need talk."

She'd never heard Nate sound so tense, almost fearful.

"I'm listening."

Nate's gaze darted around the dimly-lit packed room, his jaw tight. "Not here. In private. It's important or I wouldn't ask."

Something had gone, as Nate would say, "tit's up" to put him and Max in such a tizzy.

"Let me sneak off to the ladies' room and finish freshening up and then we can talk."

Nate nodded. "Max and I will be by the bar. He said there's a private terrace just next to it where we can talk."

"Get me a Cosmo?"

"Of course." Nate kissed her, his lips urgent as his fingers brushed her cheek. "I adore you, Paige. Please remember that."

"I adore you too."

Those were facts she wasn't likely to forget.

Paige found the restroom without any trouble, despite the horrific lighting and dark corners. Quickly taking care of business, she was just about to come out of the stall when she heard the bathroom door swing open and the sound of giggling. Voices. Young.

Holy hell. It couldn't be. She had to be mistaken.

Her.

It was *her*. Stella Riley.

This had to be what Max and Nate were so upset about. But why was she even here? She wasn't in any of the movies. Christ, was she dating some other poor bastard and planning to ruin his life too?

"I can't wait to see his face," she laughed. "I've brought the two women he had the threesome with and they're going to make it look like I ran into them by accident, only to be reminded of my heartbreak last year. I've got paps stationed at the exit to capture my anguish. His PR people threw me under the bus after I ended it and now he'll pay for that. He thinks the press and the public have forgotten his kinky night at the hotel. Well, I never forget anything, and now everyone else is going to be reminded of what he did to me. The press will be talking about his cheating and deviant sex life for weeks or more. My name will be in all the papers and everyone will want to interview me. Maybe even Oprah."

This little bitch was evil. Paige had known that already but to see - or hear - it in action was something completely different. This girl needed to grow the fuck up and move on.

"I bet he's wishing he still had you," the friend said. "Have you seen his new girlfriend? Ugly. She's like a hobbit or something."

Paige had to cover her mouth to keep from laughing. Hell yes, she was short. She was probably ugly too, but then she had brains and a sense of humor. That would last longer than firm tits and a flat stomach.

"She writes books," Stella snorted. "So boring. She's like...ancient."

Compared to this snotty little miss, Paige was pretty old. Not enough to be her mother but enough to know better. The universe didn't revolve around Stella Riley.

Paige made a mental note to kick Nate in the balls. What had he been thinking getting involved with this bitch, even if it was only fake?

"She's just his speed," the sidekick giggled over the sound of sniffing. Jesus, were they doing cocaine? Did people still do that? It wasn't the eighties anymore. "You said he was bad in bed and had a tiny dick. He's probably all she could get."

So Stella Riley was trying to pass off Nate as an actual boyfriend? Paige knew good and well the lousy actress had never slept with him.

Boy, had Stella missed out.

Smiling widely, Paige straightened her dress and shoved the door open so it banged against the other stall. If she was going to do this, she might as well make an entrance.

"Excuse me."

Paige elbowed her way in between the two girls to get to the mirror to reapply her lipstick. She was halfway through when she looked up to see Stella and her friend staring at her. Excellent.

"Stella, honey. Your mouth is hanging open." Paige pointed to the stunned girl who was wiping white powder from her nostrils. "It's not a good look for you."

Stella recovered quickly, her lip curling into a sneer. "Whatever, Grandma. This is a private conversation."

Paige's smile grew wider. She kind of felt sorry for Stella but not that much. She brought on most of her own problems. She lived for the drama.

"A private conversation held in a public bathroom while you're snorting an illegal substance. Right." Paige dropped the gold tube of lipstick back into her purse. "I just thought I'd let you know that I heard what you said and there is no way those paps are getting one picture of your fake tears. You'll have to get your name in the paper another way because you're not using him again. Those days are over."

Smirking, Stella leaned down to get in Paige's face. "He's going to leave you, you know. The whole time we were together he was fucking everything with tits. If he couldn't be faithful to me, there is no way he'd be faithful to someone like you."

Paige casually shrugged. "I'm not surprised he was getting a piece elsewhere since you two weren't even really together. But you see, that's how we're different. I keep

Nate plenty busy. I doubt he has the energy or the inclination to look at another woman. In fact, I rode his monster cock in the limo on the way here like he was the pony I never got for Christmas. I came twice and that was just the appetizer tonight." She opened the door and shot Stella one last grin, enjoying the shocked looks on their faces. "And by the way, your acting sucks."

The door swinging shut behind her, she went to find Nate and tell him she already knew what he was going to tell her. It was certainly going to be an interesting evening. Because Paige was sure Stella wasn't done trying to cause trouble. She wanted her name in the papers.

CHAPTER
Twenty-Six

"YOU SAW HER? You talked to her?"

Nate was apoplectic, pacing back and forth on the patio, his face red, while Max tried to calm him down.

"She was in the bathroom. I couldn't hide in there all night," Paige argued, keeping her voice calm. "She's brought the two women from your threesome here to the party and she's planning to pretend running into them is an accident. Some sort of amazing coincidence. She's going to cry and act all heartbroken for the paps. I guess she needs the publicity for her latest shitty movie. She wants to remind America of how you humiliated yourself last year so she can play the victim again and get her name in the papers. This from the girl who's snorting cocaine in a public bathroom."

Scraping his fingers through his hair, Nate groaned. "This is a nightmare. Shit, why is she even here? How did she get an invitation and get those girls in here?" He whirled on his heel and faced Paige. "What did you say to her?"

About that...

"I was kind of in the moment," Paige began. "Upset about what she was planning. And then she said you had a tiny cock and was lousy in bed. Well, handsome, those were some fighting words."

He shook his head, his brows pulled together. "She's not exactly my type but I don't care what she said."

"She said you cheated on her and you would cheat on me."

Nate rolled his eyes. "You can't cheat on someone if you're not in a relationship. It's not like she was interested in me. You know I would never cheat on you, right? I would never do that."

He actually sounded worried.

"That's what I told her."

Nate and Max must have read her expression, because she had their undivided attention.

"Did you say anything else?" Nate asked cautiously.

Son of a bitch. Her snarky mouth was always getting her into trouble.

"I was trying to defend you."

"That's very sweet. What did you say?"

Rubbing her chin, Paige pursed her lips. "I told her that I was keeping you too busy to cheat on me and that I'd rode your monster-sized cock in the back of the limo on the way here and came twice. Oh, and I told her she was a lousy actress because she is."

Max's eyes widened and then he burst into laughter, choking on the whiskey he'd been drinking. Nate turned a particularly unattractive shade of purple before also bursting into gales of laughter. Paige took a seat at a patio table as the two men roared, snickered and whooped, tears running down their faces.

So glad I could amuse everyone.

Nate wiped at his eyes, still holding his stomach. "Love, you are a treasure."

What?

"You're not mad?"

Shaking his head, he pulled her into his arms where she snuggled close, her cheek on his chest. "I'm not angry. In fact, I feel rather special that I have a woman who would try to defend my honor. Not everyone would do that."

Max shook his head. "She may come after you, Paige."

She'd thought about that. "I'm pretty sure she nor any of her friends and fans read much, unless it's a text or a tweet. But she can try if she wants. I really don't care. I think people are starting to see her for what she is. She's not a nice person. At all."

"No, she is not," Nate shuddered.

"So what do we do?" Max asked. "We can't let her drag you through the mud again."

His arms dropping away, Nate walked over to the edge of the patio and then back again, a visible pulse at his temple. "When it's time to go, Max, you'll take Paige home. I'll leave separately."

No, no, no.

Paige replied before Max had a chance. She wasn't going to let him face this alone. "I don't think so. I'm not leaving you to face those reporters all by yourself. We're a team now, handsome."

"No." Nate shook his head, his lips turned down. "I won't let you get caught up in the stupidity of my past. Stella is gunning for me and I won't turn you into a human shield."

He was so fucking stubborn sometimes. "I think it would be helpful to remind the press that you've moved beyond that single moment in time and with me by your side it will be easier. You and me, walking out of this joint when the party is over, heads held high and wearing a blissful smile. You know, because we're so in love and Stella Riley is a big old loser."

His mouth fell open and she didn't have to wonder why. She'd used the "L" word. She'd be nervous if she didn't think her feelings were returned but after the last several weeks she was thinking they were.

Jesus, hopefully. Otherwise she was going to look like an idiot. An idiot in love with someone who didn't feel the same.

Now she was nervous, her heart lodged in her throat and yet somehow it managed to beat wildly.

"Love?"

Max backed toward the door. "This would be my cue to leave you both alone. Don't screw it up, Nate."

"I won't." He waited until Max disappeared inside the party. "You said love. Were you saying it sarcastically?"

Not only was he stubborn, he could be a trifle thick. Good thing he was so pretty and talented.

"Did I sound sarcastic?"

Frowning, Nate shrugged as if he didn't care. "It could go either way."

Time to be brave even though her knees were currently knocking together underneath these designer duds.

"I wasn't being sarcastic."

His gaze dropped to the concrete and then he looked up again, a look of pure tenderness and joy on his handsome features. "I love you too."

The impact of his words sent her reeling and she had to grab a hold of the back of a chair to keep upright. Hopefully a human being didn't need oxygen and love at the same time because she couldn't catch her breath.

"I didn't expect this," Paige said honestly. It had come out of left field but she couldn't deny how she felt.

She loved Nate Mason.

"Me neither, but I'm happy," he confessed, and she could swear she saw his eyes tear a little. His hands were shaking and he shoved them in his pockets. "That's why I can't let you walk out with me tonight. It's my job to protect you, love."

It was her job as well but he wasn't thinking about that at the moment. She loved him for trying to protect her but this wasn't the time for chivalry. She needed to show Nate just how strong she could be for him.

"What can they say about me? That I'm a few years older than you. Truth. That I'm a boring, middle-aged writer. More truth. If they make something up, it will be a lie and we'll know that." She placed her hands on his shoulders so she had all of his attention. He needed to hear this. "I love you, Nate. That means I love all of you. The good, the bad, and the downright awful. Even all the characters you've played over the years. You did something kind of stupid last year but you shouldn't have to pay the rest of your life. Don't let Stella Riley win. She wants you to be frightened and intimidated, and then she can control you. She thinks you're afraid to walk out of here and be face to face with those girls. Let's show her she has zero meaning in our new lives."

It was a long speech and she could see the war inside of him, going back and forth. He didn't want to face the paps alone but he didn't want to expose her to what Stella might be up to.

"There's so much bad, love. If I were Kai–"

She cut him off with a wave of her hand. "Kai doesn't exist and thank goodness. He's sexy and all but he'd be hell to be in a relationship with. I'll stick with Nate, if you don't mind. Now? Are we walking out of here together no matter who is waiting to get their picture taken?"

Crushing her to his chest, he proceeded to smear her lipstick quite thoroughly and satisfyingly. When he lifted his head, he pressed soft kisses all over her face from her forehead to her chin as she giggled and batted uselessly at his broad chest with her hands.

"What are you doing? You're tickling me."

He paused his lips hovering above hers, his expression solemn. "I adore you and everything about you."

The seriousness of the moment wasn't lost on her. This meant something. "I adore you too. I love you."

"And I love you. More than you can possibly know." His throat bobbed and there was wetness around his eyes. "That you're willing to stand by me when I don't deserve–"

Her fingers covered his mouth, warm from their kisses.

He had no idea that he was worthy of her loyalty. She'd have to show him. "You do deserve it. We'll walk out of here like we give no fucks."

"Not a one," he whispered, his lips covering hers again, barely at first like the wings of a butterfly, then more as she slid her arms around his neck and pulled him closer. Every inch of her was pressed against his hard-muscled body, and everywhere his fingers brushed left a trail of fire on her skin, making her want what only he could give her.

Groaning as he reluctantly pulled away, he flicked a glance over his shoulder. "I suppose we should join the party. There are people I want you to meet. I can't wait to show off the most beautiful woman in the room."

She had to tease him a little. "You are in love, aren't you? That room is full of actresses and models. I won't be the best looking." Rising up on her tiptoes, she pressed a kiss to his lips. "But thank you for thinking that I am."

"You have no idea just how gorgeous you are. Every man in there is going to wish he was me."

Giggling, she trailed her fingers up his torso to where his pulse beat rapidly at the base of his neck. "Then let's get in there make them jealous. I know the women will be. You look especially yummy in that suit. I can't wait to take it off of you."

Nate looked of two minds about rejoining the party and she was in the same boat. A big part of her wanted to blow this off and go home to do all sorts of debauched things to one another but the more practical part of her knew they had to stay. This was his goodbye to Kai. And a middle finger to Stella.

He straightened his tie and smiled. "You are naughty. We won't stay late."

When Nate's costars heard what Stella Riley had cooked up for him they rallied to his aid. Max and a few other actors from the *Thunder* cast had Nate point out the two girls and they'd talked to them personally, asking them not to do this publicity stunt. A short conversation, some selfies, and a few dances later, the girls left by the emergency exit using Max's limo with smiles on their faces. Paige had no idea what the men had promised them but she had heard something about one of the guys attending a birthday party.

Stella kicked up a fuss but no one paid much attention to her as even the photographers were getting tired of her games.

It was two in the morning before Nate and Paige left the party but they didn't leave alone. They were flanked by Max and the other actors including the very sexy and famous Tyler Gaylord and Sam Collins.

The paps were so excited to see all the stars of the movie together in one picture, doing silly antics for the cameras and signing autographs, they forgot about Stella's victim act. There was only one line in the article the next day mentioning that she and Nate used to date and that she was also at the party. End of story. Paige had a feeling Garrett might have also put some pressure on the tabloids as well but she couldn't be sure.

The most important thing was that she'd shown Nate that love meant that she would stand beside him no matter what. He deserved that kind of devotion and he didn't have to be anybody but himself to get it.

Paige waved the morning paper in Nate's face as they sat in the hotel room eating lunch the next day. They'd slept through breakfast. "You have good friends, handsome. But I still owe you a good, hard kick in the crotch."

His brows went up as he sipped his tea. "That sounds painful. What did I do to earn that treatment?"

"Her."

"Her," he sighed. "Technically, I never *did* her, and in my defense I didn't know what she was like when I signed the contract. If I had..."

Paige waggled her eyebrows. "I'll tell you what. You can make it up to me."

"Again?"

They'd just about worn out the mattress after the party.

"I can still walk. That means your job isn't finished."

Nate ripped the newspaper from Paige's hands and tossed it away before jumping up and sweeping her into his arms.

"Never let it be said that Nathan Andrew Mason only does half a job."

Giggling, she allowed herself to be thrown on the messy bed. "Ravish me, you wild man."

They didn't leave the room until they had to catch their plane the next morning. Life was good. Oh so good.

CHAPTER
Twenty-Seven

AS MUCH AS Nate loved London - and he did with his whole heart - Paige was an American, and he loved her too. Americans celebrated Thanksgiving. She'd been planning the menu with Carrie for almost three weeks. Jason was coming home from Princeton and Paige was excited about being in her own kitchen and in her own bed. Preferably with Nate by her side.

As sweet as she was, she didn't pressure him. She simply said that she would love for him to come see her home as she'd seen his. She had gone out of her way to accommodate his schedule since they'd met so he didn't feel like he could say no. After all, he truly did want to be with her. His preference for London was well-known but he could tell she was getting a little homesick. Her calls to Carrie became longer and she'd seemed slightly melancholy for a while afterward. She'd talk about her home more and more, and her smile would be at times both excited and sad.

So he'd agreed to accompany her, of course.

Their relationship was happier and more loving than ever, he was glad to say. She was it for him. He was in love and she was all he wanted. Now he just had to convince her that he was worth taking a chance on. How to do that he didn't know but the relationship was on solid ground. They were learning to live together but there were still struggles. Like today. They had boarded their flight for Tampa - a flight he'd wanted to delay until she felt better - and were waiting for takeoff. Clearly she didn't feel well, and hadn't for several days. She'd ended up at a local doctor in London who had diagnosed her with strep throat. He'd prescribed a course of antibiotics and she'd been on them for forty-eight hours so she was no longer contagious. Nate, of course, had wanted to spoil and coddle her but Paige kept saying she didn't feel that badly.

Thankfully, in the last twenty-four hours her focus had turned to one goal and one goal only. Home. He was determined to get her there in one piece.

Paige groaned and closed her eyes, rubbing at her temple. Her face was paler than usual and her eyes had a glassy sheen to them. His girl was sick and fighting it. She needed her rest and he couldn't wait to tuck her into bed with some tea.

"Did you take your sedative?" Nate asked, rubbing his hand over hers, the fingers cold under his touch.

She shook her head. "I took some cold medicine instead. It will make me sleep and help this sore throat."

Sighing, he hated the helpless feeling that swamped him. There wasn't much he could do at the moment except feed her soothing hot liquids and hold her hand. "You shouldn't be flying when you feel like this."

"You're right but I bet you've done it when you needed to be somewhere." She looked up at him then, her fingers squeezing his. "I don't know how to explain it, Nate, but I need to be home. I need to see Jason. I know it's selfish and you wish we were in London–"

"Hush," Nate scolded softly as the engines revved and rumbled under them. At that moment, he understood this woman who always seemed in control and capable. When she was sick she was like a little girl. She wanted to be in a familiar space. "It is not selfish. I showed you London and you're going to show me your home too. I can't wait to see it and also to meet Jason in the flesh. It's going to be a wonderful trip."

He held her hand as they took off and then she fell asleep. He'd lifted the armrest so she could curl into his body and rest her head on his chest. He wanted to show that he could put her first, that her happiness was more important than his own. For so long he'd been selfish and self-centered, living for himself. Now he had Paige to think about and love. She'd stood by him at the party in Los Angeles and he'd vowed that night that he would earn that devotion. He wasn't sure he deserved it but he'd crawl over hot coals on his hands and knees to get it.

Paige's love was what had been missing.

———

It was early the next morning. Despite getting in late, Nate was wide awake before six out of habit. He disentangled himself from Paige and pressed a kiss to her forehead, tucking the blankets around her sleeping form. Her color was much better and her breathing seemed much less labored. Less than twelve hours home and she was already feeling better.

He pulled on a pair of sweat pants and a t-shirt and headed downstairs to put on some coffee, deciding to skip his run. He didn't want to be too far from the house if Paige needed anything. He could go later today if she was resting comfortably.

Nate hadn't had much of a chance to see the house when they'd arrived exhausted last night. Sun slanted in the large windows and he could see touches of Paige everywhere in the home. Splashes of her favorite color - red. Comfortable pillows and polished wood. An impressive gourmet kitchen. And books. Bookshelves crammed to the gills. He'd have to check those out and see what was there.

At the bottom of the stairs, he was about to turn into the kitchen but the fireplace caught his eye. Specifically, the framed photos on the mantle. He smiled as he saw one of Jason with St. Nick, perhaps looking all of three or four years old. There was one of Paige and Jason at his high school graduation. She looked every bit the loving and proud mother.

Reaching out, Nate lifted a fancy crystal frame from the mantle and studied the photo inside. Paige's wedding picture. No, Paige and Noah. Nate couldn't deny the man that had come before him. The couple looked young and in love, beaming with happiness. Their whole life ahead of them, naive to what lay ahead. Because she'd told him,

Nate knew that the puffy white dress she wore concealed a secret. She was already pregnant with Jason. The cut of the gown covered up the fact the she was five months along and showing.

Carefully, he placed the frame back on the mantle and reached for another. This one of Paige round and pregnant, her arms protectively over her belly. Nate's chest tightened painfully and his hand trembled as he placed the picture back.

There was only one left. A family photograph. Noah, Paige, and Jason - who was possibly around ten in the picture, all gangly arms and legs. They were all in white and red Christmas sweaters in front of a holiday backdrop. Noah's arm was around Paige and his hand was on Jason's shoulder.

They were a family. Or had been.

Paige had lived an entire life while Nate had been getting his career going. She'd written books, married, raised a child. Carpooled. Went to soccer games and teacher conferences. She'd monitored homework and fought for her marriage. She'd taken her vow of 'in sickness and in health' seriously. What had he done?

Worked. Worked some more. Partied and drank. Played the field with more women than he could remember. Lived every day in the most self-centered manner possible. He'd prioritized *everything and everyone* below his career. Who the fuck had he become? Sometimes he barely recognized himself. Was he a man that even deserved a life with Paige? He wasn't so sure he did.

"I keep most of those up there for Jason."

The family photo still in his hand, Nate whirled around at the sound of Paige's voice.

"I didn't mean to–"

She waved off his apology and came to stand beside him, her fingers lovingly brushing the frames. "It's fine. They're on display so they're not a secret. I keep these up here for Jason mostly, to remind him of his father. We had some good times." She tapped on the glass of the picture he held in his hand. "That was the last one we had taken, all three of us together. Noah was diagnosed about six months later and he got quite thin. He didn't like anyone to take his picture after that."

Swallowing a lump in his throat, Nate replaced the picture on the mantle. "They're all lovely. You were a beautiful bride and you glowed when you were with child."

Giggling, she pointed to the photo of her, late in her pregnancy. "Do you know why women glow when they're pregnant? The oil glands in our faces go into overdrive. We're not glowing, Nate. We're greasy. And if we're dragging around twenty or so extra pounds in the Florida heat we might also be sweaty. Not so romantic, huh?"

He put his arm around her shoulders. "I refuse to believe that. You were gorgeous."

Leaning against him, she gazed at the display on the mantle. "I'll offer some of these photos to Jason when he's here. I can put them into storage for him."

Nate shook his head. "No, I didn't mean for you to take them down. I was just being curious, that's all."

"It's time," she said softly. "Maybe we can put a picture of you and me up here. Start some new memories."

He wanted that so much it was a real physical pain inside of him.

"Baby girl," he said in his sternest voice, turning away from the photos and giving her every bit of his attention. His thoughts had gone to a dangerous place, one he wasn't ready to deal with. "What are you doing out of bed so early?"

"I woke up and you weren't there," she said. "I came looking for you. Plus, I need to take my antibiotic anyway."

"You're going to rest today. No arguments."

Sliding her arms around his middle, she laid her head on his chest right where his heart beat. For her. "You'll get none from me, although I'm feeling better. I was thinking of getting my e-reader and sitting out by the pool. It's supposed to be a beautiful day. You should go for a run."

"I'm playing doctor today. I can run anytime."

She batted her eyelashes at him. "Doctor and patient. That's one game we haven't tried."

"And you are in no condition to play it," Nate responded promptly. "Head back to bed and I'll bring you some tea and your medication. Then I'll start breakfast."

"Bacon?" Paige's eyes lit up. Even sick, her appetite didn't waver. She had a cast-iron stomach.

"Bacon," he conceded. "And toast, and anything else you want. Now up the stairs with you."

He knew she wasn't feeling a hundred percent when she didn't argue. He also knew this docile mood wouldn't last long but while it did, he'd show her he could take care of her. That he wasn't all about himself.

————

Paige's son Jason arrived Monday evening just after dinner. The young man was tall, the same height as Nate but with a wiry physique. The same physique that Nate had at that age. Jason's hair was dark like his father's and he had an easy smile just like Paige. Giving her a big hug when he'd come in the door, he'd lifted his much smaller mother clean off the floor. Nate thought he saw a tear in the young man's eye as well, although Jason would probably never admit it.

Paige fussed over her only child, warming the lasagna rollups she'd made for dinner. She silently urged Nate to speak with Jason as he ate, anxious for the two most important men in her life to get along. From the looks Nate was getting from her son, he wasn't sure that was going to happen.

Her phone rang and she lunged for it on the counter. "This is my agent and I need to take it. Jason, there's homemade ice cream in the fridge for dessert plus a tin of cookies on the counter."

Bustling into her office, she'd left Nate and Jason alone. This was his opportunity to make nice.

"Your mother is an amazing cook, and I think she and Carrie have some special recipes lined up for Thanksgiving."

Jason wiped his mouth with his paper napkin. "Most of the recipes are traditions from her own family. The only changes are the desserts. She tries new ones every year."

"I'm looking forward to them. This will be my first Thanksgiving."

"How long are you staying?"

So much for beating around the bush. Right to the point.

Nate could do that too.

"Paige and I are returning to London at the end of the week. I'm doing some voice work for an animated film."

Jason placed his fork on his empty plate. "And then?"

Ah. Nate was beginning to see where this was going.

"I'm not sure. You and Paige are invited to spend Christmas with my family if you like."

The young man weighed Nate's words before answering. "So if we spend the holidays with you, then are you coming back here?"

Taking a slow breath, Nate chose his words carefully. "Well, no. I have a play in London starting after the first of the year."

Jason's jaw jutted out. "And then?"

"Hopefully another movie."

Hopping up from the kitchen island, Jason rinsed his plate. "But you don't know where it will be filmed. So that's Mom's life now? Following you around like a groupie wherever you happen to be? She has a home and it's right here. She loves it here. Do you even care about that or are you just a typical egomaniac movie star? Because she loves the warm weather and the sunshine. She wants another dog, Nate. She's been talking about that for at least a year. Can she get one if you guys are running all over the world? Answer me this. Does she get anything that she wants or is it all about you?"

Swallowing hard, Nate forced himself to meet Jason's scornful gaze. He didn't much like seeing himself through the young man's eyes. "I'm determined to give your mother anything she needs to make her happy."

Snorting, Jason shook his head. "As long as it's what you want. You don't fool me. You're driving all of this and Mom is just along for the ride. You make all the decisions."

Jason was certainly Paige's son.

Nate tried again, hoping his sincerity would be enough. "I made these commitments before I met your mother and I have to see them through. I can be sued if I don't. When these are done, I'll be able to make decisions based on what we - as a couple - want. I can promise you her wishes will be taken into account. I know you don't believe this but I try to do that as much as possible."

"You want her to move to London with you."

It wasn't phrased as a question. Nate couldn't lie.

"I do," he confirmed with a nod of his head. "And your mum probably wants me to move here. A Brit in Florida and a southern belle in London. Both of us fish out of water, although your mother fits right in, I must say. Somewhere and somehow we're going to have to compromise."

Jason shoved his plate and fork into the dishwasher. "You're trying to take her away from her family and friends."

Nate shook his head and stepped closer to the tense young man. "I promise you I'm not. If I have to buy you your own home wherever we decide to live, I will. I will not take your mum away from you." He looked directly into Jason's eyes. "I know you don't believe this right now but in the not too distant future you'll have your own life and you'll start building your own family. Don't get me wrong, you'll still love your mother but you'll be busy starting your career. You might take a job far away from here. Maybe the woman you fall in love with might live somewhere else. Your mother deserves her own life and happiness, Jason. She's done all the things she should. She's been responsible and caring. Now is her time. Time to have fun, travel, live, and see all the things she's missed. She's still actually quite young and she has many years ahead of her. I think you love her enough to want that for her."

Crossing his arms over his chest, Jason leaned against the kitchen counter. "I'll always be there for Mom. She's sacrificed so much for me and Dad."

"Of course you will," Nate replied, patting the boy on the shoulder. "But what is she supposed to do while you're off at school? Or working your first job? Or getting married? Is she supposed to sit here and not change anything? Just wait for those times you come to visit? Because that would be for you, not for her. Put her first, Jason."

The young man stood straighter and nodded. "I'll make you a deal. I'll put her first if you will too."

Nate smiled. Jason didn't even realize what he was asking. Only someone that young would think that was easy or even possible. Jason wasn't always going to put Paige first and that was a normal part of growing up and separating. But Nate's relationship with her was far different.

"For the first time in my life," Nate confessed, his voice shaking with the power of his emotions, "I actually feel like that might be possible. It never has been before but I've never felt like this. Your mother is one of a kind and I want to spend the rest of my life loving her and taking care of her. I hope that we have your support but if we don't I'm still not going anywhere. I'm here to stay, Jason."

A moment passed between them and Nate felt like there was an understanding. At least there was less animosity. It was a beginning and for that he was grateful.

Paige ran back into the kitchen at that moment, her phone still in her hand, jumping around and so excited he couldn't make out a word she was saying. He and Jason managed to calm her down long enough to set her cell on the counter before she broke it. Her cheeks were pink and her green eyes sparkled with happiness.

"Darling, you look about to burst. What was the call about?"

She grabbed his arm and shook it, practically vibrating with excitement.

"They want to meet about the movie. The studio is ready to talk." She stood on tiptoe and kissed his lips. "You're going to be Flynn. We're going to make a movie together."

Wrapping his arms around Paige, Nate was so overcome with emotion he couldn't speak. Everything he'd ever wanted was right within his reach. Paige. Love. A new start for his career by playing Flynn and directing. He certainly had much to be thankful for this year and all because of this amazing woman.

CHAPTER
Twenty-Eight

FINALLY FEELING HUMAN AGAIN, Paige was making up for lost time in the kitchen. So far she'd finished a pumpkin pie and a chocolate chip cookie pie, both of which Nate seemed inordinately interested in. She'd had to shoo him away or she was sure they would have ended up in his stomach when her back was turned.

She was gathering her supplies to decorate the cake pops and Nate, as usual, was right behind her. For a grown man he liked to lick the beaters and the bowl far too much. All to help her, of course.

"What's next?" he asked eagerly as if lunch hadn't been less than an hour ago. "What do you need me to do?"

She retrieved the cake pops from the refrigerator. "We're going to decorate these. You can put sticks in them and help me dip them in the chocolate if you like. Then we can put sprinkles on them or decorate with chocolate in piping bags. You can be as creative as you like."

Frowning, he inspected the chocolate and yellow cake balls stacked in the box. "When did you make these?"

He'd missed that set of beaters and bowls and apparently wasn't happy about it. She'd licked them clean and didn't care that it hadn't even been eight in the morning. "While you were out for your run. It's easier to decorate them when they're cold."

It was like doing crafts with a golden retriever. Paws and fur everywhere. Or in Nate's case, long arms reaching across what she was working on, melted chocolate dripping on the table, on their clothes, everywhere but on the pops. Sugar glitter and sprinkles dusted the countertops, their shirts, the floor, and there was even some in Nate's hair. He was having a ball so she wasn't going to say a word. She hadn't seen this big of a mess since Jason was in grade school.

"I think we're done," Paige said with a grateful sigh. "I don't think I ever want to look at another cake pop ever again."

"Aren't we supposed to eat these on Thanksgiving?" Nate asked. "That only gives you until the day after tomorrow."

"Knowing Jason and his friends these won't make it until the day after tomorrow. I make these to keep them away from the real desserts. Those boys ate me out of house and home during their high school years."

Nate was eyeing one of the cake pops as if he wanted to bite into it right there and then. "Why didn't you just send the other boys home?"

"Because I was happy that my house was the neighborhood hangout. That meant I kind of knew what my teenage son was doing from time to time. I figured an astronomical grocery bill was the price I had to pay. It was worth it to me. Honestly, I think they would have hung out here even if I only provided popsicles and soda. They liked the game room upstairs."

Nate was giving her that smile again. "You're a wonderful mother."

"Ha! You never saw me yell or stomp around. I've been known to lose my temper."

"You're sexy when you yell."

His voice had dropped an octave and she shivered at the suggestion in his words. They hadn't since before she got sick. It had been too long.

She shoved the last of the dirty parchment paper in the trashcan. "It sounds like you have something on your mind, handsome. Care to share?"

She reached for the bowls of melted chocolate but his hand stayed her movements. "I do have something on my mind." His blue eyes had turned dark, his pupils blown wide. "You. Me. This chocolate. A blindfold. What do you say?"

Glancing down at the bowl, she could see that there was still half of the dark chocolate and white chocolate left. She did have a sweet tooth.

"I think I say yes."

———

Paige kicked off her shorts and tank top, grabbed a black scarf from her closet, and climbed into bed after closing the blinds. She didn't have nosy neighbors but there was no sense flaunting her sex life either. Nate had stayed behind in the kitchen to warm up the chocolate in the microwave but he wasn't far behind her. Flipping the lock on the bedroom door, he then placed the two chocolate bowls on the nightstand.

"So am I the blindfold-er or the blindfold-ee, love? Your choice today."

Nate's smooth as caramel voice rolled over her and she felt herself relax a little more, knowing she could safely put herself in his competent and skillful hands. Absolute trust.

"The blindfold-er", Paige replied immediately. "But let's just remember that Jason is hanging out with his friends and will be home before dinner."

That sexy as hell eyebrow quirked up. "Darling, dinner isn't for four hours or so. You certainly are an optimist this afternoon."

"I know how you are when you haven't gotten any for awhile. Just go easy on me. I don't want my son to see that I got fucked so hard I can't walk." She shook her finger at him. "And no visible love bites or bruises. I'm a mother with a sexually active son. He'll know exactly what they are. He's not a toddler anymore."

Nate chuckled and tugged his t-shirt over his head. "I love it when you get stern, and I will be careful. Jason doesn't need to know anything about our sex life."

Paige was trying hard to keep both Nate and Jason on an even keel. Change was never easy and Jason hadn't always dealt with it all that well. Just like Noah, he was a fan of the status quo. He'd pitched a fit the last time she'd rearranged the living room furniture.

Kicking his shorts away, he ran his hand up and down

his cock, his gaze hot and full of desire. Paige reached over to the bedside table and held up the black scarf.

"I think this will work. You're also welcome to use anything in here that might strike your fancy."

She'd given this a lot of thought and had decided it would be better to brazen out his discovery of her stash of sex toys. She shouldn't be embarrassed. She was a grown woman with needs that hadn't been fulfilled in a long time before she met him but the thought of him opening the drawer by accident had filled her with horror. Better to be in control of the situation and introduce it on her terms.

His brows shot up. "Is that where you keep your naughty things, love? I can't wait to see what you have in there."

He didn't have to wait. They were sitting in the drawer not three feet from where he was standing. Just look at them, laugh, and then they could move on.

"I don't consider them naughty, and there's not much there. Just a few things."

Nate didn't even glance at the drawer, instead advancing on her, snatching the blindfold from her fingers. Sitting on the edge of the mattress, he pulled her in for a long slow kiss that singed her lips and curled her toes.

"Do you trust me, love?"

Paige nodded, her mouth suddenly gone dry. "I do."

"If you say stop then everything comes to a halt. Understand?"

Nodding again, she sat very still as Nate pressed the blindfold over her eyes and wrapped it around her head, knotting it snugly in the back, careful not to catch any of her hair in it. He tugged at the material, fixing it exactly as he wanted it.

"Can you see anything?"

"Just a little light from the left corner."

He adjusted it, his warm fingers brushing her over sensitized skin. "Better?"

"Dark. Now what?"

His chuckle vibrated through his chest. "Now you lie back and be a good girl. I want you to do everything I tell you to, do you understand?"

She nodded but he tapped her chin lightly. "I need to hear your words, love. Do you understand? We don't have to do this if you don't want to."

There was no way she was stopping, already well down the road of arousal. "I understand."

"Good girl," he praised. "Now lie back and put your hands under the pillow. I want you to keep them there no matter what happens. Can you do that?"

Paige tucked her hands under the pillow as Nate pulled back the covers, exposing her naked body to the cooler air. Her nipples puckered in anticipation as she listened to his slow, even breathing in the silence. Her other senses came alive and she could smell her own arousal, the sweet aroma of chocolate, even the citrus in Nate's body wash.

"I don't think there is a more beautiful sight in the world than you lying here like the most luscious buffet. I'm definitely going to feast on every inch of you."

She didn't bother to beg as she knew he'd proceed at his own pace. Listening, she heard the spoon scrape the sides of the bowl and then warmth as a dollop of chocolate landed on her abdomen. Her body bowed as his tongue lapped at it, sending arrows of arousal straight to her clit. More stripes along her torso, more of Nate's tongue running up and down, sometimes with short flicks and other times with long, slow strokes. Each one sent her higher, making her twist and moan in the sheets. Her fingers flexed on the pillow, her grip tightening as if she could hold on to her sanity by not letting go of the fabric bunched in her hands.

A few warm drops slid down her already hard nipples and she sucked in a breath, waiting...no, pleading for the feel of his rough tongue. It was frustrating to not be able to see him, his expression, the look in his eyes, but it was exciting too. It was all up to him and her only job was to accept the pleasure he gave her.

Sucking a hard peak into his mouth, he scraped the tender flesh with his teeth as he swirled his tongue around and around until her torso was arched off of the bed, his name on her lips. She was so close to going over.

But of course the British bastard wasn't just going to let her come. He played with her for what seemed like an eternity. A kiss here. A nibble there. A long lick as he lapped up the chocolate he'd painted on her quivering flesh. She never knew where he was going to go next and the surprise kept her on the edge, teetering there. Sweat covered her flesh and the room felt hot and humid. A breath would send her over.

He insinuated himself between her legs, his shoulders pushing her thighs wide. Cool air raised gooseflesh on her arms as he hovered there, just inches from her clit. This time there would be no shock and the anticipation was killing her slowly. Without a smidgen of doubt, she knew where the next drops of chocolate were going to land and her legs shook with arousal, fierce in its intensity. She wanted to scream as the tension grew, every nerve in her body on alert. Biting down on her lip, she tasted blood in the effort to keep from screaming. She needed him right this second.

When it finally came, the heat was a sweet relief. This time she did scream his name as his mouth and tongue devoured her, his face pressed in the most intimate of spots. Her thighs clamped onto his head as she rode his tongue to one orgasm after another. They all began to run together and it felt like her body didn't belong to her anymore. He was the maestro and he conducted this orchestra in complete control.

It might have been minutes or hours later when he swiftly climbed up her body and impaled her on his massive cock. This time she couldn't keep her hands under the pillow; she had to grab onto his shoulders and hold on for dear life. He was thrusting into her like she was sending him off to battle, grunting and gasping with the effort to pound her into the mattress.

She wouldn't come again, her body too spent, but she caressed his back and dug her heels into his very fine ass as she whispered filthy dirty things into his ear, urging him on. As his peak hit, she could feel every muscle in his body go rigid as her name fell from his lips. He collapsed on top of her, his breathing ragged and labored, his skin covered in a fine sheen of sweat.

Eventually he levered off of her and eased the blindfold from her eyes. She blinked a few times against the light before looking up into the worshipful gaze of the man she loved.

"We did good?" he asked, hope in his tone. "The trust stuff. It was okay?"

"It was better than okay. We've got to put that down on the list of things to do again."

His smile was dazzling and she marveled how she could still be surprised when she saw it. She didn't think she'd ever get used to it. The buzz of his phone broke through the intimate moment they were having and she groaned, pushing at his shoulder. She was becoming used to the phone interruptions, hers and his.

"That's yours."

Groaning with the effort to move, he reached onto the nightstand and checked the screen. "It's Max. I'd better take this."

"Tell him I was starting to like him but if he interrupts sex again he's on Santa's naughty list."

"It could have been worse. He could have called five minutes ago."

Chuckling, Nate stood and padded naked into the bathroom, phone pressed to his ear.

Dozing for a few minutes, she was roused by Nate sitting on the edge of the bed. "Darling, are you awake?"

She rubbed her eyes and sighed. So much for her nap. "I am now. How's Max?"

The look on Nate's face didn't say happy things. "He's not good. Alana was supposed to come to London so they could make one last try at reconciliation. Now she's called and she is not coming. He's devastated."

Paige pointed to the phone Nate was holding. "Is he still on the line?"

He nodded. "He's on mute. I think he's been drinking. He wanted to save his marriage but she won't even try."

Some people didn't appreciate what they had and Paige had a feeling Max's wife was one of them.

"Tell him to get the first flight out and get down here. Charter a jet if he has to. We don't want him to be alone."

Nate's face lit up, his smile full of gratitude. "Are you sure, love? I was afraid to ask."

"I'm sure. Tell him to get his ass down here. We'll have him cheered up in no time. Or we'll have him drunk. Just tell him we can definitely do one of those things."

How did one cheer up a famous Shakespearean actor without sex? Paige was going figure out the answer.

———

The kitchen smelled wonderful. Turkey, stuffing, potatoes, sage, and cinnamon all combined to create one delicious sniff. Max had drifted in and out of the kitchen but always with a drink in one hand. Frankly he didn't give a fuck if it was too early to drink alcohol. He was going to do whatever he wanted. Now he was hiding in Paige's office and hoping no one noticed he had disappeared.

It was nice of Paige to invite him but he shouldn't have come. He was bringing everyone down with his foul, gray mood. He knew enough about America to know this was supposed to be a happy holiday with everyone feeling thankful for all they had. He wasn't feeling particularly grateful about anything.

Wait...he did have one thing to be thankful for. His lawyers and family had made him have a prenup with Alana. It was going to save him millions.

It wouldn't save him any heartache, though. Nor would it restore his shredded dignity. That was gone forever. He'd pleaded with the woman who had cheated on him to give their marriage another try. He still had a nasty taste in his mouth from saying the words. She'd destroyed their love when she'd been unfaithful but he'd been willing to see if he could fall in love again. She'd pretty much laughed in his face.

"Dinner is in about half an hour."

Carrie stood in the doorway of Paige's office wearing a blue apron over her casual sundress. Even at the end of November, Florida was almost eighty degrees.

"Thank you." He held up his whiskey glass. "I think I need a refill."

He tried to stand but the room spun and he had to grab the arm of the chair. Carrie was instantly at his side, helping him sit back down as she took the empty glass from his hand. He protested but she shook her head. "Relax, Hamlet. I'll get you a refill."

He scowled, not sure if the American girl was serious or if she was teasing him. "I've never played Hamlet but I did play Richard the Third."

She nodded and reached into the drawer of a desk, pulling out a bottle. "I know. Paige and I went to see it at the local movie theatre for the National Theatre showing. You were amazing." She held up the whiskey bottle. "This isn't as fine as what you were drinking. It's from my own stash but I think you're far gone enough that you won't be able to tell the difference."

Max cleared his throat and sat straighter in the chair, trying to look as sober as possible.

"Are you insinuating that I am in my cups?"

She handed him the refilled highball glass. "I'm not insinuating anything. I'm saying it straight out. You're soused, dude."

"I am not a dude," he said stiffly. This was why Paige made fun of him. "And thank you for the compliment."

She shrugged and leaned back against the desk. "You brought a rawness to the role that I appreciated."

"You read the Baird?"

Laughter bubbled from her pink lips and her cheeks turned the same shade. "I only know what I read in high school. Romeo and Juliet and Hamlet. That's it. They were kind of depressing. It didn't make me want to read more."

Max found himself smiling for the first time that day. "They are tragedies. But you went to see it anyway."

"Paige wanted to go. Then she spends the entire trip home telling me how she would have rewritten it to have a happy ending. So basically I get the best of both worlds. She has a good imagination."

"You should try one of Shakespeare's comedies," Max suggested but Carrie pulled a face.

"I get hung up on the language and it pulls me out of the story. I think I'll stick to regular novels." No one said anything for a long moment and the silence seemed to thicken between them. "I'm sorry about your marriage."

Max stiffened, shocked that Nate and Paige had revealed something so personal. It wasn't that he didn't trust Carrie. He did. Obviously if she worked for Paige she knew how to be discreet but it was just one more person who knew his humiliation.

"I know what you're thinking," she said, breaking into his thoughts. "They didn't tell me. You did."

Scowling, he shook his head. "I did no such thing."

"You did," she declared with a smile. "Last night you were drunk and mumbling something about women, cheaters, and prenups. I got the meaning behind the words pretty quick. I am sorry. She doesn't deserve you."

That was an interesting observation. Carrie didn't even know him.

"Maybe I deserved this," Max challenged. "Maybe I was a real arsehole to be married to. Maybe I cheated on her first."

"You didn't." Carrie slid down into the office chair. "If you had you wouldn't be this upset. You might have been an asshole though but that still doesn't mean it was okay to cheat. That's not cool at all."

"No, it's...not cool."

It was also painful as hell. Like his heart was ripped out of his chest with her bare hands.

Giggling, she reached for the bottle and held it up, but he shook his head. He needed to sober up a little before dinner. "You sound funny when you say *cool*. I don't think proper British gentlemen are supposed to use that word."

"I'm not all that proper," he shot back, letting his gaze rake her from head to toe. Maybe a rebound shag was just what he needed. "And being a gentleman is a real pain sometimes."

It was then that he saw her left hand. Why he hadn't noticed before, he didn't know. But there it was.

A diamond engagement ring.

Nothing ostentatious. Just a regular, normal engagement ring for a regular, normal couple. Probably less than a carat, and he would know. He'd spent way too much time picking out Alana's ring, knowing it would be photographed by every tabloid in the world.

"You're getting married."

She smiled and held up her hand. "I am. We've been dating for four years so I guess it's about time."

"Are you commitment shy?"

She shook her head. "Not me. Mark. He's been married before so he wasn't sure he was ready to do it again until recently."

Max had to stifle the urge to tell her to run, very far and very fast. Marriage and commitment was fraught with opportunities for heartbreak and pain.

"Congratulations," he said instead. Manners had been hammered into him from an early age. "I'm sure you'll be very happy."

She was regarding him with amusement. "No, you're not sure at all. You think I'm going to be miserable. That's okay. I get that you're in a mood. I'd be the same if I was you."

He tossed back the remainder of his whiskey and set the glass on the desk. "Paige promised to feed me and get me drunk. That's only one out of two."

Carrie laughed and stood, offering her arm. "Then by all means let me help you to the table. Dinner will be served very soon. You don't want to miss out."

Sadly, Max was sure he'd already missed out. His chance at happiness and love was gone.

CHAPTER
Twenty~Nine

FRUSTRATED, Paige tossed the skirt on the bed. She was running out of time and needed to be dressed for her meeting, but she had a big problem.

Nothing seemed to look right. This was just about the biggest meeting of her life and her clothes were all wrong. What had she been thinking when she'd packed for New York?

"Darling, after your meeting do you want to go to lunch?"

Nate froze in the middle of the hotel bedroom, his gaze taking in the pile of clothes on the bed. She was sure she looked a sight as well, standing in her bra and panties. He'd been patient with her excitement since she'd received the call right before Thanksgiving and had even offered to accompany her here on their way back to London. Of course she'd jumped at the chance to have him by her side. He might not be attending this meeting with her but they were a team making this movie together.

"I don't think they'll let me in the restaurant dressed like this."

He placed the script he was reading on the bed and approached her carefully, like she was a wild horse about to bolt. "Don't like anything you packed, love?"

Taking a deep breath, she picked up the skirt she'd just tossed away. "I hate every single thing I packed. It's all wrong and I'm an idiot who only wears pajamas all the time."

Those last words were choked out as a lump lodged in her throat. She had no idea what to wear to a Hollywood meeting. A bank meeting? Sure. But big studio executives? She was clueless.

Rushing to her side, he pulled her into his arms, dropping a kiss on her temple. "You are not an idiot, love, and you wear some rather fashionable jammies. Now let's take a look at what you packed. I've been to many of these sorts of meetings and I'm sure we can find something here that will be suitable. Did you bring a skirt or dress?"

"I brought two skirts." She held them up for his inspection. "Black and red."

He picked up an eggshell colored lace blouse. "This with the red skirt and the black pumps. Very classy and elegant."

"You're a freakin' genius." Paige stood on her tiptoes and pulled Nate down for a kiss. "I'd been eyeing that combination but I wasn't sure if it was appropriate. Man, Treetop, you made my day."

"I'll bank the points for the next time I'm in the doghouse."

She pulled the shoes from her suitcase and placed them by the bed. "Are you planning to be there any time soon?"

Tossing the rest of the clothes back into the dresser drawer, she laid the outfit onto the bed but Nate moved closer, his hands cupping her sensitive breasts.

"It's a crime to cover up these beauties. They should be displayed like the work of art they are."

Biting her lip against the surge of desire, she had to stifle her moan as his thumbs brushed her nipples. "Are you suggesting I walk around topless?"

"Only for me."

His lips pressed against the curve of her breast, his tongue snaking out under the edge of the lace. They were only headed one place if they kept this up and she needed to make that meeting on time.

"Let's put this on hold, handsome." She gently pushed at his arms. "I can't be late. This meeting it too important. For both of us."

He stopped back reluctantly and sighed, his gaze still glued to her boobs. He was a breast man through and through.

"You're right. Finish dressing and I'll walk you downstairs and to your car."

"I don't have a car. I'll just get a cab." He was smiling that I-have-everything-under-control-smile again. "You ordered a car service for me, didn't you?"

"I did," he nodded. "I just wanted to make sure you're taken care of today when I'm not around to do it."

There were times this coddling and spoiling stuff was pretty good. "Thank you. That was very thoughtful."

"I know you're nervous but you have no reason to be,

love. They want your books and you have control of the negotiation. Remember that. You have what they want."

She slid the skirt over her hips. "I hope you're right. I want this deal. For us, handsome. I can't wait to work with you."

"We're an unbeatable team."

––––––––

Paige met the two movie executives in a tall office building just off of Park Avenue. She was ushered into a conference room with a large oval table, plush leather chairs, and a pretty female assistant in the corner who she was told would take notes. Paige's stomach tumbled with nerves but she managed to smile and shake their hands as her agent Kris introduced her. Burt Ellis and Earnest Thorpe.

Wait...Burt and Ernie?

"Paige, we are so excited to finally meet the woman who created these amazing stories," Burt gushed. Or was it Ernie? She'd been too nervous to pay attention. "This is going to be a very important film. I can feel it. A movie that everyone will want to see."

That was quite the overstatement but she was happy to see their enthusiasm about the project. That boded well for the rest of the meeting.

"Thank you, I'm excited as well." She fiddled with the hem of her blouse under the edge of the conference table. It gave her fingers something to do. "I have a lot of ideas about the movie."

Ernie leaned forward, a grin on his face. "We absolutely love, love, love the ideas your agent forward to us, plus the sample pages of the script. Pure gold. No, make that Oscar gold."

They really were laying it on thick. While she thought her books were good, they weren't the heavy literary works that won Academy Awards. She wrote feel-good stories that made people cry and smile.

She nibbled at the muffins they'd placed on the table but stuck to water instead of coffee. She was already jittery and overexcited.

They bantered back and forth about their ideas for the production, even discussing ways they could market the movie to the masses. They didn't need to discuss money as she wouldn't even be here if the dollar figure wasn't fair. This was all about creative control and so far they appeared to be open to her vision, but then they hadn't discussed all of her ideas. Better to ease in and pick her battles. She wouldn't win all of them, of that she was sure.

Paige thought she was home free when she saw Burt and Ernie exchange a look that wasn't a happy one. Well, crap.

"There is one thing," Ernie began, shifting in his chair. Even he didn't want to talk about it from the looks of things. "You've chosen Nate Mason as Flynn and also slated him to direct. We have some concerns about that."

A quick look at Kris's face told Paige that this was the first she was hearing this too.

She didn't panic, instead crossing one leg casually over the other, although her stomach twisted into a knot. "What concerns do you have?"

Burt held up his hands in almost surrender. "We understand that you and he are in a relationship." He used air quotes when he said *relationship*. Really? Air quotes? "But we believe he lacks the star power needed to bring in the crowds that this story deserves. If you're set on someone from the UK, let's talk about Maxwell Hayes."

"Max? Trust me, Max is not Flynn. Not even close."

Ernie's brows went up. "You know Hayes? That's even better. We can sweeten the deal for him with the directing. He can sell tickets."

Paige shook her head. "Flynn is Nate. Nate is Flynn. He is my first and only choice."

Burt sighed and seemed to regroup. "We like you, Paige. We like your work. But after last year, Nate just isn't an A-lister, if he ever was. When we market this movie, we want people buzzing about the story. All people will be talking about will be Nate's PR nightmare."

"He's rehabilitated." Paige argued. "No one talks about Stella anymore."

"But they will," Burt shot back. "Otherwise, he's just not that interesting. He runs, he reads boring English litera-ture, and is – I mean was – something of a playboy. What else do they have to talk about?"

"His large body of fine acting," she answered, keeping her features as schooled as possible. "Nate is a great actor. Possibly one of the best in the business."

And her mood had just gone to hell. She had taken a swing to the dark side. Heaven help Burt and Ernie.

Kris decided it was time to pop into the conversation. "I think we can all agree that we want a great movie to come from this project. I think we can also agree that Paige's cooperation hinges on making any casting and directing decisions."

Ernie's head bobbed in agreement. "We completely understand but we all want to make money here. Nate is an immense talent and I agree that he may be one of the best actors of our time. But he's had two box office flops in a row. He can't put people in the seats and that's a fact."

Paige had had enough.

"First of all, he was born to play this role and he's going to do an amazing job. As for the movie flops, the first one was a terrible film but Nate received excellent reviews. The consensus was that the actors deserved better material to work with. That one is on the writer and director. As for the indie movie, that was never going to be a big grossing film. The story is too niche for that. Once again, his acting was reviewed positively. He received an Emmy nomination a few years ago, so his acting must not suck." She leaned forward and looked Burt in the eye. "Who do you want to see in the role? Who is your dream casting?"

His smile widened. "I'm so glad you asked. We think Sam Collins would be perfect and have that star-power draw that we need. I think we can get him too if we give him points on the back end."

"Sam Collins," Paige repeated, giving Kris a look of disgust. Sam was a nice man and a great actor but he wasn't the Flynn type in the least. "Isn't he a little busy making Scorsese films?"

"We heard that he wants a break to do something lighter," Ernie crowed. "He's looking specifically at book adaptations."

"Who told you that?" Kris asked, her brows pulled down into a frown. "I haven't heard that."

The two men shifted in their seats, clearly uncomfortable with the question. Burt glanced at Ernie before speaking.

"Actually it was Stella Riley."

Stella Riley. Paige should have known. That girl needed to mind her own business.

"I didn't realize she and Collins were that close," Paige replied tightly, knowing full well that Sam couldn't stand that woman. "What else did Stella say?"

More fidgeting and fussing but Paige and her agent simply sat there patiently waiting. They wanted answers. This time it was Ernie who broke first.

"We saw Stella at The Ivy yesterday at lunch. She reminded us that Nate has a history of bad judgment. We can't have someone like that starring and directing in one of our movies."

Paige couldn't control her reply. "Might I remind you gentleman that the bad judgment Nate showed was dating...Stella Riley? If I were you, I wouldn't make the same mistake of trusting anything she has to say."

Burt cleared his throat and Ernie took a long swallow from his water bottle but they weren't saying anything else. Frankly Paige didn't want to hear more of their excuses.

This was every nightmare she'd had about this project only now she was living it in full living color. Taking a deep breath to steady her voice, she placed her hands flat on the table before speaking. She had to say this exactly right.

"Gentleman, this is what I was trying to avoid. The entire reason I've fought so hard for creative control was to stay out of discussions like this. Sam Collins? He's a great actor but he is all wrong for this. In addition, I'm not sure how Stella Riley became a consultant on this project especially considering that her own acting career is made up of one good role in a romantic comedy and then low budget horror films for the rest."

To Paige's relief, Kris straightened in her chair and took control of the meeting. "Gentleman, I need to speak with my client. Would you mind if we took a little break?"

Both men seemed relieved, and they all stood, Paige and Kris excusing themselves to the ladies' room. Paige freshened her makeup while Kris returned a few texts. When the older woman was finished, she tucked her phone back in her handbag and leaned against one of the sinks.

"Talk to me, Paige. Tell me what's going on in that brilliant writer's brain of yours."

Rubbing her temple where a headache was forming, Paige wasn't sure Kris was going to want to hear it.

"I'm frustrated," she finally confessed. "I feel like I've been lured to New York on false pretenses. They know what I want and they acted like everything was great but it wasn't. They're taking advice from Stella Riley of all people. Do you think one of them is dating her? Then they sprung this shit about Nate on me at the last minute. I'm pissed off, I guess."

"They never mentioned it to me either," Kris said with a harassed sigh. "I'm as angry as you are because these guys know better, but they're trying to take advantage of you. They think you want this movie more than you want control, but I think they're wrong."

This was why Kris was Paige's agent. She understood.

"They are wrong. I'd rather not do this at all if it can't be done my way. I've heard too many authors lamenting what Hollywood did to their books. I don't need the money or fame and frankly, I don't need the hassle. Anyone who would do this isn't someone I want to trust with Flynn."

Kris gave her a shrewd look. "And Nate? Is he a deal breaker?"

Lifting her chin, Paige nodded. "If they don't want him, they don't want me. He and I are a team and we're going to make this movie together. We've talked for hours about what we want to do, and we've made so many plans. I won't sell him down the river because these two guys can't see any farther than their own hands. If they want the books so bad, there has to be others out there that also want them."

"Maybe. Are you prepared to walk away knowing that this movie might never be made?"

She didn't even have to think about it.

"Yes," she stated, putting every ounce of certainty she could into her answer so there would be no question in Kris's mind. "I'm prepared to do that without an ounce of regret. Are you angry with me?"

Kris laughed and checked her hair in the mirror. "You mean am I going to miss the huge commission that I would get for selling this to Hollywood? Of course, but I have to say that I admire your intestinal fortitude. You know what you want, Paige, and you're not afraid to do the hard stuff to make it happen."

That's where Kris had it wrong. Putting Nate in the role and making this movie with him was the easiest thing Paige had ever done. This wasn't about love, although she did love him more than she'd ever imagined. This was about Nate Mason being the perfect person to play Flynn and direct this film. It was more a business decision than anything although she was sure no one was going to see it that way.

"I know what I want," Paige said. "I was happy before all of this movie talk and I'll be happy if it all goes away."

Or better yet, find someone else to help them bankroll the movie.

"I'm not giving up," Kris warned her. "Let's go in there and see if we can make it happen."

It was clear Burt and Ernie had also spent their break retrenching and they weren't inclined to budge. But it also became clear to Paige that the two executives thought this was simply a bargaining tool she was using and not a deeply held belief. They were destined to be disappointed.

"I just can't see Nate Mason in that role," Burt said, his hands folded on the table. "We can't go forward with him as part of this project."

Paige shot Kris a quick glance before replying in case the other woman wanted to do the talking, but she nodded in acceptance that this was her client's show.

"I think you need to know that I am prepared to walk away from this deal if my choice cannot be accommodated." She turned to Kris. "Is there anything left to discuss?"

The agent shook her head, a smile playing on her lips. "No, not really. I think we're done here."

Paige turned back to the two men who had both gone quite pale. "It appears we have nothing left to say. Thank you for your time, gentleman."

She and Kris began to rise and the execs seemed to

wake up from whatever stupor had come over them. Both men waved her back in her seat but she decided to remain standing until she heard what they had to say.

Burt spoke first. "You can't walk away from a deal this big."

They didn't want to negotiate. They simply couldn't believe she was walking away from millions. She already had money and she didn't spend all that much. What she wanted was to see her work on the screen, but she wasn't going to trust just anyone to do it.

She relaxed and smiled for the first time that day. The conversation was over and she had nothing to be concerned about. She wouldn't be making a movie with these men. Thank goodness.

"Actually, I can."

Turning on the heel of her black pump, she walked out of the conference room after shaking their hands, taking a deep breath of relief. She hadn't had the best vibe from them but if they'd given her what she'd wanted she would have signed. Now she didn't have to wonder if she'd done the right thing. She knew she had.

Kris didn't speak until they were in the elevator. "I think you just shocked the ever loving shit out of them. I doubt they get turned down much."

"Then it was time," Paige said proudly. "I don't have any regrets. I did the right thing. I could tell they wanted to turn my book into a Hollywood disaster just from the ideas they floated. By the way, thanks for that. You know, in there. Backing me up. I know you worked on hard on this and I don't want you to think I'm not grateful."

The doors of the elevator slid open and they exited into

the large lobby. "I'll be honest with you, I almost tried to talk you into it. But then I realized you were truly fine if the movie wasn't made. And I have to admit it was fun to walk out like that. They looked positively sick."

There was just one thing Paige needed to make sure of before she let Kris go back to her office.

"Can I ask you a favor?"

"Sure, what can I do for you?"

Paige ran her fingers through her tangled locks. "Don't tell Nate about today. He doesn't need to know that the execs didn't want him or that Stella stuck her nose in this. He's had enough of a smackdown to his ego lately. No need to make it any worse."

"No problem. Honestly, Ellis and Thorpe aren't going to be running to the press to tell them they lost the book because a little slip of an author wouldn't play ball. They're going to pretend it was all their idea and that they changed their minds. Only you and I will know the truth. But what are you planning to tell Nate?"

"I'll just tell them they couldn't accommodate my vision for the movie which is the truth. Keep it vague. If he asked more specific questions, I'll tell him about the script they wanted and the locations. That was horrifying enough."

Paige followed Kris out of the high rise and onto the busy sidewalk. Her agent turned to leave and then paused, swiveling back. "If you're having second thoughts, I can go right back upstairs and talk to them. You don't even have to go. I'll do all the groveling. You've worked so hard and I just want you to have what you want."

It was sweet of Kris but Paige was just as sure now as she was ten minutes ago.

"I wouldn't do anything different. I have no regrets then or now."

Kris pulled her into a big hug, unexpected behavior from the savvy agent, before heading down the sidewalk to her Fifth Avenue office. "I wish I could clone you a dozen times. Tell Nate I said hi."

Paige - and Nate - would find a way to make this movie. Their way.

CHAPTER
Thirty

EARLY MORNING SUNLIGHT filtered through a crack in the drapes. A quick glance at the bedside clock told Paige it was barely seven in the morning. They had flown back to London from New York yesterday and she was feeling every bit of the jet lag. She wasn't someone who jumped out of bed all smiles ready for the day like Nate but for some reason she was wide awake with no hope of going back to sleep. Her mind was already whirling, thoughts and emotions making it hard to drift back to dreamland. A new book was beginning to take shape and her imagination wasn't going to let her rest easily until she put it on paper.

She sat up carefully, not wanting to wake Nate and allowed herself the luxury of looking at him. Really looking. He was so full of energy, like a little puppy, that he rarely stood still. At this moment he was at peace, his expression one of sweet repose.

With his mouth open - snoring and drooling.

Okay, he wasn't the most serene of sleepers, but he was all hers. Her gaze started at the top of his head and those adorable curls that she loved to run her fingers through. Nate would joke that she needed to be careful or his hairline would recede even farther. She didn't care about his hairline or if he was completely bald. He'd be just as beautiful either way.

Her fingers itched to trace the elegant lines of his face - his nose, his scruff covered chin, and those impossibly high cheekbones. His head was turned to the side so the cords of his neck were exposed, his Adam's apple tempting her to kiss or nibble. She restrained herself and let her gaze wander lower.

His lean but muscular torso, his flat male nipples that she'd traced with her tongue so many times. And those abs. Sweet baby Jesus, she wanted to lick every ridge of his stomach and then follow that treasure trail...

Ooooh! What do we have here?

Nate's morning wood didn't have a damn thing to do with her but that didn't mean she couldn't give him a lovely wake up call.

Easing the sheet down, she licked her lips at the bounty she'd exposed. He was long, thick, and half-erect. She could work with that. Bracing her weight on her palms, she leaned down to give the head a lick, then swirled her tongue around and around before sliding down and then up. He let out a grunt but didn't wake and she watched in fascination as his cock grew longer and harder before her eyes.

She wrapped one hand around the base and her mouth around the head, moving them in unison as the fingers of her other hand played with his balls, already pulled tight to his body. This wasn't going to take long.

Flicking her tongue, she tightened her lips determined to make him come even as his hips lifted up from the mattress and he pushed deeper into her mouth, nudging at the back of her throat. He was moaning now, his fingers tangled in her hair, and guiding her exactly where he wanted her to be. Even half asleep, the British bastard had to be in control of their sex life. Luckily she was happy to let him do it.

"Baby," he choked out. "I'm going to–"

Of course he was. That was the whole point of this. She doubled her efforts and he thrust faster, his breathing more like gasps. With one last final stroke he pushed himself deeply into her mouth, his entire body bowed and tensed as his hot seed hit the back of her throat.

The one thing that she loved was watching his face as he orgasmed, his cock buried in her mouth. His eyes were squeezed shut, his head thrown back, his teeth gritted together as a string of expletives fell from his lips. Nate could talk dirty with the best of them but his language took a real turn for the gutter when she gave him head. If he'd been awake the entire time, he would have been talking nasty to her and loving every minute of it. She'd never known anyone who could mix Shakespeare with limericks from Nantucket, but he could.

Wiping her chin, she slid up beside him as he struggled to catch his breath. He finally opened his eyes and a grin spread across his face.

"That was quite a wakeup call, love. What did I do to deserve that?"

His long arms enfolded her, his chin resting on the top of her head while his fingers began caressing her spine. It appeared he had more on his mind than a morning run.

"Just being you," she replied cheekily, pressing a kiss to his chest. "Isn't that enough?"

"I won't argue. When a day begins like that, you know it's going to be a good one."

Paige decided she'd have a little fun with this.

"Absolutely. I thought it might be a good way to send you off for your morning run."

She scooted away from him and sat up as if she expected him to get up and get dressed and really go for that run. If he did, she'd never forgive him.

His forehead wrinkled and he propped himself up on his elbow. "Run? I can do that anytime today."

"You should get it over with. Get it out of the way."

His fingers trailed up the calf of her leg, a mischievous smile on his face. "Later."

Paige shook her head but was swiftly losing this game. One touch from him and she was well and truly lost. "I don't want to be the reason you get out of shape. You should go now."

He'd already explained to her that his fitness routine for the play he had coming up in the new year was much more relaxed than for some of the other roles he'd had in the past. He had to stay about the same weight so the costumes would fit - which was why he ran five days a week - but he didn't have to bulk up and eat massive amounts of protein either. He simply needed to be sensible.

Those devilish fingers slid to her inner thigh and she

couldn't hold back the squeak of pleasure and surprise when they brushed over that most sensitive spot between her legs. This was the great thing about sleeping naked and the worst thing. Every part of him was available but every part of her was too.

He chuckled and delved those long digits deeper, finding her quite wet and ready. "My lady, I think you doth protest too much."

Time to give in and let him think it was his idea.

"Well...if you insist."

The next thing she knew she was flat on her back, her legs thrown over Nate's shoulders, and his face buried between her thighs. Half giggling and half moaning, she thrust her fingers in his curls as his tongue circled her clit, scraping the sides with his teeth and making her hips buck. He teased and tormented her until her voice was hoarse from begging to be allowed to come. This was one of his favorite games - keeping her on the edge until she couldn't take it anymore. No matter how much she swore she wouldn't plead, he always won. But she won too because her orgasms were always bigger and stronger when he did.

A white-hot bar of arousal had taken up residence in her abdomen as she sought her release, chased it desperately. Her fingers clawed at the sheets and she said his name over and over like an incantation, a spell of witchcraft.

Because he was so much bigger than she was, he could simply lift her and place her where he wanted her to be. He did that, rolling her to her stomach and lifting her up onto her knees. They'd never used this position before but it was hot to be manhandled in such a way, firmly but gently, his own desire for her so strong that he had to have her right now, this minute. Positioning himself behind her, he leaned down to whisper in her ear.

"Brace yourself, darling. This might get a little rough."

———

Nate buried himself balls deep in one stroke, the sensation rocketing through his spine and straight to his cock. His fingers tightened on Paige's hips and despite coming only minutes before he was ready to blow again.

So much for more control as he got older. This sexy little woman was going to be the death of him. Every time he had her it only made him want her more. He imagined it would be like this for the rest of his life.

He was one lucky bloke.

With each stroke he bottomed out, her walls clutching him greedily, like wet, hot velvet. He'd kept her waiting, not letting her fall over the precipice so she was already close to climaxing, those muscles milking him.

The pressure was beginning to build in his lower back and his balls, a shimmering tide of pleasure blurring his vision. He reached back and landed his palm smartly on Paige's creamy bottom cheek, leaving a vivid red handprint behind. Her body jumped and she moaned as her channel clamped down on him, sending shocks through his overloaded system. With his other hand, he landed another blow to the untouched cheek, leaving another handprint on the pillow of her bottom. If the gush of honey that followed was any indication, his naughty girl liked her spanking.

He leaned over her back to whisper words of encouragement right in the shell of her ear. "Do you like that, baby girl?" He gave her another smack. "Answer me or I won't let you come."

He would let her come, of course, but this was part of their game. She looked over her shoulder, her expression contorted with a mixture of pleasure and pain.

So fucking gorgeous.

"Yes," she replied, her words breathless and soft. "Yes, I like it."

He couldn't hold back any longer, the pressure was too strong.

"Such a good girl," he praised as his fingers found the swollen bundle of nerves that would send her into the stars. "Come now. Come."

Paige screamed his name as she climaxed, every muscle in her body tightening. His own orgasm roared through him like a freight train and he thrust in one last time, holding himself there until he was spent and empty. They fell together in a damp tangle of arms and legs, Paige already giggling as he pulled her close. At moments like these, he needed to feel every inch of her beautiful body pressed to his. He could feel her heartbeat thumping in time to his own as the musk of their coupling hung in the air.

This was how it was supposed to be. This wasn't the sex that he was used to with the other females of his past. This was mating, claiming. Deeply primitive, his instincts firmly in control. This was more and it was everything. He prayed she felt it as well. Every cell in his being was crying out to make her his and his alone. To protect her from harm. To bring her happiness every day. To give her everything in his power and then give some more. He wanted to spend the rest of his life with her.

He wanted to make her his wife.

He *needed* to be her husband.

He brushed her hair back from her face and pressed a kiss to her nose. "Paige, love. I have something to ask you."

She nodded. "Hmmm...okay."

He gathered his courage and the words tumbled out. "Will you spend Christmas in London with me and my family?"

Her lids fluttered open and for a moment he was lost in her emerald green eyes, but then she smiled, her fingers caressing his jaw. "I will."

For now it would have to do.

CHAPTER
Thirty-One

PAIGE PATTED her stomach and fell into the couch cushions with a groan.

"I ate too much. Why didn't you stop me?"

Back in London, they'd met Max this morning for brunch and the restaurant the men had chosen was a buffet. Paige had filled up on chocolate chip waffles, lemon-poppy seed muffins, bacon, ham, and some lovely croissants. She'd even managed to down some dessert - a light coconut custard.

Now she was miserable.

"Stop you?" Nate marveled, his hands on his hips. "How does a man tell the woman he loves that she's dancing with one of the seven deadly sins?"

"Gluttony?"

His brows rose. "Sadly it wasn't lust, although I think you could make a case for sloth right about now."

She wrinkled her nose at him. "You're mean, Mr. I-Can-

Eat-Anything-And-Look-Like-A-Runway-Model." She nudged his leg with her foot. "Say that again."

"Lust? Or Sloth? I have a feeling if I'm not careful I might see Wrath as well."

"You got to see so much lust this morning we were late to brunch. No, I meant say *it* again. You know."

His expression softened and he knelt down between her legs. "I love you."

She sighed and ran her fingertip along his jawline, enjoying the scruff that tickled her fingertips. "I love you too. So much."

He'd said it every day but she didn't think she'd ever tire of it.

He shook his head. "I love you more."

"You're so competitive. We love each other. This isn't a contest." She lay down on the couch and closed her eyes before muttering, "But I totally love you more."

"You don't, but I'm going to let that go. Is that how you want to spend the afternoon with Mike and Amy? Lying on the sofa, bemoaning a brunch buffet? It's a bit different than our original plans."

Shit, she'd forgotten all about that. She'd agreed to go see a movie this afternoon with the other couple.

"I'd like it noted that I said a buffet wasn't a good idea. Now let me go upstairs and freshen up so we can get ready to go. You know I hate to be late."

Nate only laughed. "You hate anything where you can't wear pajamas."

He was beginning to know her so well.

———

Paige was halfway up the stairs when his phone went off. Garrett, his publicist. Maybe there were new pictures of him and Paige in the tabloids. She needed all the publicity she could get after her meeting with the New York executives. They'd wanted to change too much of her book for her to be able to sign on. "Hey, Garrett. What's going on?"

"Nate, I'm sending you a blind item I came across. I'm pretty sure it's about Paige's meeting with the studio guys a few days ago. Did she say anything to you? I thought you would want to know."

"Okay, let me open it."

He clicked on the link and began reading.

A certain blonde bestselling author who is dating a hunky Brit had to put her foot down yesterday when meeting with the studio brass. Sources confirm that said author was blindsided by studio demands that Brit boyfriend not star or direct in the movie based on her bestselling series. The brass said he was tainted and couldn't fill the movie theatre seats. The author took her book and agent and walked right out the door. There would be no compromises. She and boyfriend are a package deal. Looks like she lost out on millions because of true love. Will she regret it? Only time will tell.

"Son of a bitch," Nate muttered under his breath, his heart hammering in his ears. "This is definitely the first I'm hearing of this. Do you think it's true?"

"I don't know," Garrett confessed. "Half of these blind

items are true and the other half are bullshit. She didn't say anything at all?"

Not one fucking word.

"She said that they wanted too many changes to the story plus there were location issues as well. Fuck, I never wanted her to put her career on the line for me. Jesus, she walked away from millions."

What had she been thinking? Nate couldn't wrap his mind around her actions. This was what Paige had dreamed of.

"She knows what she wants. I've heard of these guys and they were trying to intimidate a newbie. Good for her that she stood her ground."

Good for her? Losing out on this deal couldn't be called good. This was madness.

"She lost this because of me... I'll never forgive myself."

Doubtful Paige would ever forget that he'd cost her the chance of a lifetime. She might pretend that everything was all sunshine but inside she had to be crushed. Her relationship with him shouldn't come with this high of a price tag.

He wasn't worth the sacrifice.

"I'm sure she knows what she's doing, Nate. She had her agent there and I doubt Kris Lawson was going to allow Paige to walk away from a great deal. The only reason I brought it to your attention is that I thought it was important for you to know that Paige fought for you."

Something she shouldn't have had to do. This was his own fault. His own stupidity. Stella, the gift that kept on giving.

"Thanks for letting me know, Garrett. I really do appreciate it. I'll talk to Paige."

"Let me know if we need to spin this in any way. Right now it's a blind item but it could blow up on us. We don't want anyone thinking the studio didn't want you."

Except that was the exact truth if this little article was to be believed.

"I'll let you know. Thanks again."

Nate hung up the phone and headed straight upstairs, taking them two at a time. He and Paige needed to have a little chat.

———

Paige was in the bedroom pulling a sweater over her head when she heard Nate's footsteps on the stairs. He was impatient to go to the movies but they had plenty of time. She'd allotted thirty minutes for the ten-minute walk to the theatre. She'd been thinking they might stop at the coffee shop for a hot chocolate and a slice of their lemon cake. Nate might not think it was cold but she did. Winters in London were much different than what she was used to.

"I'm ready, handsome." She smoothed down her hair and slipped on a pair of leather loafers. "But don't worry, we have loads of time."

"Good, because I think we need to talk before we go."

She hadn't noticed his expression but she did now. His jaw was tense and his lips a thin line. Her beloved wasn't happy and ten minutes ago he'd been over the moon.

"Okay," she drew out the word. "What do you want to talk about?"

He shoved his phone in front of her face. "Garrett sent me this."

She read through the blind item, heat suffusing her cheeks. Jesus, that girl in the corner taking notes must have leaked this. Kris was sure that Burt and Ernie wouldn't do it.

"Nate, I can explain."

She heard his indrawn breath and he turned sharply away. "Christ, do you mean it's true? Did you walk away from a multimillion dollar movie deal?"

Well, yeah. But she'd had a good reason. Pacing back and forth, muttering to himself, Nate was acting like she'd shot someone in the streets. This was not a tragedy; it was just a temporary setback.

"Will you please sit down and let me explain? I'll start from the beginning."

Jerkily he sat, but his hands couldn't seem to settle, landing first on his thighs, then the mattress, and finally crossed over his chest. Great, terrific body language. He wasn't that open to her explanation.

"Kris and I met with the two execs. Burt and Ernie, of all things. They gave me the usual snow job. Blah, blah, blah. They love the books, they love the script. We went through my list of ideas and they gushed some more. It was all good but then they started with their own ideas, which were horrifying. Toward the end of the meeting they sprung the issue on us. They felt like you couldn't fill the seats after the two box office bombs. Then they said the narrative would be all about you and your threesome instead of the movie. I told them that you had received great reviews for your work on those films and the tickets sales weren't your fault. I could see they were going to continue to argue so I just cut them off at the pass. This was why I'm fighting for control. Then they admitted that Stella Riley had put these ideas into their heads which told me that they absolutely couldn't be trusted with my movie. So, I told them basically that if they didn't let me make the decisions I was ending the meeting."

He looked up, his usually clear blue eyes almost gray. "Stella? Bloody hell. That girl is a menace to society. I wish I'd never met her. And so you just walked? That's it?"

Paige smiled at the memory. "We'd both stood and I had my purse over my shoulder. This was too important to give in."

Nate stood and grabbed her shoulders, his expression full of anguish. "Have you lost your mind? You may have lost the chance to make Flynn a reality."

She wasn't sure what Nate was angry about. "If not this studio, then another one. This is why I didn't sign the first contract offered to me months ago. I need the control. I certainly can't trust these guys. They have lousy judgment."

Whirling around, he stomped back and forth, his chest heaving as he scraped his fingers through his hair. Finally he stopped and turned to her, his jaw tight.

"You walked away because they didn't want me?" She started to speak but he cut her off with a wave of his hand. "It doesn't matter why they didn't want me, Paige. It doesn't matter where the idea came from. Jesus, woman, I'm not worth losing millions over."

He was but he wasn't the only reason she'd walked away.

"I already have money."

His cheeks turned red and he snorted in derision. "You've blown what might be your one and only chance to get this movie made over me. I earned every bit of what they said and then some. I'm the one who made that mistake. You will not pay my price or suffer because of what I did."

"I don't feel like I'm suffering, Nate. You're the one upset here, not me. I'll make the movie when the time is right. Don't you want to play Flynn anymore? Don't you want to direct?"

If he'd changed his mind, he hadn't said anything.

"Of course I do. But the thought of you losing out because of my being an idiot is too much to bear. I won't have it."

He was being so sweet and yet so dimwitted at the same time. There was no way she was going to do this movie without him.

"We're a team," she argued. "You said that yourself right before I left for the meeting. We do this together or not at all."

He looked at her squarely, tilting her chin up so she was staring into his eyes. "You should have launched me. Told them you'd look at other actors and directors."

She shook her head. This was what he'd been trying to say in his roundabout, longwinded way? "Not on your life. You're Flynn. I told them that. As for directing, you and I are in sync about this movie. We're a team and we're going to do this together. Us against the world, handsome." She tilted her head, a horrible thought occurring to her. "Is that what you would have done if the positions were reversed? Would you have launched me, as you put it?"

He smiled then, but it was sort of sad and cynical. "It's a nasty, cutthroat business and it's survival of the fittest, love. You have to put yourself first. You may never have this opportunity again."

Perplexed and confused, he still didn't understand what love and commitment meant but she was going to show him. This was his first serious relationship since he'd become a star.

"I'm putting us first." There was no way she could make this movie without him. "This isn't about us as a couple, Nate. This is about you being the perfect person to play Flynn and how in sync we are about the film. This is about business, not love."

His dubious expression clearly said that he didn't believe her and she didn't have any more words to convince him. Time would show him how serious she was about this. When he saw a week or a month or a year from now that she didn't care about the movie, he'd understand that this was no sacrifice.

Checking his watch, he exhaled noisily. "We're late for the movies, but I want you to know this discussion isn't over."

He could talk until he was blue in the face. She was at peace with what she'd done that day and she'd do it again in a heartbeat. Money and fame didn't matter. She had everything she could ever want right here with Nate.

CHAPTER
Thirty-Two

AMY SIDLED close to Paige as Nate and Mike waited in line for popcorn, drinks, and candy. No movie was complete without Paige getting her salty and sweet fix.

"What's up with Nate?" Amy whispered, her gaze on the man standing next to her husband. "He looks like someone peed in his breakfast cereal."

Indeed, Nate did look like he'd had better days. His expression was cold, his answers to every question short and curt. He hadn't calmed down at all from the conversation earlier.

"He's upset," Paige sighed. "We had a little fight before we left the house. He's mad at me because he thinks I've done something stupid and I don't agree. His last words before we left the house were that the discussion isn't over. I have so much to look forward to."

Amy and Mike were good friends - and actors themselves - but she wasn't comfortable revealing that the studio executives didn't want Nate for the movie. Unfortunately, her keeping it a secret might be for naught if that blind item was anything to go by.

Amy's brows went up in amazement. "Did he actually use the word stupid? Because if Mike did that, he'd be regretting it."

"He did," Paige confirmed with a grimace. "I know why he thinks that way but I'm upset that he doesn't trust me. He doesn't trust...us. I know this is all new to him but it's frustrating."

"Nate's amazingly naive when it comes to relationships," Amy agreed. "In the last six years I've seen him with dozens of women but never like he is with you. He worships the ground you walk on, my dear, but he's also a trifle dense about how things work. Like how he shouldn't call the woman he loves stupid, unless of course he's contemplating celibacy."

"Technically he didn't call me stupid. He called my decision stupid. I can't go into the details but I do understand where he's coming from, but he refuses to see my side of it. He thinks I'm making some huge sacrifice for him and I don't feel that way at all."

Amy nodded, a smile playing on her lips. "It's these Shakespearean actors. I've got one at home myself, you know, but it can be hard for us American girls to truly understand. Our boys read all these classics and they start to think the stories are some sort of documentary instead of what they are. Dramatic entertainment for the masses. Nate is simply playing his hero's part. He thinks the only one sacrificing anything should be him and you're the beautiful lady-in-waiting that needs rescuing from the dragon. That's how they see themselves, for heaven's sake.

Like knights in shining armor slaying the enemy and writing poems to their lady-loves."

Good Lord, was that true? Did Nate think he needed to be some romantic hero for her?

"I'm no damsel in distress."

"Neither am I," Amy declared. "And I hear that chain mail chafes. But that doesn't stop our handsome heroes from wanting to save the day, then lift us onto their white charger and ride off into the sunset with us looking up at them with stars in our eyes."

Holy crap on a cracker. That was one ridiculous scenario.

"So what do I do? My late husband wasn't like this at all."

If anything, Noah had wanted Paige to save him, not the other way around. Everything in their marriage had somehow been her responsibility.

Amy glanced over at Mike. "After ten years of wedded bliss to my knight, I find that it's just easier to let him save me. Or at least let him think that he has."

Paige shook her head. "That's not really an option, I'm afraid. His version of saving me is my version of giving in."

"Then you might be screwed."

There had to be a part of Nate she could reason with. "Life is not a Greek tragedy. He has to get over this. I'm sure with time he'll see both sides."

Mike and Nate were headed their way, arms laden with snacks.

"Men are known for their reasonableness and flexibility," Amy deadpanned. "I'm sure Nate will see the error of his ways and admit that he was wrong. It happens so often in relationships."

Crap.

———

Nate took another long swallow of whiskey, feeling the burn all the way down to his stomach. It had been two days since he and Paige had fought about the movie deal and she'd dug in her heels. She wasn't going to change her mind even though he'd tried to convince her this might be the only chance she'd ever get to make the movie. There might not be any other opportunities. Period.

The only reason she wasn't upset was because she didn't understand Hollywood, but he did. In her writer's mind she'd pictured another studio stepping up to the plate, giving her all the control she wanted including Nate starring and directing, and they'd all get their happy ending.

Just like all of her stories.

Nate feared there would be no happily ever after for this tale. As time passed, she'd come to resent and then eventually hate him when it hit her all that she'd given up. For him. *Him.*

"You've been glowering for the last half hour," Max said, slapping his beer down onto the table and jarring Nate from his dismal thoughts. They were having a drink at the pub and catching up. "What's going on?"

Nate's first inclination was not to talk about what had happened but this was Max, his best friend and even more, a person who was in the same business. A few years older than himself, Max had walked in Nate's shoes. Hollywood could be nasty, cold, and unkind and Max had been its victim a few times so of all the people Nate knew, Max would understand. Hell, he might even be able to give some good advice.

Nate sure as hell didn't know what to do about the situation. Paige wasn't going to budge and he wasn't going to change his mind either.

"Paige and I had an argument and we haven't quite resolved it," Nate said, easing into the heart of the disagreement. It was a touchy subject for him, talking about how the studio didn't think he was good enough. It was a blow to the ego.

"Give her whatever she wants," Max said bluntly. "Whatever it is, Nate, give it to her."

Easy enough to say but did he mean give her what she should want or what she said she wanted? Those were two different things.

"It's not that simple–" Nate began, but Max cut him off with a wave of his hand.

"Whatever she wants, mate. You will never find another woman like Paige. Your number one goal should be to make her happy."

She was one of a kind. The kind of woman Nate had dreamed of finding all his life but had given up hope. Max was right. Her happiness had to be his number one responsibility.

"All I want in the world is for her to have everything she wants," Nate replied, desperation in his voice. He'd wracked his brain trying to figure out what to do. "I don't want her to have to give up her dreams because she's with me."

Max's eyes narrowed. "Her dreams? Nate, never take those from her. Never."

"I'm not trying to but it's complicated." Nate bowed his head. "The studio doesn't want me. They told her no movie deal unless she chose another lead and director."

Inhaling sharply, Max fumbled for his beer. "Jesus, I'm sorry. That had to be tough to hear. There will be other movies though. If this film does well for her, she'll get more say on the next one."

Even Max assumed that Paige would go ahead with the deal sans Nate.

"That's just it." Nate groaned and scraped his hand down his face. "When they told her she couldn't have me in the lead, she walked away. She and her agent said no to the deal and walked out of the meeting. She said there would be other studios and that we were a team. That we'd make the movie together or not at all."

He would have laughed at the shocked look on Max's face but it wasn't that funny. His friend was so astonished his mouth was moving but no sounds were coming out.

Nate pointed to Max. "That's about how I reacted but then I got angry. She gave it all up for me. She said she doesn't care, but eventually when she realizes what she sacrificed she's going to wish she hadn't done it. She'll hate me and I don't think I can wait around for her love to turn to loathing. I love her too much to let that happen. I want her to have her dream and that's the movie."

"I don't– I don't know what to say. I'm...stunned, frankly." Max took a deep drink of his beer. "That she was willing to give all that up for you speaks of great love. Shit, you're one lucky son of a bitch. I've never been loved like that."

"For how long though?" Nate asked hoarsely. "I can't take this from her but I can't convince her to get rid of me and move forward with the deal. She's all about us doing this together and I can't talk her out of it. She's ruining what might be her only chance and here I sit idly by watching and doing nothing. I've tried to talk to her these last few days but she shuts me down immediately."

Max drained the last from his glass and signaled the waitress for a refill. "If you can't change her mind then all you can do is support her decisions."

"Even if I know that sooner or later she's going to wish she hadn't sacrificed her dream for me? She'll see that I'm not worth it eventually. Fuck, few men would be worth giving up what she's worked for. Nothing good is going to come from this."

Another beer was slid in front of Max. "Damned if you do..."

"And damned if I don't," Nate finished. "Either she hates me now or hates me later."

Max shook his head. "She doesn't hate you now. She loves you."

"It's that love that's keeping her from making the deal."

His brows pinched together, Max shook his head. "Are you suggesting that Paige fall out of love with you? That's not going to happen. I've never seen a woman so devoted to a man. You two are truly in love. The real, forever kind."

Yes, Nate would love her forever. He'd be an old man in a rocking chair reminiscing about the love of his life.

The love he'd die for if he had to.

This movie was his dream too. A handpicked role and a chance to direct. It would revive his career and that was something he'd worked his whole life for. His success was riding on this part. So was hers in a way.

One of them could have it though.

What was Nate willing to sacrifice for the woman he loved?

"I love her, Max. More than I love myself, and that's fucking saying something, because I'm a selfish, self-centered git who has put everybody second to my precious career. Friends, family, and definitely relationships. But there isn't anything I wouldn't do for her."

"It doesn't seem like there's anything you can do. The decision is hers to make."

Throwing back the rest of his whiskey, Nate made his own decision. He'd promised her son Jason that he would put her first and that was exactly what he was going to do. For once in his self-indulgent life, Nate Mason was going to think about someone other than himself. There were worse things than being alone. The one person he loved above all others could hate him. That would truly be painful.

"It is her decision to make," Nate agreed. "But I can show her what she's chosen."

CHAPTER
Thirty-Three

ANOTHER RED CARPET. Another party. But this time Nate was acting completely different.

It had been tense around the house the last few days. He'd been trying to convince Paige to have her agent call the movie executives back and she'd kept repeating her first answer.

No.

It wasn't going to change. The longer she thought about it, the surer she was that she'd done the right thing. Her sixth sense had been on high alert during that meeting and her little voice had been telling her to turn around and run. She'd done the right thing calling that deal off. She'd tried explaining that to Nate but he'd been stubborn and pig-headed the last three days. He just stomped around the house and growled. For the most part she'd ignored him but he had her full attention tonight.

Every time she'd seen him at this party, he'd had another young beauty on his arm gazing up at him adoringly. At first she'd rolled her eyes at his blatant attempt to rile her up but now it was becoming downright hurtful. He'd ignored her all night and surely people were noticing his behavior. He was being an ass and she didn't have the patience for it. Time to grow up and act like an adult instead of a spoiled and pampered movie star who had his every whim catered to. Except by her.

Frankly, she'd had enough of this shitshow. He might be acting like a jerk but she didn't need to stand here and be a witness to his foolishness. The longer she stood here, the less respect she had for herself. Just what kind of woman did he think she was? Some passive little ingénue that hung on his every word? Fuck no.

Determined to put an end to this awful night, she tucked her purse under her arm and strode over to where he was holding court, a bevy of females surrounding him.

Prince fucking Charming, he was not.

Nate had his back to Paige so she had to tap him on the shoulder to get his attention. He whirled around, his cheeks pink from the alcohol he'd consumed and his balance slightly off.

Great, he's drunk.

Tensing, Paige steeled herself, determined not to show any weakness. She'd never seen Nate inebriated but she'd seen other men in that condition and they hadn't impressed her with their common sense and decorum. She wasn't going to argue with a drunk. There was no point to it and if what she thought was true, Nate had orchestrated all of this tonight because he was pissed and acting out.

"Darling, are you having a good time?"

He had a drink he didn't need in one hand, the other

arm around the smirking skank who was currently looking Paige up and down, probably wondering what Nate saw in her. If the woman had the poor taste to ask, Paige wasn't above telling her that Nate loved how she gave head.

"Actually I think I've had enough fun for one night. I'm going back to the house."

Paige didn't imagine the woman's hand clinging to Nate a little tighter, pulling him closer and smiling more invitingly. He scowled and seemed to have to think about what she said as if she'd spoken a foreign language. One of the six he didn't already speak.

"Home? But it's early." He suddenly seemed to notice the appendage he'd grown since they'd last seen one another. "Darling, have you met Bethany Sinclair? Bethany, this is Paige Mitchell. Paige, this is Bethany."

Bethany nodded coolly and Paige almost burst out laughing. Did this woman actually think she'd stolen something from Paige tonight? Like the man standing between them was a designer purse or a great pair of shoes? People weren't objects and they came and went as they pleased. That's why she'd chosen to go.

Paige ignored Bethany. This wasn't about her anyway, not really. This was about Nate being a jackass.

"I'll just take a taxi. You can take the limo whenever you're ready to leave. Good night."

Turning on her expensive high heel, she marched to the front entrance and out onto the sidewalk feeling rather proud of herself. She hadn't lost her temper or made a scene. So far, so good.

She was about to head for one of the taxis lined up when a large and masculine hand landed on her arm.

Well, shit. She'd thought she was home free.

"What is your problem?"

Slowly, she turned to look at him, his question shaking her resolve to stay calm. She only had one problem right now and that was him. He'd been testing her patience all week and she didn't have much left.

With the light of the streetlamp she could really see his face, unlike inside the club. His color was high and his eyes were red-rimmed. Drinking really didn't look good on him. He looked old and worn, not nearly the cinema heart-throb he was supposed to be.

"I'm sick to my stomach if you must know. Now let go of my arm."

If anything his fingers tightened and he leaned down, his usually soft blue eyes a sharp shade of gray. His breath stunk of whiskey and cigarettes. When had he snuck a smoke? He knew that she hated it. "Don't be difficult. We came together, we leave together. Do you want the press to start talking?"

Paige almost fell off her Jimmy Choos. He had the nerve to talk about the press? Was he drunk *and* stupid?

Her gaze darted around the sidewalk where a few people milled, having a smoke or climbing into a cab. "This isn't the best place to do this. Let's go home."

Nate was looking down his patrician nose at her. Honest to God. She'd read about it in books but had never actually seen anyone do it, but here he was with an arrogant haughty expression that defied logic. Did he think he had the moral high ground here?

"I'm not ready to leave," he whined. "I want to stay and have fun. That's your problem—you're no fun."

He hadn't thought that when he was fucking her on every horizontal or vertical surface in his house the last few months but then she had to remind herself this was all part of his plan. He was pushing her into a confrontation so he could get his way.

"Depends on your definition of fun, Treetop. Now I'm going. Are you staying?"

His hand dropped from her arm and the fucker sneered. *Sneered.* Shit, he'd pulled out all the stops for this. "Go home then. It's much more enjoyable without you."

Maybe a saint or a smarter woman could have walked away but Paige was neither of those. She was human and when stabbed, she bled just like anyone else. She should have turned her back and walked away but her mouth was in charge.

"Bethany looks like she knows how to party. You better get back in there before she finds another guy who's better-looking and has more money."

That smug smile was back on his face and she wanted more than anything to smack it off.

"You're jealous," he said so condescendingly it made her want to hurl. What was it about the British accent that could make something sound so pompous? "Really, darling, you're going to have to get used to women flirting with me. If you can't take it, then perhaps this relationship isn't going to work out."

Pressing two fingertips to her temple, she would have sworn there and then she'd just had some sort of stroke. He couldn't have said that. No way.

But as she played his words backwards and forwards she realized he had. He was going a hell of a lot further than she'd thought he would. This was the plan and he wanted them to have it out, right here and now.

Alrighty then.

"Nate, I have been dealing with women flirting and throwing themselves at you since the day I met you and I think I've been doing a damn good job with it. You see, that doesn't really bother me all that much. What burns my ass is when my boyfriend, the man I've been sharing a bed and my life with, spends the last few hours flirting back. In front of me. In front of your friends. In front of the press. You said you'd never humiliate me but tonight you did. You deliberately hurt me tonight because you're mad."

If she thought Nate might back down and apologize, she was wrong. She should have remembered he'd told her he had a temper. He bent over so they were nose to nose.

"I can do anything I fucking want. I'm Nate Mason. You're so uptight and anxious, such a control freak. Every fucking thing has to be your way. I just wanted to have some fun tonight but you couldn't allow that, could you? You can't stand for anyone to do something without your permission."

Silently reminding herself that this was all to provoke her, she held onto her temper by a slim thread. This was not the time or the place for her to blow her stack. Her brain couldn't stop her body from reacting, however, and a red tide of heat swept over her, making her legs jelly and her heart race. She was literally shaking with rage. It was only through years of keeping her cool that she was able to speak somewhat rationally.

"Only a child thinks they should be able to do anything they want, Nate. Real adults know that isn't possible. As

for having fun, no one is stopping you. Rock on or whatever. I'm done with this conversation. You want me to
scream and make a scene so you can justify what you did
here tonight. You're frustrated and mad because you think
you know me better than I do myself. News flash. I'm not
as dumb as the women you've dated in the past. You're
about as transparent as your skank-friend's dress."

She turned and grabbed the door handle of a taxi but
she wasn't quite fast enough.

"Go. I'm going back to Bethany. At least she appreciates
me. Go back to the suburbs and your boring pathetic
existence."

For fuck's sake.

She whirled back around, her temper battering at the
bars of its cage like a wild animal desperate to be let out.
He'd taken one step too far. What had started out as Nate
lashing out for imagined slights had turned into something
far different. He was angry because she wouldn't listen to
him. Well, she was listening to him now and not liking
what he was saying in the least.

"My poor baby, you don't feel appreciated? I don't
adore and worship you enough, like one of your fangirls?
Welcome to the human race, you asshole. Nobody is
appreciated enough. You're spoiled," she hissed, no longer
able to control all the emotions that were threatening to
spill out and make a mess. Angry tears pricked the back of
her eyes and her hands shook with the effort it took not to
slap him into next week. "A spoiled little mama's boy who
needs everybody to love him and tell him how great he is.
If all you want is a woman to tell you how handsome and
sexy you are, how great of an actor you are, and never,

ever call you on your bullshit, then you're absolutely right. This relationship could never work out. Go back to what's-her-name because I don't have the time or energy to prop up your king-sized ego twenty-four seven."

This time she did manage to wrench the taxi door open and stumbled into the back seat. Nate didn't come after her, simply standing there on the sidewalk as the cab pulled away and into traffic. Tears she'd been holding in began to fall, her body shaking with sobs she couldn't control. She turned to look out of the back window. To see him one more time.

He'd gone back inside.

CHAPTER
Thirty~Four

WORN OUT AND NOW DRY-EYED, Paige shoved socks and underwear into a bag along with the jeans and shirts she'd already packed. She'd changed out of her cocktail dress and high heels and into a pair of trousers and a sweater. The dress was pretty but just looking at it made her wince. It would be forever tainted after tonight. Shoving her cosmetics on top of her panties, she looked around the room for anything she'd forgotten. She was only packing for a day or two, needing the space to think. She couldn't stay here and deal with his drunken ass when he finally stumbled home, probably smelling of whiskey and Bethany's perfume. Sitting around and waiting for a man to come home simply wasn't her style. Depending on the outcome of her time away, she could always come back and pack the rest of her things if she needed to.

She'd cried and now she had no more tears to give him. The man she'd seen tonight wasn't worth her time or mourning.

But in their time together she'd seen a man who was worth it but he'd not been in attendance tonight. Did he even really exist or was he some creation that Nate put on when he needed something or someone? Had she been played by one of the greatest actors on earth? Had anything between them been true?

Will the real Nate Mason please stand up?

How this entire situation had spiraled out of control like this she didn't have a clue. Yes, they'd argued and hadn't been able to put it behind them, but nothing had prepared her for the way Nate had acted tonight. It was almost as if he hated her.

Maybe he did. Every time he looked at her was he reminded that the studio didn't want him? His ego was fragile. Had this been too much for him to handle? She'd tried to make him see that it didn't matter but it might matter a hell a lot. To him. He couldn't see that this was just a temporary setback, not a permanent situation. She simply couldn't be with him while he was wallowing in self-pity, lashing out indiscriminately. Watching him self-destruct would destroy her.

He had money, fame, women, and their dissolving panties. He was living the dream even though he wanted more. Maybe that was his problem. More. He couldn't get enough of what he had. He wasn't grateful or satisfied. Ever.

If she were honest she was a little disappointed he hadn't come after her, begging for forgiveness, and she hated herself for giving a damn.

Out of the corner of her eye she spied his light-blue t-shirt draped over a chair. It was one of her favorites and it brought out the blue in his eyes. She picked it up and buried her face in it, inhaling deeply and drinking in his heady scent. He smelled better than any one person she'd ever met and she wasn't sure why. He used regular soap, deodorant, and cologne that he bought in a store. Maybe it was his personal chemistry. Whatever it was, it was like a drug. She shoved the t-shirt in her bag, not allowing herself to think about what the action meant.

Opening the closet, she pulled out a pair of tennis shoes and tossed them into the bag and then started to zip it up before another thought occurred to her. She reached back into the closet and found those ugly grey-suede shoes he loved to wear. She hated these shoes and had told him so often. She shoved them in the bag with all her things before heading downstairs. It was petty and immature but that was the mood she was in.

The taxi was waiting for her on the curb, courtesy of the promise of a huge tip, but she still needed to hurry. He wouldn't sit there forever playing games on his phone. She passed by the kitchen and then backtracked to the corner cabinet where Nate kept the liquor. He didn't keep much on hand. Just a few bottles of wine but he'd taken to keeping flavored vodka for her and she grabbed both bottles and stuffed them in her bag. Then she uncorked the two wine bottles and poured them down the sink. If anyone was going to have a drink tonight, it was going to be her. He didn't deserve any more booze and she hoped he had a painful hangover tomorrow.

With one last look around she exited the house, making sure to lock the door behind her. Heading for the taxi, she stopped briefly at the garbage bin on the curb. The trash service would be by in the wee hours of the morning to empty it. She threw open the top of the bin and pulled the grey shoes from her bag, tossing them in. It was where they belonged.

She kept the blue t-shirt.

She shut the lid tightly and climbed into the cab.

"The Savoy, please."

———

The house was empty. Nate had known it would be. That was the point of the show he'd put on tonight but it had quickly gotten out of hand. He hadn't meant to hurt her like that, but then it was probably the only way she would leave him. She had to be pushed. Hard. Even when she was leaving the party she hadn't intended to break things off with him. She was simply planning on cooling off. He couldn't allow that to happen so he'd turned brutal until she had no choice but to hit back, if only in defense.

He hadn't realized just how painful watching her walk out of his life was going to be. It felt like someone had ripped his heart out with their bare hands. The agony was immeasurable but he'd done what he thought was right. Paige deserved to have her dream and she couldn't if she stood by him. Now that she'd seen the worst of him she could move on, make her movie. She'd get over him.

He'd never get over her. Tonight had been the hardest thing he'd ever done.

The evening had been like some terrible nightmare that

only got worse when he woke up. The one person in the world he wanted to reach for and hold and he'd shoved her away. She wouldn't be offering him any comfort. He was solely responsible. But he'd kept his promise to her son. He'd put her first.

She'd been partly right about the stunt he'd pulled tonight, but she'd also been wrong. He didn't give a rat's ass about Bethany and he hadn't fucked her tonight. When he'd seen her at the party, he'd known she was the perfect vehicle to push Paige away.

Stumbling up the stairs, he saw that the closet door was open and Paige's knicker drawer wasn't shoved in all the way. A quick perusal told him what he'd hoped and feared; she'd packed some belongings and left. The house felt colder without the warmth of her love and he shivered as a chill ran up his spine.

He collapsed back on the bed and rolled over so he was lying on her pillow, her scent surrounding him as if she was still there but there was nothing to hold onto. No warm, inviting curves to cuddle with. He was alone and wasn't that what he'd intended at the beginning of the night? Mission accomplished.

She would have stood by him no matter what. He wanted her, had fallen in love with her, so he had to force her to do it. Make a clean break and don't look back. Funny how he'd done that in the past but somehow he had a feeling he'd hurt himself far worse than ever before. Paige wasn't just anyone. She was special. The hole in his heart was so huge he had no idea how he was even still alive. He was shocked it was still beating. He had prayed for numbness but instead he'd felt every slash of the knife acutely.

Now what do I do?

His alcohol-soaked brain didn't have any answers, however. But he did have one last thought before he passed out from too much whiskey and sheer exhaustion.

If I did the right thing, why does it hurt so fucking much?

CHAPTER
Thirty-Five

MAX HOVERED near the front door of Nate's house, impatient to leave. "Are you coming for a pint or not?"

Nate dug deeper into the foyer closet, just as anxious to be going. The house felt empty without Paige, the echoes reminding him of what he didn't have anymore. A drink was exactly what he needed. Several of them. "I'm looking for my shoes. Once I find them, we can go."

Frowning, Max leaned over Nate's shoulder. "Why would they be in there? Have you checked your bedroom closet?"

Frustrated, pissed off, and exhausted from not sleeping, Nate sprang to his feet. "Of course I've looked there. I've looked everywhere. The closets, the drawers, the back porch, under the beds. Hell, I even checked my suitcase even though I know I've worn them since my last trip. It's like they've walked away on their own. They've disa–"

Nate slapped his head as a thought occurred to him.

"I'm a bloody idiot. She took them. She took my fucking shoes. She did it again."

How was he going to live the rest of his life without Paige to make him laugh?

"So wear a different pair. And what do you mean she took them? Paige?"

Nate laughed, falling back against the wall. It was the first funny thing in four long tortuous days. "Yes, Paige. She hated those gray shoes and she took them."

Max shook his head. "I don't understand you at all. What happened between you and Paige? You both seemed so happy and now she's staying in a hotel and neither one of you are talking."

Nate was doing plenty of talking but now it was to the houseplants after he'd had too much to drink. So far, the ferns didn't give a fuck that he was going to be alone until the day he died. He'd thought he'd known what misery was but he hadn't a clue. His world was a living, breathing hell that he simply tried to survive each day, hoping that perhaps the next day might be better. That hadn't happened yet.

"I did what was right. Maybe the first time in my life, and it would be nice to have my best friend support me in this."

A dubious expression on his face, Max crossed his arms over his chest. "Just what am I supporting?"

"I told you. My doing the right thing. It was your advice that helped me see what needed to be done."

Holding his hands up in surrender, Max shook his head. "My advice? I don't remember what I said but here's some more. You need to swallow your pride and call her, beg her to come home."

Nate had been fighting that urge every second since that night. All he wanted was to see her, hear her voice, and smell her skin. It was like a fever in his blood. He'd dialed her number a thousand fucking times but never put the call through. She deserved better even if it was killing him inside. He'd had to make due with calling her assistant Carrie to make sure Paige was all right. It wasn't the contact he craved but it was better than nothing.

Feeling tears burn the back of his eyes, Nate swallowed the lump that had risen in his throat.

"I can't beg her to come back because I'm the one that pushed her away."

Max blinked a few times. "You? But...why? That's daft. You were happy. I know you were."

"I was," Nate agreed, falling into an overstuffed chair. He'd been so fucking exhausted lately, his limbs, head, and heart all hurting. "But eventually she would have come to hate me and I couldn't let that happen. You said so yourself, mate. Don't take a woman's dreams away from her. This was me giving hers a chance."

Lowering himself onto the sofa, Max slowly exhaled as if holding onto his temper very carefully. "Why don't you tell me what you think you've done? Then I'll tell you how crazy you are."

Slowly, with several interruptions by Max for clarifying questions, Nate described the argument he and Paige had had and how they couldn't agree on what she should do. Then he reviewed their own conversation almost word for word and that had led to Nate's decision to push Paige away. For her own good. He even mentioned his promise to Jason. His description of his behavior that evening drew a pained groan from Max and by the time he was done his friend was holding his head in his hands, barely able to breathe.

Eventually Max raised his head, looking at Nate as if he had lost his mind. "You have fucked this up ten ways to Sunday. What were you thinking? You deliberately hurt the woman you love."

Nate didn't feel great about that but he'd been saving them even more heartache down the road.

"It would have hurt worse a year or two from now. Fuck, by then we might have been married. Tell me how much fun a divorce is."

Max blanched at the mention of the 'd' word. "I get your reasoning, truly I do. But this wasn't the way. Don't you see that Paige was willing to sacrifice the movie for you?"

"She shouldn't have to sacrifice anything for me." Nate argued. "Shit, I'm not worth it."

Hopping to his feet, Max paced the small living room. "She thinks you are. Hell, we all do. You're a good person who thinks his characters are more interesting. News flash. They're not. You should be grateful you have a woman that loves you as much as Paige does. Not many women would give up that chance."

This conversation was going nowhere. "You were the one that assumed she would make the movie without me, remember? Now you're saying it's okay that she doesn't. Which is it?"

Halting a few feet away, Max appeared to be holding

onto his temper by a thread. "It's however she wants it to be. It's her fucking life and you don't get to pull the strings. Isn't that what she was so angry about that first night you came home? That you were trying to control her? You're doing it again, only this time is far worse. You're acting like she's a child who doesn't know what she wants but she does. Clearly, she wants you although at the moment I cannot imagine why. You're a fucking idiot."

That first night in London seemed so far away. He lived a lifetime since then, but he did remember her reaming him a new one that night. She didn't like to be manipulated.

"I did this for her own good," Nate said a trifle desperately. "I want her to have her dream."

Max scraped his hand down his face, his eyes sad. "Maybe...maybe she had a new dream she hadn't told you about yet. Maybe her dream was something about you, her, and a future. Did you ever think of that?"

He hadn't. He'd been too busy giving her what she'd said she wanted. She'd been so desperate for that movie deal she'd agreed to a PR relationship with him along with all the red carpets and parties that went along with it. She'd told him of her ambition. An ambition that matched his own.

"I did the right thing."

It was all he could say. It had practically become his mantra since that night, the only thing that kept him from losing his mind completely. He'd sacrificed for the woman he loved. What was nobler than that? The problem was that being a hero sucked. If he'd known how much this was going to hurt he might not have done it.

The gloom that Nate had been trying to deal with took over again. He didn't love easily and now that he'd fallen, he was in all the way. For life, it looked like.

Paige Mitchell had done the one thing all his friends and family thought couldn't be done.

She'd made him want to be a better man.

———

Paige sipped her hot chocolate, preparing herself for the grilling of a lifetime. After avoiding almost everyone's calls except Jason and Carrie, she'd finally agreed to meet Amy at a nearby cafe. From the look on Amy's face when she walked in, she had a million questions and they were all about Nate.

"So go ahead," Paige said with a sigh. "Just tell me one thing before you do. Will everyone be hearing about what I say today?"

Amy shook her head. "Not if you don't want. If Mike asks me, I'll just tell him it was girl talk."

Chuckling. Paige picked up her fork and tried the red velvet cake. "Right, like that's going to work. I don't mind, really. So get to it. You look like you're about to burst."

Amy sucked in a breath and nodded. "First, can I say that you look marvelous, dear? I wasn't sure what to expect, actually. But you look good. How are you feeling? Are you ready to talk to Nate?"

No beating around the bush. Paige admired that.

"That's two questions so I'll answer them separately. As to how I look, well, you should have seen me a few days ago. I spent the first forty-eight hours in the hotel room feeling sorry for myself, not showering, and crying in spurts and fits, mostly because I was also drinking a large bottle of vanilla-flavored vodka. Hard liquor makes me melancholy."

Amy's well-shaped brow lifted. "You obviously showered this morning."

"Yesterday and today, actually. I had to go shopping and buy a six-pack of panties. I don't mind wearing jeans or a sweater more than once but I draw the line at underwear. I didn't pack for more than a few days. As for how I feel? Like I've been run over by a truck. I ache everywhere, but mostly my heart." Paige stared out the window to the passersby on the sidewalk. "I'm so angry and hurt."

"Have you talked to him?"

Paige took another bite of her cake, the sweetness cloying on her tongue. Even food didn't taste the same since that night. That asshole.

Paige shook her head. "No, and I don't know what we would say. Intellectually, I know why he put on that little play at the party but my heart is a different story. He was deliberately cruel and even though I don't think he meant any of it - I hope - I can still hear his voice ringing in my ears and saying those horrible things. I'm not sure I can forget it."

Amy looked near tears herself. "Do I even want to know what he said?"

"I wish I didn't know. Let's just say he called my life pathetic and boring and that I was no fun. I can't help but wonder if perhaps he wanted me gone. That I was a daily reminder that the studio didn't want him. Maybe he's glad I'm gone."

Amy signaled to the waitress for a tea refill. "I'm sure he didn't mean any of it. He's ass over tea kettle for you, girl. If any man in the world was in love, it's Nate."

Paige wanted to believe that but he hadn't made it easy.

"Yet he didn't have any trouble finding nasty names to call me. There wasn't much of a struggle there."

"Would anything else have pushed you away?"

Stirring her chocolate, Paige thought about that question. She'd been torturing herself with it for days and she still didn't have the answer.

"I doubt it," she finally said. "Nate did what he had to do, but what has he accomplished? We're apart. That's bad. What does he think he gets from all of this? Did he think I was going to change my mind because he was an asshole? It doesn't make any sense."

Amy placed the spoon next to her cup. "Maybe, just maybe, he doesn't get anything from this. Maybe this was about what you could have."

The lightbulb went on over her head. The gorgeous, sexy Shakespearian idiot. He was trying to be a goddamn knight in shining armor.

"The movie," Paige groaned. "I don't even want the damn thing now. Those guys gave me the willies. Even if they begged me to do it with Nate on board, I wouldn't sign the contract. I heard Stella Riley checked herself into rehab over the weekend which tells me Burt and Ernie don't have great judgment. That little voice in my head is screaming at me to stay far away from them."

"You're a writer. You should be used to the little voices by now."

"This one is a pain in the ass."

"So what are you going to do?" Amy asked. "Go back home? Talk to him? Can you forgive all the mean things he said and get your relationship back on track?"

Answers? Paige had none.

"I don't know. I go back and forth. Part of me is all - hey, he did something stupid but I probably will too at some point so I should forgive him. Another part is like - he's a child in the body of a grown man and he's going to continue this behavior for the rest of his self-absorbed life. I can't let him manipulate me when he doesn't get what he wants. That entire evening was a study in passive-aggressive behavior. Will he do this every time we have an issue? Because I don't think I could take the stress. The whole thing gives me a fucking headache." Paige looked Amy in the eye. "Do you think I should forgive him? You know him well."

Amy rubbed her chin in thought. "Relationships are hard and complex. People do stupid things but they can learn from them. The question is are you willing to put in the work of repairing your relationship?"

It would be work too. Hard work.

"That's something else I don't know," Paige admitted. "I love Nate, I really do. He has so many wonderful qualities that I admire and would want in the man in my life. I just fear that he'll repeat this behavior over and over every time we argue. So I've holed up in the hotel room writing."

Like the coward she was.

"How's that working for you?"

Paige gave up on the cake and placed the fork on the edge of the plate. "Terribly, thank you very much. At some point I have to make a decision and I have to talk to Nate. Normally those things wouldn't be an issue."

She wasn't happy with Nate but she was even angrier with herself. This indecisive shit was for the birds.

Amy reached across the table and patted Paige's hand. "I just want you to know that I'm on your side no matter what you decide."

It was Amy's expression that gave her away. "But you think that I should give him another chance?"

Sighing, the other woman nodded. "Nate needs you and I think you need him."

"I think you might be right but I'm still pissed as hell right now."

"Is that what you're going to say to Nate when you finally see him?"

She had no idea but there was one thing she did know. If he touched her she'd do anything for him.

CHAPTER
Thirty-Six

THREE DAYS BEFORE CHRISTMAS, Paige found herself miserable in New York City. It turned out that walking a red carpet was much more fun when she did it with Nate. Despite Helen and Carrie hovering close by, Paige didn't feel as relaxed and comfortable as she did when he was there. It was hard to make small talk without Nate's effervescent charm and perfect manners. She'd struggled all evening at the movie premiere and now she simply wanted to go back to the hotel. She had an early flight in the morning. She'd be glad to get home to Florida, lick her wounds, and finally make some decisions.

"You aren't going to the after party?" Helen asked as they stood on the freezing cold sidewalk outside the theatre waiting for their limo. "You should go. Have some fun."

Paige rolled her eyes and elbowed Carrie, who was giggling behind her hand. "I had fun last night, thank you very much. This one took me to a male strip show and I have never been so mortified in my life. She kept giving them money to dance all up in my business. I'll never get that oil out of my dress. It's ruined."

"I'll buy you another one," Carrie said in her sing-song voice. She'd been a rock of support for Paige this last week.

"It was Prada."

"You pay me well."

Carrie earned every penny and then some.

"Besides, I have a flight at the butt crack of dawn. I need my beauty sleep."

Not that she was sleeping well these days. Nate filled her thoughts night and day. She missed him more than she'd ever thought possible. She lay awake at night trying to figure out what to do, how to work this out. So far she'd come up with nothing.

Helen's gaze darted back and forth between Carrie and Paige. "I'll give in gracefully as I can see I won't win." She leaned in to hug Paige. "If you need to talk, just call. I can make sure you never have to see him again if that's what you want."

Paige literally couldn't imagine never seeing Nate again. As it was, she'd gone cold turkey and it was driving her insane. Turned out the British bastard was addicting. She ached from missing him and it was only getting worse.

"I don't know what I want yet, Helen. But I will have to see him eventually. He's Flynn."

The older woman curled her lip. "You don't owe him anything."

This wasn't about debts.

"He's Flynn," Paige said firmly. "He's the only one in the world that can bring him to life."

Helen sniffed disdainfully but nodded in agreement. "If you say so. That's what we're fighting for here—your control. And we're getting closer too. I think they're ready to cave, hon. It's going to happen. This new studio wants you desperately."

It didn't feel as important or wonderful as Paige had thought it would. Everything seemed better when she was with Nate.

How freakin' pathetic.

The limo pulled up and Paige and Carrie climbed in. On the way back to the hotel they chatted about the celebrities they'd met and the movie they'd seen. By the time they reached the room, Paige couldn't wait to kick off her high heels and that's exactly what she did. After changing into pajama pants and a t-shirt, she sat down on the couch and propped her laptop on her knees. There was little point in trying to sleep.

Carrie came out of the second bedroom of the suite and sat down across from her, reaching for the three-ring binder on the coffee table between them. It was an inspiration book for Flynn's series. In it were all sorts of photos - homes, cars, rooms, clothes, furniture, even pictures of Nate. Those photos were how she pictured Flynn now. Golden hair. Goatee. Sexy as hell.

Tapping one of Nate's photos, Carrie made a clicking noise with her tongue. "You have to talk to him eventually."

Paige looked back down at the screen of her laptop. The last thing she wanted to talk about was Nate. She was physically exhausted from thinking about him night and day.

"I know."

"Do you?" Carrie challenged. "I'm not so sure of that. You're acting like you can just ignore this entire situation and it'll work itself out magically. That's probably not going to happen."

"I have to talk to him," Paige parroted. "I got it. Next subject."

Carrie's expression turned uncharacteristically stormy and she slapped the coffee table hard with the flat of her hand to get attention, making Paige jump at the sound.

"You have to talk to him," Carrie almost shouted. "This is not healthy. You're miserable, he's miserable. What in the hell are you waiting for?"

Unbidden tears pricked Paige's eyes and she shook her head in denial. Why was she reacting so strongly to this? It didn't make any sense. "Stop it, Carrie. Just stop it."

"You have to talk to him."

Throwing her laptop aside, Paige headed for her bedroom. She didn't have to listen to this. None of it.

"You have to talk to him," Carrie repeated, hopping up from the couch and giving chase. "Don't run from this."

Stopping abruptly and whirling around, Paige couldn't hold back her emotion any longer. Tears slipped down her cheeks and she didn't bother to wipe them away, too overcome to deal with them.

"I know. I fucking know. What I don't know is why I'm so upset."

Carrie's own eyes were filled with tears. "Do you know? For real? I've never seen anyone throw away happiness with both hands like you are right now. It's such a waste. You love him more than you want to breathe but here you are, stubborn as hell, not dealing with this. He did something fucking stupid but he did it because he loves you so goddamn much he can't think straight. He may never think straight, Paige. He may always do dumb shit. Are you going to stop loving him for that? He's in a great deal of pain right now. He loves you, you know. The only thing that's keeping him going is that he did it for you. For you, and I have to tell you, with the way you're acting now I don't think you deserve his sacrifice."

Paige loved him so much. She did know she needed to deal with this, but how did Carrie? Heat rose in her cheeks as she realized they'd been conversing behind her back.

"Have you been talking to him?"

Carrie shrugged. "He checks in with me to make sure you're okay and to see if there's anything you need. He was worried about you tonight going to the premiere by yourself. You should let him know you got through it."

Nate was worried about her? Paige numbly wandered back to the couch and dropped down onto a cushion. "I'm not even going to yell at you for talking to him behind my back. But I feel I need to point out to you that he wanted me to leave. Now suddenly all this is my fault, according to you."

Carrie sat down next to her. "What Nate did that night is Nate's fault. He's responsible for his own actions. It was a shitty thing to do but it wasn't done with malice. It was a completely and totally misguided attempt to give you what he thought you wanted. Let me ask you a question. If Noah had pulled what Nate did that night, what would you have done?"

There was no answer to that question and Carrie knew it.

"Noah would never have done that."

Laughing, Carrie shook her head. "No, he wouldn't have. He wasn't the sacrificing kind of guy. Noah was a good person, but he expected to be catered to. He blamed others - namely you - for his own faults. You keep saying that Nate is spoiled. I think perhaps you're thinking of someone else."

Tears pricked the back of Paige's eyes. Her marriage had been far from perfect but it hadn't been bad either. It had been...difficult. Noah wasn't the romantic, cuddly, nurturing type. He'd expected Paige to be extremely independent, not needing much praise or compliments, and certainly no romance or flowers.

"Maybe he wanted me gone so that I don't remind him of the fact the studio didn't want him."

Carrie shook her head. "Now you're grasping at straws. If the thought of you hurt his delicate male ego, then why is he texting me to make sure you're okay?"

That was actually kind of sweet. "How long has he been doing that?"

"Since the day after the party. He sent me a text and said that you two had argued and you moved out. He thought you might need my support."

The hot tears she'd been trying to hold back spilled over and down her cheeks, salty on her lips. "He's always worrying about me. He fusses when I don't sleep enough or get lost in my work and forget to eat."

Rolling her eyes, Carrie snorted. "Wow, what an asshole. He sounds like a real jerk. Good thing you left

London because I bet he would have kept that up for the rest of your life. All that lovey-dovey shit would get old after awhile. I bet he kissed and hugged you a lot too, didn't he? The bastard. Did he say you were pretty? That's the worst. I can't stand that. You had a lucky escape, my friend. Men like that cannot be trusted."

Laughing through her tears, Paige scrubbed at her cheeks. "I get it. Jeez, I'm a terrible person and Nate is wonderful. I've broken his heart and I'll burn in hell."

"I never said that." Carrie wagged a finger in front of Paige. "Nate has to own what he did as well. You both are idiots and selfish. Walking around with all this love between you while the rest of the world can only dream about having a person loving them that much. Then you both go and waste it, tossing it aside like it was nothing when you and he know better. You know what it's like to be alone yet you walked away. I get that you left him for a few days to lick your wounds and regroup. But it's going on two weeks now. Enough is enough. Do you love him or not? Because if you don't you should step aside and let him find someone who does."

The ache in Paige's heart wrenched more tears from her eyes. She was so fucking tired of crying. "I love him. I swear that I do. I was just so fucking hurt. He was trying to control me and then he pulled that crap at the party. I was angry."

Carrie put her arm around Paige and patted her shoulder. "You had every right to be angry. Nate pulled a dick move and he needs to make that right. Let me ask you a question. Do you think that your issue with him is unrecoverable? You'll never be able to work it out?"

"Honestly I'm not really all that angry anymore. Mostly I just miss him."

Carrie snorted and stood, heading for the wet bar in the corner. "Trust me, he misses you. So what's the plan? Misery for a lifetime with Nate or misery for a lifetime without him?"

He missed her. It was a start. "It wouldn't be misery."

"Ladies and gentleman, I think we have progress here."

There were still problems that had to be resolved.

"He has to stop trying to manipulate me. He needs to let me make this decision about the movie."

Carrie popped open two soda cans and handed one to Paige. "I think Nate is so desperate without you that he'd probably agree to just about anything if you'll come back and forgive him. What's the worst that can happen? You talk to him and you come to an impasse. Then at least you'll know you tried. You can walk away with some sense of closure."

Just the word "closure" made Paige's stomach twist into knots. She didn't want this to be the end, but they could have a new beginning. A more honest one. They'd both been so scared that they weren't enough. Nate had pushed her away because of his fear and she'd let him because of hers.

There was only one thing for Paige to do at a time like this. The urge was strong for the first time in days.

Write.

"Carrie, thank you. Go get some sleep. I'm staying up. I know exactly what I need to do to fix and finish this book."

Dragging her laptop back onto her lap, Paige's fingers itched to type out the words that were already fighting to get out. Flynn was talking and she was finally, after all this time, really listening. He had so much to say.

"Will you think about what I said? I used all my psychology classes here."

Barely listening now, Paige tapped at the keys, lifting one hand briefly to wave at Carrie.

"Absolutely. I'm all over it. Will do."

Things were becoming clearer. First things first. Finish the damn book. Then get a flight back to London. It was time to show fear who was boss.

CHAPTER
Thirty-Seven

"NATE, are you going to join us in the living room? Faith suggested we play cards."

Nate stared out the kitchen window that overlooked the back garden, draped in shadow as the sun began to set. He'd tried hard to not let his mood bring down his family's holiday but it felt like he was fighting a losing battle.

Without Paige by his side he was like a rudderless ship. Every day he fought the urge to call her and apologize. Beg her to give him another chance, but it was too late. She'd moved on. He'd seen pictures of her smiling at a red carpet movie premiere, looking so incredibly beautiful. If she was happy, that was all he could hope for. That's why he'd done this. He simply hadn't known how painful it would be. He'd lost the love of his life.

Turning toward his mother, he pasted a smile on his face. "Sure, but if I win I don't want to hear her complain."

Her head tilted, Elaine studied him, her blue eyes soft

with love. "It's okay to miss her, Nate. I would be worried if you didn't. But it will get better with time."

He took a ragged breath and placed a hand over his aching heart. "I don't think it will. It's only getting worse."

"You could call her."

He was tempted, so very tempted. He'd taken to listening to the last voicemail she'd left him before they'd fought over and over again just to hear her voice. He was sad and pathetic. He'd even told his agent he didn't care about getting another movie role once the play was done next year. He just wanted to slink away and lick his wounds.

If Paige felt even half of this, he could believe that she didn't care about the movie if it meant she lost him. It was only now he was seeing her side. But once again...

Too fucking late. He was too stupid to be with Paige.

"I can't do that, Mum. She could do better than me."

Elaine smiled and pulled her son in for a hug. "I might be biased but I don't think she could find a man that loved her more than you do."

"Is love enough?"

He was afraid it wouldn't be.

"Love can be if it's combined with a few other things like patience, understanding, kindness, and commitment. If you can do that you've got something very powerful, son."

He scraped his hand through his curls. "My track record isn't a good one."

"Have you ever felt this way before?"

"No, never. It's unlike anything I've ever experienced."

She smiled and patted his arm. "Then I don't think past

performance is indicative of future behavior. For what it's worth, I believe in you."

"You're my mum. You have to," Nate chuckled.

"I don't have to," she said stubbornly. "I can see all the good in you. You've done some selfish and self-centered things. You've sown some wild oats. More than your share, that's for sure. But I think you know that your life could be so much more if you allow yourself to see yourself in a different way. You don't have to be alone."

The ringing of the doorbell saved him from having to reply. Thank goodness, because he didn't know what he would have said. He had sown wild oats. He had been selfish. But for a moment he'd dared to think he could be more than a self-centered, egotistical movie star.

He desperately wanted to be the man Paige thought he was.

"Who could that be?" his mother asked as she bustled to the front door, Nate on her heels. It was probably one of the neighbors over to wish them a Happy Christmas. His mother had lived here for years and was quite close to the people on her block.

Faith and Jack were sitting in the living room and she'd jumped up to get the door but Elaine waved her away. "I'll get it. It's probably Rupert from down the street. He always stops by before church and brings me some lovely chocolates."

"He's sweet on you, Mum," Faith teased, getting an elbow from Nate for her trouble. She elbowed him back just as hard, getting him right in the ribs just like she had when they were children.

"Shit," he hissed, not wanting his mother to overhear him. "Your elbows are pointy."

There was the sound of voices from the foyer and his mother came back into the living room, a big smile on her face and her blue eyes sparkling.

"Nate, you have a guest."

He didn't have a clue who else it could be. He stomped into the foyer and with one glance at who stood there, his heart stopped dead in his chest before coming to life and beating like a timpani. For the first time since that awful night he was able to breathe again.

"Paige."

Her name came out choked but it was with happiness. She was here and all his doubts were battered over the head by one simple truth. He loved her beyond all measure. He'd do whatever needed to be done. This woman held his heart in her dainty hands.

"I hope it's okay that we came." She wrapped her arm around Jason, her gaze darting from Nate, to his mother, and then back again. The color on her cheeks was pink and she appeared to be as nervous as he felt. "I think we have some things to work out. I missed you."

Just three words and he almost fell to his knees in gratitude, weeping at her feet. She'd missed him and that meant more than she'd ever know. He shoved his hands in the pockets of his trousers so she wouldn't see them shaking.

"I missed you too."

He didn't realize that he was just standing there like a statue until she held out her arms in welcome. They flew together, their bodies and lips colliding as if they'd been apart years instead of a few weeks. It had only felt like a century or two.

The kiss didn't last long but it was a promise of sorts. They were going to find a way to work this out. Being apart wasn't an option any longer. They'd figure out how to be together.

Eventually she pulled back and reached up to cup his jaw with her hands. "Is there somewhere we can go to talk?"

Yes, they needed to talk.

"My room," he said before finally giving Jason some of his attention. "Jason, let me introduce you to my family. Do you play cards?"

CHAPTER
Thirty-Eight

HE COULDN'T BELIEVE Paige was here. In the flesh. He kept reaching out to touch her, run his hands down her arms or through her hair just to remind himself this wasn't one of his dreams. That she was allowing him to do so was overwhelming. The last time he'd seen her she'd been hurt and angry, walking out of his life.

"Not that I'm complaining, love, because I'm thrilled that you're here...but how? Why? I thought I'd never see you again."

She sat down on the edge of the bed and he sat next to her, their hands entwined. He could smell her shampoo, that scent that had driven him half mad since she'd left, and feel the softness of her skin. There was a part of him that feared this was some break with reality until she leaned over and kissed him, soft and sweet and over much too quickly.

"I thought that too," she sighed. "I'm still kind of mad at you."

She had every reason to be. He'd been ruthless in pushing her away.

"I'm sorry, love. I'm so, so sorry." Once he'd started speaking, it seemed like he couldn't stop. "I was so afraid that you'd hate me for giving up your dream of making Flynn's movie. I hated the thought that in a few years you'd resent me and wish you hadn't chosen me. I couldn't take seeing that. I just couldn't."

His voice broke, a huge lump in his throat making it difficult to catch his breath. Her fingers tightened on his and he could see the tears welling up in her eyes and her lips trembling with emotion. From the agony on her face, she'd been as miserable as he was.

"I know. I know why you did it and now I know why I let you push me away. I guess maybe I was a little scared of not being enough too."

"You're more than enough," he rushed in to assure her. She was everything. He'd learned that while she was gone.

"I need to finish this, handsome, or I may not say it at all. I'm pissed that you tried to control me. You can't do that anymore, even when you think you know better than me. Next time we just wait until we're not mad anymore and talk it through. It may take several conversations and a bunch of arguments but we'll work it out. The alternative is not to be together and I don't want that."

He hung his head, ashamed of his own actions. "I can only apologize profusely. I shouldn't have done it and I was ruled by my fear. Your happiness is the most important thing in my life, love. I'd do and sacrifice anything to give you what you need."

"I know that and I'm so grateful to have found someone

like you, but you need to know that you don't have to save me or sacrifice yourself. You're already my hero."

"I promised Jason–"

"Wait," she interrupted, her brows pinched together. "Jason? What did you promise him?"

Paige looked extremely unhappy at this revelation. Too late Nate realized he should have kept his mouth shut but he wasn't thinking straight with her so close to him.

"He was concerned about our relationship and I promised him that I would always put you first. I meant that then, and I mean it now."

Her lips tightened at his reply.

"He questioned you about us?"

"It was at Thanksgiving," he explained, wanting to take her focus from Jason. None of this was the young man's fault. Nate owned this mess. "This isn't about Jason, love. This was my decision and mine alone. He loves you and wants the best for you, plus he looks to you for security and stability. It was a natural concern and we talked about it. I think he and I are good. At least we were. What does he know about the last two weeks?"

The frown she'd been wearing disappeared and her entire demeanor relaxed.

"Nothing. He was at school until a few days ago and when he asked about coming here to London for Christmas I just told him I was still deciding."

His chest didn't feel large enough to hold his heart. "Thank you for deciding in my favor."

"I think I would have eventually been here but Carrie sort of gave me the push I needed," she revealed with a smile. "She said I was throwing away my happiness with both hands. She also said that we were selfish and stupid for turning our backs on love when we both know what it's like to be alone. She made a good case."

He was going to go out and get Carrie the greatest Christmas present ever. He owed the younger woman more than he could ever repay. Because Paige loved him, he had a future.

Nate pressed baby kisses on her cheekbone and temples, making her laugh and giggle some more. The doubts that had plagued him for the last twenty-four hours didn't stand a chance when Paige was this close to him. "I've been thinking about this movie thing." He felt her stiffen next to him but he plowed forward. This was something that needed to be settled between them. "I have some contacts in the business and Max does too. If we make him a producer on the film, we might be able to raise the money we need to get it done. I talked it over with him a few days ago and he wants to branch out behind the camera as well. We can make this work. We can be together and get the movie made."

"That would work." She leaned over and pulled her cell phone from the side pocket of her purse on the floor. "Or we could go with this new offer that Kris sent me right before I got on the plane. They're excited to have you star and direct plus I get my creative control. You know the business better than me so I'd like your advice as to which way we should go."

He read through the email with growing amazement. There was another offer just as Paige said there would be. She got her happily ever after. If Nate had his way, she always would.

"We can talk about the pros and cons, but now we have options."

She nuzzled against him, her body warm and delicious. "I love you. Next time we're mad at each other, let's not do anything rash, okay? Let's just give each other the silent treatment like other people in love."

He rested his chin on top of her head, and pulled her closer. "I love you too. I promise no drama from here on out."

She tugged at his arm so he would let her go. "We're in love. We're not dead. We're going to fight. We're going to stomp around the house. The trick is to remember what we have together and to place that above it."

"I can't think of anyone or anything that would be more important than my wife."

He hadn't even realized he'd said it until he looked down into her face, her eyes wide with shock. Her mouth was open and she was trying to speak but only a squeak came out. He felt the heat rush into his cheeks. This wasn't how he'd wanted to broach the subject.

"About that...I guess you could say that I've been thinking about us...and commitment for awhile now. Definitely since Thanksgiving and maybe before. You know, happily ever after and forever."

He was babbling and he needed to cease immediately. He snapped his lips closed and tried to breathe. In and out. It was like waiting for the executioner's ax. She might react with revulsion at the idea of him being any sort of husband to her. They were only just back together.

"Marriage," she whispered, her voice tentative. "You've been thinking about marriage?"

"Specifically with you," he rushed on, not sure what to say next but knowing he needed to say something. "I know you said you didn't want to get married but I said the same thing too. I'm actually thinking that it might not be a bad idea. You. Me. The rest of our lives."

"It does sound good." She frowned and pushed at his shoulder. "This better not be a proposal, handsome. In your childhood bedroom while we're making up after a nasty fight. It lacks romance and finesse."

He shuddered at the thought. "Certainly not. I wasn't thinking we'd rush into it or anything. I kind of thought it could be there for us when we were ready. Maybe in a few months or maybe in a year. We'll decide." He got nose to nose with her. "But believe me when I propose you're going to be swept off your feet. I'm the king of romance and I'll prove it to you."

She held up her hands in surrender. "I believe you. So we kind of just sit with this then? Knowing that's in the future. I like that idea. It feels...warm and good."

He took her hands in his, lifting them to press a kiss to the knuckles. "I never thought I would have this. I didn't think this kind of love truly existed."

He'd surprised her; he could see it in her eyes that shone with tears yet to be shed. Licking her lips, she took a visible breath.

"It's not only real, it's ours. We have to take care of it. Nurture it."

He kissed her tenderly and then more passionately as emotion took over. "Thank you for giving me another chance." He kissed the tip of her nose and turned to lead her out of the bedroom and back down with his family. He couldn't wait for them to get to know her, but she stood her ground not moving from that spot in the middle of the room.

"Love? Don't you want to go downstairs?"

"In a minute." Her smile was gone and in its place was a sober expression that had him worried all over again. Had she changed her mind so quickly? Was he more trouble than he was worth? "I just want to say something first. I love you and I feel so lucky that you love me. But you need to know one thing. You can't keep going back and forth like this, whipping me around like the Scrambler at the state fair. One minute you're all in and the next you think that maybe we shouldn't be together. From now on, I need you to be committed to me."

Nate nodded vigorously. "I am, love. Totally and completely."

Tears slid down her cheeks and he reached to wipe them away, a lead weight on his chest. "I can't take this back and forth, Nate. It hurts when you pull away. I can take the doubts and fears but I can't take this whiplash again. Believe in yourself, believe in us. But God, Nate, believe in me and my love. Stop making my decisions for me. It's not for you to decide whether I'd be better off without you or making some movie. As sexy as you are, you don't get to run my life. If I hadn't come here today we might have ended things without giving me a voice. That can't happen again."

He'd been hurting her by trying not to hurt her. He had some making up to do.

"You're right. All of this was rather high-handed, wasn't it? I wouldn't want you to do the same. End things because you thought I'd be better off," he conceded. "I'd be hurt and angry and lonely."

He used the hem of his shirt underneath his cardigan to dry her tears. She laughed and tucked it back into his waistband. "Merry Christmas, handsome. Here's to the first of many holidays together."

He wasn't sure he'd ever felt so happy in his entire life. One thing was certain, his favorite Christmas memory had changed. The bicycle was now definitely second.

"Happy Christmas, love. I'm so glad you're here."

"Merry," she said, a mischievous glint in her eye. "It's Merry Christmas."

His beautiful American wife-to-be. The love of his life and beyond.

"Happy," he corrected softly. "You're in England. Christmases are happy here."

She slid her arms around his neck and pulled his head down to hers.

"They certainly are."

CHAPTER
Thirty-Nine

SIX MONTHS LATER...

Paige and Carrie sat on the back patio of her Florida home ticking off the last minute details for the wedding. Tomorrow was the big day. Strangely, Paige didn't feel nervous so much as anxious about everything going well. There was a part of her that was looking forward to declaring her love and commitment to Nate in front of their friends and family.

"Flowers?" Paige consulted her own list.

"Check," Carrie grinned. "They'll be here around noon. Along with the rental company who have promised to have the tables and chairs set up by the pool before one."

The ceremony was scheduled for five-thirty with dinner afterward. The Florida weather had indeed cooperated and it was a lovely eighty-five degrees and sunny today and predicted again for tomorrow. Warm weather for a wedding but Paige loved it.

"Music?"

"I have a selection of boring classical crap and also some fun party tunes set up on your old iPod and we can plug that into the stereo system since you have speakers outside."

"Nate likes that boring classical crap," Paige giggled. "But I hope you let him choose some of the fun music as well."

"I did." Carrie rolled her eyes. "He has terrible taste."

Nate had other fine qualities though.

"Okay, let's talk catering."

"They'll be taking over the kitchen early tomorrow. I confirmed cocktails and finger food for before the ceremony and then more cocktails while you and Nate take a few pictures. Then they'll open the buffet for the guests at six-thirty." Carrie looked up from her planner. "Are you sure you don't want a real photographer? I'm good with selfies but not much else. I could make some calls. I'm sure someone would love to take pictures at the wedding of a movie star and a bestselling author."

Nate stuck his head around the doorway to the kitchen, his blond curls sweaty from his run. He looked absolutely gorgeous. She still sometimes couldn't believe he'd chosen her out of all the women in the world. Thank heavens she'd said yes to that stupid contract, otherwise she might never have known what it felt like to be this deeply in love. The fact that he clearly adored her didn't hurt.

"And that's exactly why we're not going to have one."

Frowning, Carrie shook her pen at him. "You'll regret not having pictures."

Swallowing down half a bottle of water, Nate groaned as he collapsed into a chair next to Paige. "We are going to have a photographer. It's a friend of Garrett's who knows better than to sell our pictures to a tabloid. He's talented and discreet and he flew in this morning. I got a text from him confirming his arrival. He'll be here tomorrow after-noon to take whatever photos we'd like. I also asked him to video the ceremony."

Nate had promised to handle this item on the to-do list and she hoped this "friend of Garrett's" was as good as promised. "So that's taken care of. I think there's just one more thing. The most important thing at the wedding."

"The officiant?" Nate said with a smile.

Oops. Two things left.

"Uh, I was thinking the cake, but sure. Let's talk officiant."

Laughing, Nate patted her hand and leaned over to give her a peck on the lips. Any other time he would have done more but he never liked to get her sweaty. "The cake is a close second."

Carrie tapped a page in her planner. "The minister we'll be here by five at the latest and he's already signed the NDA so we're set there. He's a big Kai fan so prepare to sign an autograph, Nate."

"Duly noted. Now about that cake?"

"One four-tier chocolate and vanilla with a white-chocolate filling in two of the layers and a salted caramel in the other two. Yum. And might I say I saw a picture of the cake you chose. Very classy but different too."

Instead of the traditional white cake, Paige had wanted a chocolate frosting and Nate had wholeheartedly agreed. The tiers were decorated with gold accents and fresh flowers. It was too big and over the top for the simple wedding they were having but she hadn't been able to control herself when it came time to order it.

"Thank you, but it was Paige's idea. She has excellent taste."

"This from the man that tasted every single cake, filling, and icing flavor they made."

Chuckling, Nate drained the last of his water. "I think it was my favorite part of the wedding preparations. Or maybe it was the honeymoon plans. I can't decide."

Paige nudged his bare calf with her toe. "Speaking of honeymoons, I don't suppose you want to give me any more details other than the destination?"

He tapped his chin in thought before shaking his head. "I don't think so. It will be better as a surprise."

"I hate surprises."

She really did and he knew it.

"This isn't a surprise appendectomy, darling. It's a honeymoon to Paris. Happiness and fun are pretty much guaranteed. Even if I told you where we were staying how would that help you? You've never seen it before."

That was true. "I could look it up on the Internet."

"And the restaurants?"

"Ditto."

He leaned closer, a mischievous smile on his lips. "I'll give you a little preview. They'll be speaking French."

Carrie hid her face behind her planner but Paige knew she was laughing.

"It's like you've never met me before."

Carrie peeked over the book. "It's like he doesn't even want to have sex on that honeymoon."

Nate stood and dropped a kiss on top of Paige's head. "Now that the two of you are ganging up on me, I'll head upstairs to take a shower. What time do we have to be at the restaurant?"

They'd rented out the backroom of a fancy restaurant on the water for tonight's shindig. Just dinner and some fun for all the guests so they could get to know one another.

"Six." Paige checked her phone. "Are you heading to the hotel to see your mother and sister after your shower?"

They'd arrived yesterday and had been quite enthusiastic about the weather and the beach. They'd talked about staying a few extra days and going to Disney.

"I am," Nate confirmed. "Unless there's something you need me to do here."

Paige shook her head but Carrie - who was the epitome of organized - checked her list.

"Who is picking up Max at the airport? He arrives at noon. I'd do it but Paige, her mother, and I have spa appointments at eleven. We'll be there all afternoon."

Dammit, she needed to go get dressed. Leaving the house required more than pajama pants and a tank top.

"I've got that covered," Nate said, checking his texts. "He didn't want to be a bother when he knows we're busy the day before the wedding so he's ordered a car to take him to the hotel. By the way, I'm taking Jason with me. I think he'll be more comfortable with the men than hanging around here with the ladies."

Nate and Jason had bonded and were now best pals. Nate had even given her son advice about dating, which had scared Paige a little bit but it seemed to be working out. Jason was planning to fly back to Princeton for summer semester on Sunday but she and Nate were already discussing getting a new house in London to accommodate their growing family. She wanted Jason to feel welcome wherever in the world she and Nate might live.

"He's talking about becoming an actor instead of a doctor," Paige huffed at the man she loved. "I don't suppose you know anything about that?"

"It's just a phase," Nate declared with a smirk. "You know you did forget one thing on your list. The dress."

Nate had been snooping around the house all week trying to see her dress before the big day. Little did he know it was at Carrie's, away from his prying eyes. Lace and organza, it was simple but not plain.

"I didn't forget. It's bad luck to see the bride's wedding dress before the wedding."

Scowling, he shook his head. "Actually, I think it's bad luck to see you *in it* before the wedding."

She gave him a breezy smile. "Just in case, I'm covering all the bases."

"Speaking of covering all the bases, can I file my objection one more time about tonight?"

Paige took a fortifying drink of her iced tea. Nate was like a dog with a bone on this subject.

"You may file your objection," she replied calmly. "But you won't win. Even your mother and sister agree with me."

He wasn't a happy camper. "We're going to spend the rest of our lives together so explain to me one more time why we have to spend tonight apart?"

They'd mutually decided not to have sex this week, thinking it would make the anticipation of the wedding night more special, but Nate thought this was taking things too far. He'd been complaining all week about how he couldn't sleep without her next to him and although she didn't sleep great without him either, it was a tradition. One last night in a bed alone.

"It's our last night of being single. You and Max can stay up all night and talk if you want. You can read, drink, or watch television. Whatever. It's your last night of freedom."

Nate had already promised her no strippers or a bachelor party and she'd promised the same.

"But I don't want my freedom anymore. That's why I'm getting married, and I can do all those things with you."

He was making too much sense but this last night was, for some reason, important to her. One night wasn't too much to ask.

She pressed her fingers to her temple and sighed. "Nate, it's just a silly tradition, okay? Can you just go with it?"

He rubbed the back of his neck and nodded, although his expression was glum. "Yes, I can. I'll just miss you, that's all. I guess I better get in the shower."

He jogged into the house and Paige admired the rear view as he went. She was actually marrying this wonderful man. She hoped she would never take him for granted a single day in their life.

Carrie closed her planner with a decisive snap, pulling Paige from her daydreams. The assistant had a huge grin on her face. "Stop mooning over him and get dressed. We have a spa day with your mother."

"This is really happening, right? I'm really getting married. To Nate."

Carrie hopped up from her chair. "You are, you lucky dog, even though I think he's luckier. You're going to be happy. Not all the time because that's unrealistic. But you two are going to make it. I can tell."

Paige smiled at her best friend and maid of honor. "I think you're right."

"Haven't we come a long way since the day you met Nate?" Carrie teased.

She had, and she was ready to be happy.

CHAPTER
Forty

MAX WANTED to bang his phone repeatedly onto the bar until it was smashed into a million tiny pieces. Then maybe his soon to be ex-wife wouldn't be able to get a hold of him. She'd randomly called him this evening to let him know she had a truck backed up to the house they'd shared in London and was loading it full of their belongings.

The house she'd abandoned months ago, along with him.

Instead of losing his temper, he'd coolly responded that he was glad to see all the rubbish go that would have reminded him of her. Now he could start fresh and she could have the castoffs from their marriage and think of him every day.

However, when he'd hung up it was all he could do not to sling his mobile into the nearest brick wall. He didn't give a shit about the furnishings. It was only things and he could buy more. It was the feeling that he would never be free of Alana. If it wasn't her calling him to brag about something shitty she was doing to him, it was the press taking sides in their divorce. He supposed he should be happy that most were on "Team Max" but it was small comfort that so many people felt sorry for him. Like he was a stray dog without a home or a family. A mutt nobody wanted.

He'd thought about going out to the London clubs and picking up some lovely young thing but that wasn't what he wanted. He'd long grown tired of the single life. He wanted to settle down, have a family. Sleeping with a woman he barely knew wasn't high on his list of things he wanted to do.

He shouldn't have even come to Nate and Paige's party tonight but he was the best man. Max had to make sure that Nate and Paige actually tied the knot. Knowing one or both of them, there was a very real possibility that someone might get a case of cold feet. If they needed a push down the aisle Max would be there to do it.

Stepping outside the back door of the restaurant for a cigarette he shouldn't be smoking but desperately needed, the warm breeze tousled his hair and he pushed it out of his eyes. It was longer than he liked it but he needed it for his next role.

He lit his cigarette and looked out at the water, realizing he wasn't alone. Soft crying was coming from the end of the small dock that overlooked the water. At first, he thought to turn around and leave whomever it was in peace but then he recognized the sapphire-colored dress as belonging to Paige's assistant Carrie. A sweet and efficient young woman with expressive light brown eyes that contrasted with her fiery red hair. Paige swore up and down Carrie was a miracle in human form and kept her organized and on time.

"Are you okay?" Max approached the woman carefully, not wanting to pry but not feeling comfortable just leaving her here by herself. "Do you want me to get Paige for you?"

Carrie's head jerked up and she shook her head. "No, please don't. I don't want her to know that I'm out here crying. I don't want to ruin her wedding."

"I'm sure she wouldn't think you were ruining her wedding. Are you sad that Paige is moving to London?"

Max was aware that their future domicile had been a bone of contention between the happy couple and he was glad they'd come to some sort of compromise.

"I'm happy for her," Carrie said quietly. "This doesn't have anything to do with her."

He knew enough about women to guess. "Is it some bloke? Your fiancé? I'll go inside and tell him he doesn't deserve you."

He'd thought he might get a chuckle but instead she burst into a fresh spate of tears, her shoulders shaking with sobs. Startled and worried, he placed his arm around her shoulders and tried to say something soothing.

"It's okay. It's going to be alright. Do you want to tell me about it?"

Sniffling, she dabbed at her cheeks with a tissue but there were already tracks of mascara under her eyes. "I don't have a fiancé. Not anymore."

He glanced at her left hand which was still wearing a ring. "You two probably just had a little row. It will be okay in the morning."

She snorted rather indelicately. "It won't. He's left me for his ex-wife. They're getting back together. I've suspected something was going on with him for quite awhile. He told me last week but tonight he called me." She held up her phone. "He wants his ring back so he can exchange it for another one. You know, for her."

Clearly this fiancé was an idiot. Plus, the infidelity was a personal pet peeve with Max. If a person wanted to be with another person, they needed to man up and just say so instead of sneaking around.

"What a horse's arse," Max growled. "That's a man that doesn't deserve to have a good woman. You're well rid of him."

"I know that. I really do. But now everyone—"

She broke off and turned back toward the water.

"Let me guess, you think everyone feels sorry for you," Max said. "I know exactly how you feel."

Looking over her shoulder, she frowned. "You think people feel sorry for you?"

He shoved his hands in the pockets of his trousers. "Are you Team Max or Team Alana? Jesus, I hate that shit. I've seen the way people look at me, like I'm a big fucking loser because I couldn't keep my wife happy."

He'd made her smile although he wasn't sure what she found so entertaining. "Max, I'm not sure that people feel sorry for you. I think they feel sorry for her." She held up her hand when he started to protest. "In that, they think she's been an idiot for leaving you and going to him. That relationship has trouble written all over it, let me tell you. Personally, I think you've escaped and should be celebrating. Whatever the divorce is costing you, it's worth it."

He straightened at her words. It *was* Alana's loss. He'd treated her like a queen and she'd never appreciated it. "It's not so bad. We had a prenuptial but as we speak she's loading up all our belongings from our home and taking them away in a truck."

"You could send your lawyers after her."

"I could...but frankly I just want to be done with it. I never wanted this war in the press. That was all her. She wanted to humiliate me."

Carrie looked at him curiously. "That seems harsh. What happened?"

Lifting his chin, he shook his head. "Everything seemed good until after the wedding. Then we started arguing like cats and dogs over the littlest things. She did say I drove her to cheat."

"Ouch," Carrie replied, her brows pulling down. "That's a shitty thing to say. You know, I never liked her acting and this publicity can't be good for her career."

It was through his contacts that Alana had landed her last two movie parts. "You might be right, although she's of the opinion that all press is good for her career."

"Then she should be winning an Oscar this year," Carrie said sarcastically. "She's all over TMZ with that skeevy guy. If that was her type, what was she doing with you?"

Max highly suspected marrying him had been a savvy career move. "Availing herself of my moviemaking contacts. Good luck to her."

Carrie stepped toward him. "I'm sorry you're going through this. It makes my problem seem kind of small."

Rubbing his chin, Max shook his head. "Hardly. Your problem is important to you. Besides, this isn't a competition. Who's the most miserable tonight? That's not a contest you want to win."

She laughed and blew her nose with a fresh tissue from her purse. "True. So we both are trying to hide something from Nate and Paige. Neither one of us want them to know how unhappy we are. Well, your secret is safe with me."

Max inclined his head. "And yours with me. We make quite the pair, don't we?"

As soon as the words came out of his mouth, a light-bulb went off in his head.

An idea.

Maybe a terrible idea.

But it would benefit them both greatly.

Did he dare?

Would she even agree?

He was tired of being the object of pity, and she didn't want that either.

He could help her. She could help him.

He liked the idea more with every passing moment.

"Carrie, I'd like to talk to you about something. You're familiar with the word showmance, right?"

CHAPTER
Forty-One

PAIGE COULDN'T SLEEP. It wasn't all that surprising. Tomorrow was her wedding day, after all. They would set off for Paris the day after then make their home in London, although now that the West End play was done they'd be jetting off to Los Angeles so Nate could work on a new movie. Carrie would be staying at their London home while they were gone. She would be searching for her own flat nearby so they could continue working together.

Throwing back the covers, she slid her slippers on before heading downstairs. Maybe some hot chocolate would help her sleep. Warm milk and all that. Jason was a heavy sleeper so he was probably snoring in his room with his earbuds still in. Carrie, who had been acting strangely since the party tonight, had gone home to sleep despite her protests. She'd volunteered to stay in the guest room but Paige had been adamant. She'd be fine. One last night as a single woman.

Opening the refrigerator, Paige grimaced at the

crammed shelves. Since people were in and out of the house all weekend, she and Carrie had cooked and baked up a storm in case anyone got hungry. It meant that everything had been re-arranged and the milk was now in the old fridge that was located in the laundry room.

Flipping on the light in the utility room, she was blinded for a moment and had to squint until her eyes adjusted to the brightness. Her gaze landed on the doorframe and it felt like a fist squeezed her heart until she had to gasp for breath. Reaching out, her fingers lightly traced the pencil markings on the wood.

Jason - 8 years old.

Jason - 9 years old.

Jason - 10 years old.

A sob caught in her throat as she remembered each birthday as if it were only yesterday. Every birthday morning after moving into this house, she'd hustled Jason right to this spot and measured his height. With the pencil she'd marked how much he'd grown and labeled it. Why had she stopped doing it? Was it when he'd towered over her?

Allowing her fingers to caress the marks one more time, she smiled. She had a whole new future ahead of her and it was fantastic. What she'd had here would never be forgotten but nothing she did would bring it back. The only constant in life was change—or something like that. She had so much to look forward to. They weren't planning to sell this house. If she wanted a walk down memory lane she could come here anytime. Nate had promised they would visit as often as possible.

Snapping off the light, she closed the door to the

laundry room and stood in the center of her kitchen. Hot chocolate didn't sound as appealing as it had. She knew now why she hadn't been sleeping and it wasn't bridal nerves. It was excitement. She didn't want to miss a minute of her future.

Was Nate sleeping? He'd swore he wouldn't if she wasn't beside him but then he was a trifle dramatic on occasion. Maybe he and Max were drinking and laughing, talking about fun times. The past. What was it about milestones that made one ponder their life and choices?

Nate had been right. Sleeping apart was stupid. There was only one thing she wanted. Him.

Decision made, she turned and headed back, past the washer and dryer and into the small mud room where she shoved her feet inside her tennis shoes and wrapped a light jacket over her pajamas. Her purse and keys were also hung up on a hook so it only took mere moments before she was in the driver's seat of her car and backing out of the driveway.

She pressed the accelerator and the car exited the garage but didn't get far. Bright headlights appeared in her rearview mirror and she slammed on her brakes just in time.

Shit and fuck. She'd almost backed into something.

Her gaze flew to the rearview mirror and all she could see was the chrome grill of a pickup truck but it looked suspiciously like the one Nate had driven to the hotel earlier.

Her door flew open and she was practically lifted out of the seat. "I almost killed you. Are you okay?"

Nate. She'd know that voice - albeit panicked - that

scent, his touch anywhere even if her eyes were closed. His hands were running up and down her arms and legs, checking for injury but the hilarity of the situation was the only thing that had smacked Paige in the face. She began to laugh, softly at first but eventually holding her stomach as he braced her against the side of her sedan, a disapproving look on his face.

"Care to tell me what's so funny? I thought I'd almost killed or injured my bride-to-be. Where were you going at this time of night?"

She wiped at a tear that was rolling down her cheek. Didn't he see?

"I'm laughing because it's funny," she explained, trying to straighten up. He was glowering down at her as if she'd farted in front of the Queen. "Because I was coming to see you, and I'm guessing you were coming to see me. We couldn't stay away from each other even one night. I love you so damn much and I just couldn't wait for our married life to start. I didn't want to wait until tomorrow so I was coming to see you tonight."

A smile slowly spread across his so-handsome face. "I feel the same way. I love you more than I ever thought possible. Let's start our lives together. If I could marry you right now, at this moment, I would."

She grabbed his hands, rough from his workouts and the gardening he'd done since they had arrived in Florida. "We can. I promise to love you, and cherish you, and maybe now and then obey you if I think you're right. I promise to learn to make a proper pot of British tea but I'll never eat Scotch eggs. I promise to love you more every day and I promise to remember that nothing is more important than our family. I promise to listen and I promise to talk even when I don't want to. I promise to be your partner, your friend, and your lover. As long as we both shall live."

Tears shown in his blue eyes but they were happy ones, just as hers were. His fingers tightened on hers and he lifted them to his lips, pressing reverent kisses to the knuckles.

"I promise to worship and adore you, my love. I promise to love you for all of eternity, in life and in death. I promise to run baths for you and rub your shoulders after a long day. I promise to play games in the bedroom with you and only you. I promise to never forget what it felt like to lose you. That is my solemn vow."

"I now pronounce us gorgeous husband and slightly crazy wife," Paige giggled. "You better kiss your bride."

The kiss felt like more. More love, more hope, more passion, and more tenderness. It was a long time before he lifted his head.

"Darling, I love more than words can express. But I think we need to pull the cars into the garage and go to bed. We have a big day tomorrow."

Shrugging, she nestled closer, placing her cheek on his chest where she could hear and feel the heavy thud of his heart underneath her ear. "We can but tonight is really our wedding night. I feel married to you already."

The vows tomorrow were a formality. They'd made the commitment.

Nuzzling the top of her head, he pressed a kiss to her temple. "Me too, love." He pulled back and frowned. "Are you in your pajamas? You were coming to the hotel in your jammies?"

"I couldn't wait." She glanced back where the two vehicles had nearly collided in the driveway. "You couldn't either."

He shook his head. "I needed you and I was willing to risk your wrath. I thought you'd take pity on me and let me stay since it was so late."

"Staying apart was silly. You were right."

He rolled his eyes and gave her a gentle nudge toward the door to the house. "Write this day down. Paige admitted I was right. Film at eleven. Now go inside while I pull the cars into the garage."

Her first instinct was to protest, insist on helping him, but he had such an expression of adoration on his face. He wanted to do this, he needed to care for her. It was a little thing, letting him pull the car into the garage. She was learning.

CHAPTER
Forty~Two

PAIGE SNUGGLED under the covers as Nate joined her in the bedroom, tossing both sets of keys on top of the dresser along with his phone. He tugged his hoodie over his head and went to work on his belt buckle.

It was like the best strip show ever.

Of course he noticed her avid gaze.

"See anything you like?"

Propping herself up on an elbow, she inspected the man she'd just informally married from head to toe. Damn, she was a lucky woman.

"Everything. Every single thing." She waved at him to get on with it. "You know I didn't get a bachelorette party or a stripper."

That brow quirked slightly and a smile played on his lips. "Really? That's strange because I had a wild stag party with dozens of strippers and booze."

She sat up and gave him her best mean look. "You better be kidding."

"I'm kidding." He unbuckled his belt and placed it next to the keys on the dresser. "Max and I had a few drinks and looked online for possible homes for you and I to buy."

"You looked at real estate the night before your wedding?"

The white t-shirt, at least two sizes too small, was tossed to the floor revealing every yummy inch of his muscled torso.

"I did and I think I have two or three possibilities for us to look at when we get back to London. We'll have a day before we leave for L.A."

She laid back against the pillows. "You want to buy me a house but all I want tonight is a stripper. I'm a bride, it's tradition."

Smiling indulgently, Nate took a step back to the middle of the room. "A tradition? Far be it for me to get in the way of that. Sadly, though this is the best I can do."

It was a good thing she was young and healthy because if she hadn't been, there was a real possibility she might have a stroke then and there. Nate was rotating his hips in a circular motion, every once in awhile giving them a thrust into the air, while he watched her reaction closely.

The Brit bastard knew what he was doing.

Flushed and flustered, Paige took a few deep breaths to calm her racing heart, not to mention what was going on in parts farther south. Holy hell.

She smirked at the tent in his jeans. "Looks like someone is happy to see me."

"I'm always happy to see you, love, but you have to admit it's been a long week. We're married now, yes? It's our wedding night."

For a moment she was going to say no, but then that would be a lie. They'd said their personal vows to one another. Whatever they said in front of their family and friends would simply be the icing on the cake. She was committed and so was he.

"It is," she confirmed, still mesmerized by his gyrating body. "What do you intend to do about that?"

He stopped and seemed to ponder her question before ripping at the zipper of his jeans, stripping them off his legs. "Having my wicked way with my wife, of course."

Dive bombing into the bed, he'd somehow landed right between her legs. She didn't have time to wonder if that was by design as he pawed at the covers, yanking them down to her ankles and baring her naked flesh.

Okay, I had an idea or two while I was waiting here.

"Love," he purred, a smile gracing his movie star visage as his gaze caressed every curve of her body. "This is certainly a pleasant surprise. Promise me you'll sleep nude from now on."

For the life of her, she couldn't think of one reason why she hadn't been doing this all along. He was a genius.

"I promise, but you have to promise to keep me warm. I'm a little cold here, husband."

"We can't have that."

The promise in his smooth as honey voice sent electricity through her veins and down to her already curled toes. His large frame covered hers and she reached up to run her fingers down his chest and over his ridged abdomen, delighting in every dip and plane she discovered. That this man was all hers was mind-boggling and she winged a silent prayer up to the heavens that they lived a long, happy life together. She'd do everything in her power to make that come true.

His lips caressed hers before gliding across her jaw and down her neck to that sensitive spot where her pulse beat. He left behind a trail of fire that sent white-hot heat straight to her core even as her nipples puckered in anticipation. They too were rewarded with his talented mouth as he lapped at the tight buds, swirling his tongue, his breath warm on the damp tips. He scraped his teeth on the sides and she arched her back, pressing herself against his steel-like shaft. Groaning at the friction, his hands went to her hips as he pushed her thighs wider.

"Yes," she hissed as the tip of his cock rubbed up and down her slit, just teasing her entrance. A coil of arousal began to tighten in her abdomen and flames licked over her skin. "I love you."

His head dipped down and his lips grazed her ear, making her quiver with need and want.

"I love you, my beautiful wife. In all this world, never doubt that truth."

At this moment she would have believed anything but then he was pressing slowly and inexorably inside of her, stretching her, and it never ceased to take her breath away nor send her close to the precipice. Velvet over steel, he rubbed that sweet spot deep inside of her, the one no other man had ever seemed to bother to find, and his name escaped from her lips.

With increasingly ragged breaths, he pulled out slowly before slamming back in, bottoming out and sending arrows of pleasure straight to her extremities. She wrapped her legs around his lean waist and her braced her hands on his shoulders as his hips snapped, pressing his groin against her swollen clit.

"Open your eyes, my love. Look at me."

His whispered words were warm against her neck, sending goosebumps skittering across her skin. Forcing her lids open, she found him regarding her, his blue eyes dark with arousal, his pupils blown wide. But what she saw in his expression was more than she'd ever believed existed. He radiated love, passion, devotion, and deep promise. It took her breath away and she had to blink rapidly to keep a tear from escaping down her cheek.

Their gazes locked, he pistoned in and out of her, moving them both closer to heaven on earth. When her climax washed over her, she clung to him like a life raft in a turbulent sea. Solid and real, he was the lighthouse to her ship, the oasis in her desert. He was everything and she'd never get enough of this beautiful, kind, talented, and flawed man.

Collapsing, their damp bodies pressed together, she ran her fingers down his spine and then back up over his muscled shoulders until their fingers tangled together. His own hands were exploring as well, tickling her ribs and stroking her hip until she sighed with contentment.

"I'm sorry you didn't get your bachelorette party, love."

She giggled, burrowing her face against his chest. "I'm not really all that upset about it anymore. This was much better. Feel free to strip for me as often as you'd like."

"Every night."

Her fingertips traced his jaw and then his lips as she felt his steady heart beat under her cheek. "All I need is you."

"You have me."

She did and she wouldn't take it for granted.

———

The day of Nate's wedding was as sunny and warm as promised. He and Paige had a leisurely breakfast with Jason, Carrie, and Max, chatting about Nate's upcoming film and Max's upcoming play. The day seemed to fly by as the caterers, then the florist, and then the photographer showed up.

The rest of the day was a whirlwind and before he knew it he was standing under an arch of fragrant flowers watching the most beautiful woman he'd ever seen in his life walking toward him. Dressed in white lace, her green eyes sparkled with happiness as she smiled just for him. They didn't take their eyes off one another, as if they were the only two people in the world. This moment was just for them and no one else.

He repeated the vows and Paige dutifully did the same but he could tell she was thinking the same thing he was. They'd already said their promises last night. It was their little secret, something only between the two of them.

When it was time to kiss the bride, Nate bent her over his arm dramatically and she laughed even as their lips met. The guests clapped and cheered at his antics, their joy truly genuine. Nate the lonely womanizer had finally settled down and Paige the workaholic widow had found a second chance at love. It would have been the perfect story for one of her romance novels but this was the real thing.

There was music, delicious food, flowing champagne, hugs and kisses, and much happiness. His mum kept breaking into tears and wrapping her arms around him as if she was sending him off to war instead of a honeymoon. Max kept clapping him on the back and calling him a "lucky bloke", which he was.

Even across the room Paige would catch his gaze at random moments. He couldn't seem to tear his eyes from her, loving the graceful way she moved and how when she smiled it was heartfelt and lit up her whole face.

He'd almost blown this. All of it. If she hadn't had such a warm, generous heart, he'd be out in the cold. No wife. No love. Just the gnawing feeling in his gut that he wasn't enough. It would have eventually eaten him alive, leaving him a shell of a man. Empty and bitter.

Paige had brought the sun into his life and she'd dragged him kicking and screaming out of that dark place he'd grown accustomed to. She'd saved him in her own way.

Striding across the lawn, he grabbed her around the waist and twirled her in his arms until they were in the middle of the dance floor. This gorgeous bundle of woman in his arms was smiling up at him as if he was the greatest thing ever created.

"Thank you."

Her brows went up and her smile grew wider. "You're welcome. What am I being thanked for, might I ask?"

"For being you. For loving me. For forgiving me. For not giving up."

"I'll never give up."

Resting his forehead against hers, they swayed to the soft music. "You didn't have to."

"That's where you're wrong, handsome. Believe me when I say this was a done deal the day I met you. I have the strangest feeling we were meant to be. Some force kept pushing us together and wouldn't let go."

Nate chuckled and brushed his lips against hers. "That was love. The forever kind."

"Forever, that sounds nice."

He wouldn't accept one day less.

I hope you enjoyed Nate and Paige's story! Read Max and Carrie in Swinging On A Star!

Thank you for reading A Kiss For The Cameras!

About the Author

Olivia Jaymes is a wife, mother, lover of sexy romance and mystery, and caffeine addict. She lives with her husband, son, plus two spoiled dogs in central Florida, spending her days with handsome alpha males and spunky heroines.

Visit Olivia Jaymes at
www.OliviaJaymes.com